WITHERSHYNNES
CHEATING THE WIND

SUSANNA M. NEWSTEAD

HERESY PUBLISHING

First Published in 2022
by HERESY PUBLISHING
Newbury RG14 5JG
www.heresypublishing.co.uk
© Susanna M. Newstead 2022

A CIP catalogue record for this book is available from the British Library.
Paperback ISBN 978-1-909237-15-5

Based upon the map of Bedwyn 1820   Some names are older or later

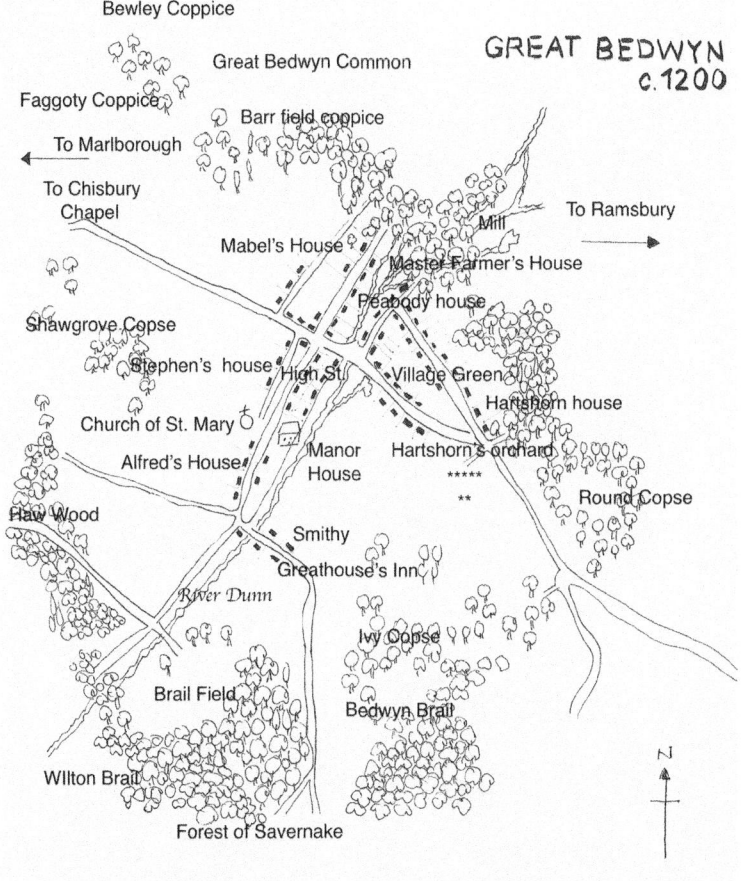

Bewley Coppice

Great Bedwyn Common

GREAT BEDWYN
c.1200

Faggoty Coppice

Barr field coppice

To Marlborough

To Chisbury
Chapel

Mill

To Ramsbury

Mabel's House

Master Farmer's House

Peabody house

Shawgrove Copse

Stephen's house

High St.

Village Green

Hartshorn house

Church of St. Mary

Alfred's House

Manor
House

Hartshorn's orchard

Round Copse

Haw Wood

Smithy

Greathouse's Inn

River Dunn

Ivy Copse

Brail Field

Bedwyn Brail

Wilton Brail

Forest of Savernake

N

Not to scale and not intended in
any way to be totally historical.

© Susanna. M. Newstead 2021

GLOSSARY AT END OF BOOK

CHAPTER ONE ~ IF PIGS COULD FLY

BEDWYN, SAVERNAKE FOREST AUTUMN/ WINTER 1212

Johnny Chatterwell ran across the rough grass of the meadow behind his home, his feet slopping around in shoes which were too large for him. His heart was hammering, his mouth was dry.

"Arrgh!"

His mother popped her head from the door of their cottage and looked out. One by one, three other heads appeared underneath her own. First, Gertrude, aged eleven. Second, Matilda, aged ten, and third, Alfred, nine, watched wide eyed as Johnny, the youngest at eight, skidded around the corner.

"Argggh!"

"Whatssup?" shouted Gertrude, straightening up and coming out of the house. She was undoubtedly the nosiest child.

"Hush your yelling, Johnny!" said Mistress Chatterwell. "Yer father's still asleep.

"I seen it—I seen it!"

Mistress Chatterwell stood up tall which wasn't easy as she was merely four feet and nine inches. "Seen what, you clod head?"

"A pig—a pig!"

Johnny received a buffet around his head. "Pigs are two a penny round here you idiot. It's nothing to yell about."

"No. Not pigs what can *fly*!" said Johnny, oblivious to the slap and out of breath.

His mother took him by the arms. "You been at the Christmas ale? I told you..."

"No—no—come with me, I'll show you."

Johnny ran off across the meadow once more, pausing now and again to hop and replace the shoe on his bare foot.

His mother harrumphed, "Go with him and get him back, Gertie. It's Sunday, we need to be at the churchyard soon. Even if it isn't mass."

She turned into the house, "Alf, go and wake yer Da. Gently, if he ain't already awake."

Matilda, or Tildy as she was known, looked up at her mother's careworn and old before its time, face. "Pigs, what can fly?"

"It's Sunday, the lad has told a lie on Sunday."

"That's bad i'n't it, ma?"

"Tellin' lies is bad on any day but speshly on Sunday." She unwound her head cloth and retied it, not knowing quite what to do with her hands. Then she disappeared into the house.

If we had been able to follow little Johnny and his sister across the field, we would have seen a small river winding its way through fertile meadows; stands of bare birch trees swaying in the wind and one lone old oak tree standing in the garth of a cottage where the patch, full of seed heads and drying and decaying plants, was thrashing about in the stiff breeze.

The two children came to the river bank but they could go no further without crossing the water or running up the bank and making a long detour round.

"Where was it?" asked Gertie, scanning the sky.

"Up there. Not too high."

Gertie looked at her little brother. "It was a cloud, you ninny!" she yelled at him in disappointment.

"Twas not."

"Twas!"

"Twas not. It was a pig what had wings and it was flying around up there." Johnny pointed to a patch of sky. "It was flyin' about plain as the nose on my face."

His sister took hold of that nose and tweaked it.

"OW!"

"That'll learn you not to tell lies."

Johnny rubbed his nose. Oh how he'd love to give his sister a kick up the bum but he knew she was bigger and stronger than him and he'd never managed to win a fight with Gertie. "S'not a lie."

"Now that's two lies!"

She reached for his nose again but he ducked, losing his footing and falling backwards, his foot leaving behind his unlaced shoe once more.

"Argh! Look!" On his back he had a view of the sky over the oak tree. He pointed up. "It's a pig—and it's flying!"

Gertie followed his gaze.

The pig swooped over the tree, flapped its quite large wings, which were somehow strangely familiar, and disappeared to the back of Mistress Wetherspring's cottage.

"Oh—no—it can't be!" yelled Gertie, falling over like her brother.

"It is—it IS!"

"Pigs can't fly!"

"You just seen it, ain't you?"

"With my very own eyes," said Gertie, scanning the sky again. Then she rubbed those eyes and looked again.

Half a furlong, half a foot and half an inch away, Mabel Wetherspring was just coming around the corner of her cottage carrying a bucket. And limping slightly on her right ankle.

"Let's go and see if Mabel saw it."

"If Mabel saw it, then ma will have to believe us."

They ran along the riverbank and crossed at the little wooden bridge which allowed them passage to the other side of the bank.

"Mistress Wetherspring! Mabel! Mistress Mabel!" they yelled as they ran at a pace along the little lane.

Mistress Peabody stuck her head out from her door. "Children please—not on the Lord's day!" she said. "Even if we can't celebrate it."

"Sorry mistress," said Johnny, "But we gotta go." They ran on in silence.

The kerfuffle had brought Master Lovegrove from his shippon. "Children nowadays! No discipline!" he said.

His neighbour Master Whitelock was just exiting his house. He pulled down his Sunday cotte and tightened his belt. "Good day neighbour."

Lovegrove nodded and vanished into the darkness of his cow shed.

Mabel had known she'd been seen, but had no idea the children were bearing down on her. She took the bucket and began to strip some of the seed heads from certain plants in her garden. It was a chilly day; she'd not be too long out here without a cloak and besides, the priest would be waiting for his congregation in the churchyard by the preaching cross; all that was allowed now since the Interdict had prevented the clergy from doing their jobs and preaching *in* the church. The doors had been locked since March 1208 and there would be no proper service.

Johnny skidded to a halt by her bucket.

"Johnny! What—the—?"

"The pig, mistress."

"Did you see it?" asked Gertie. "It went over your house."

Mabel raised her fair eyebrows. "A pig went *over* my house?"

"It flew—on wings—b...big wings," stuttered Johnny. "You...you *must'a* seen it."

"I'm afraid the only pig I've seen lately was Master Hogg's big black boar. And that was last Thursday."

"Aw, you must'a seen it."

"I am sorry children, but no. I must have been looking the other way."

"Pigs can't fly, can they?" said Johnny breathlessly.

"Well, they might be able to jump but I doubt they could clear the roof of my cottage." She looked back at it as she spoke. It was a small single storey flint and daub cott on a stone platform, with two windows to the front and a small oak door. A good straw thatch topped it making it look like a well risen loaf.

"We saw it—both of us."

"Well if you say you saw it—then you did."

"We aren't lyin'."

"I am sure you aren't, especially on a Sunday."

"Mistress, do you think *certain* pigs can fly?" asked Johnny.

"Well I have never seen one but, there are some very strange things in this world, Johnny, and flying pigs might be one of them, I suppose."

"Pigs are too fat to fly," said Gertie, now doubting what she had just seen with her own eyes.

Mabel took a child under each of her arms. "A bumble bee is fat, Gertie, but we all know it flies very well."

"Yes but…"

"Let's think what it *might* have been, shall we?"

Johnny pulled away. "It was a flying pig. I saw it several times."

"And what were its wings like Johnny?"

"Big, like a eagle…"

"An eagle? Well, we have no eagles here in the forest."

"The Lord's got a eagle."

"Ah Johnny, I think you'll find that's a saker. It's very big, yes. But not as big a bird as an eagle," said Mabel.

"It looked like a kite," said a ruminating Gertie, *now* convinced that she had indeed seen a flying pig.

"Well that might be just what it was. A kite taking a pig from Master Hogg's pen."

"They wouldn't do that. They don't like live prey," said Johnny authoritatively. "And Master Woodman said that kites don't like confined spaces."

"Well then, maybe the kite had found a wild piglet dead and was tidying up. It might have looked as if the piglet had wings but..."

"NO!" Both children yelled at her. "It was a pig with wings."

"Very well. it was a pig with wings and you'd better be on the lookout for it again."

"Oh we shall!"

"Now, I think your mother will want you at home. It's nearly time for going to the churchyard," said Mabel, ushering them out of the gate.

They looked back just once at the small smiling woman and vanished up the lane.

Mabel Wetherspring let out an enormous breath.

"Flying pigs indeed!"

She put her bucket down by the door and entered her cottage. Once there, she fell down on her stool and laughed and laughed and laughed until she almost cried.

*****

Mabel Wethersping was a rather unusual woman. At the age of thirteen she had discovered that she could change her body into any animal she fancied, simply by raising her arms and spinning three times to withershynnes—against the direction of the sun—and telling herself that she would like to be this or that.

It had been quite a shock at the time. But now eight years later, she was used to her skill and rather took for granted that she could become a bird or a bat or a butterfly.

What she had not realised until today, was that it was also possible to become a trifle—shall we say—mixed up?

Once, when she was learning about her new found skill, Mabel had accidentally turned herself into a fly. She had been desperately trying to avoid being seen by someone she knew and had hastily repeated instructions to herself without actually realising that her body would do exactly what she'd said.

"I want to fly," rather than, "I would like to be able to fly" had been interpreted by the magic of her transformation as, "I want to *be* a fly." It was not a wise move and she'd narrowly escaped becoming dinner for a spider that day.

Today something of the same had happened.

She'd fancied, before church, an early morning wheel about the skies as a kite, those large grey headed, russet brown birds often seen riding the clouds, cheating the wind high above the downs or the forest glades.

It had all gone well to begin with. She had stretched out her arms, spun twice to withershynnes whilst saying, "I would like to be..." when around the corner of her house came one of Master Hogg's porkers at lightning speed. He had obviously been saved from the autumn slaughtering and had escaped the pen. No one was chasing him. They hadn't yet found that he'd gone.

Her third and final turn was accompanied by the words, "A hog!" which was rapidly followed by a hasty, "No! A kite."

Into her brain came the picture of a pig, the little pig she had just seen, round, red and lively. Her tongue, however, lagged behind and the word kite was begun as her body began to transform into a small pig.

She felt herself grow four short legs. Ah well—she could easily turn herself to withershynnes again and rectify her mistake. Her nose lengthened, her eyes retracted into little folds, her ears grew bristly and erect.

Then she felt the wings unfolding on her back—powerful, red, long feathered and black tipped.

She chuckled to herself and looking around realised that the round bottom of the piglet with its curled tail, had become a rather nice forked and feathered tail.

Now, Mabel was somewhat of an inquisitive sort and just in that moment, she wondered if it was possible that this body might lift itself from the ground on such wings and navigate the air currents with this amazing forked tail.

She lifted off.

"Whee!" Higher and higher she flew. She had to admit that it was not as easy to fly as a '*pite*' or a '*kig*' or whatever she had become. She'd been a red kite many times and flying had been effortless. Height could be obtained very easily and speed built up without too much flapping of wings. Roaring through the skies on the wind was easy as a kite.

As a pigkite or a kithog—or whatever it might be—she had to flap harder and turn more carefully steering her larger lump of a body and heavier bones with precision, with her v shaped tail.

It was tiring and after one or two passes around her garth, Mabel decided on a quick landing and re-transformation.

She hadn't banked on Little Johnny Chatterwell seeing her.

Her piggy eyes spotted his open mouthed face staring up at her as she flew over her lone oak tree. One or two more passes, Mabel began to realise that landing as a pig on four little black trotters was not going to be easy. She flew about so that she might slow down.

Then Gertrude had come out of her house, had joined her brother and she too had seen her.

There was nothing for it.

She *had* to land and get back to herself again.

She put out her feet, pulled up her wings, ran along on her trotters, tippy-toe and used her tail to make a brake on her speed.

"Ouch!" One little foot didn't quite make the ground as gently as she might have liked and buckled under the weight of bacon—or was it ham?

Mabel rapidly turned to deosil—with the direction of the sun—and said, "I wish to be Mabel Wetherspring again."

Her ankle ached but that was all she had to show for her demonstration and she quickly picked up her bucket and rounded the end of her cottage. 'Serves me right,' she thought. 'Concentrate, Mabel, next time you want to change—the Lord only knows what you might become!'

After church and for the rest of the day, she spent time with her drop spindle, musing upon what she *might* become, if she did such a thing again.

"A dorse, perhaps—a mixture of horse and deer." She giggled; that would be a fine thing but upon reflection, the two were very similar and to be really clever, you had to find some animals which would never be mistaken for each other or ever come together.

'A snake and a peregrine!' Now there was a thing, thought Mabel. What would that look like? The tail of a snake and the head and torso of a bird, complete with vicious beak. Ah no. There were no really interesting large snakes hereabouts. The forest adders were small shy creatures and anyway, peregrines were known to eat small snakes.

'What about a mixture of a lion and a falcon?' Ah, Mabel had never seen a lion up close. Or anywhere actually.

She closed her eyes and, carrying on with her spinning, she tried to picture a lion as she'd heard they looked. She remembered someone had told her that at the Priory of St. Margaret in Marlborough, there was a depiction of a lion on the underside of a seat in the chapel. Might she just have a little fly over there and take a look? She knew that the monks at the priory were still using their church even with the Interdict. She was sure she'd be able to get in somehow to have a peek.

In her next breath she dismissed the whole thing as a foolish enterprise. Why would she want to waste her time and energy trying to become a beast which no one had ever seen? Well, no one around here.

Oh, but it was tempting. Yes, a lion and falcon with large wings— like the dragons she'd heard had terrorised the countryside around the area in the north of the country—that would be such fun.

Folk were in their homes. It was quiet and dark came early in December. If she was to have a go at a Lalcion, as she'd named it, she'd have to do it now.

She ran down to the river and found a clear pool—there was no point in doing this if she couldn't see herself, now was there?

Quickly looking around to make sure she wasn't overseen, she turned to withershynnes three times and began on the first turn, 'I wish to be an animal with the body of a falcon, the wings of a dragon and the head of a lion.'

As she made her last turn she thought, 'Oh this is foolish. Downright foolish and surely against the laws of nature.'

Her head grew broad and her teeth multiplied. Thirty huge and sharp teeth filled her growing mouth. Her brow widened and her eyes grew large. At the same time she felt a wriggling on her back and two large leathery wings suddenly erupted from her—; pointed and strong—they were heavy and Mabel almost fell with the weight of them.

Feathers began to sprout all over her torso; a tail of brown feathers developed from her spine. She stretched like a cat and unfolded the wonderful wings.

Did she dare to look into the clear water of the still pond? She hadn't realised she'd closed her eyes. She opened them to an amazing sight. A brown eyed cat stared at her, larger than any she'd ever seen. 'Well, well, a lion is a cat—who knew?'

She turned sideways. Oh the wings were absolutely splendid and the body beautiful with its feathered variations in colour, black, brown and tawny.

Once more she looked around. She'd just fly into the forest and back, just to see how it felt.

She stretched her gorgeous wings and flapped. The tips were rather like a bat's, scalloped and striated. The wings had to fold forward first and the air had to be scooped under them. It was a little like being a large bird—a swan or a heron, perhaps—both of which Mabel had practised.

The muscles of the torso were strong but even so they strained to pull the wings back and forth. Suddenly she was a foot from the ground. More languorous flapping and she was a yard in the air. She flapped harder. Now she was approaching the trees at the edge of the river. 'Argh, I must gain height.'

She pulled the wings right back and, trying to remember how she'd flown when she was a goose, she scooped the air underneath them. Touch at the front, scoop to the back. She missed the trees and carefully drew up her two legs with their dagger-like claws beneath her body.

Over the trees at the edge of the river she flew.

Whoop Whoop, went the sound of her huge wings. Her equally large lungs took in huge breaths to power the wings and lift the body higher. Her stately lion head lifted and looked up at the sky.

"Whee!" she said, except it came out as a huge roar.

Over the Peabody house, towards the village mill she flew. Master Farmer came out of his barn building to look at the sky. "Jesus Christ!" he said.

Mabel moved on—over the trees by Master Miller's house. He was just exiting his door and he saw her. He'd obviously heard Master Farmer shout for he too looked towards the sky. He crossed himself and fell to his knees. "Lord save us!" he groaned.

Now she'd left the village of Bedwyn behind. Here it was all trees and isolated meadows with grassy patches of scrub and no houses. Mabel looked down and breathed out in order to take in another huge breath to shout in elation.

From her mouth came fire. Oh no. She hadn't meant that! A gout of flame spouted into the darkening sky. "I never said I wanted to breathe fire," said Mabel to herself. She'd better be careful or she might set fire to the forest. It was dry and crispy at the moment for they'd had no rain for weeks. And it was nearly Christmas; the trees were almost denuded of leaves and the branches in many places, bare. Dry leaves would go up like tinder.

Now, Mabel knew that the longer you stayed an animal, the more difficult it was not to behave like that animal. It took a lot of willpower to retain the human in her. She wheeled around the blackening sky and contrary to her own human Mabel wishes, she took in a breath and let out fire once more.

Oh how satisfying it was. She flew higher. Below her she saw the little river Dun winding its way towards the larger river Kennet. The stately oaks were like little plants below her. She turned on her side and glided over the river. Below, Master Farmer's cattle, disturbed by this 'thing' flying above them and breathing fire, thundered about their field in absolute terror.

'OH, NO! I hadn't meant to frighten the cows,' said Mabel to herself as she veered off back towards Round Copse and Bedwyn village.

The village was in uproar. Master Hartshorn was in discussion with the reeve, Master Head. Stephen Meadow came out of his house and happened to look up. Mabel couldn't help it. She roared. She wasn't terribly fond of this stupid man who had made her childhood a misery. 'Just a little shock for him eh?'

"Grrrrraaaaarrrrgh!" she yelled.

Everyone flew into their houses.

'Oh this is wonderful!' said Mabel's beast brain. Her human brain said, 'Ah, time to stop terrifying them all now.'

She wheeled over the trees by her house and landed on talons which gripped the ground fiercely and scraped up the grass. She stomped into the trees. She couldn't afford to let the villagers see her changing.

Mabel stretched her wings once more, made sure she was alone and turned clumsily to deosil. 'I wish to be a woman again.'

She was running out of the trees as Mistress Peabody came skidding into her garth.

"Mistress Wetherspring, are you alright? It seems the beast has made for the trees close by your cottage."

"I am fine, Matilda. Truly. I saw it and gave chase."

Mistress Peabody was followed by the men; Stephen, the reeve, the miller and Master Farmer, joined by Master Hogg and Master

Corngold, the ploughman. Master Lovegrove came up to them at a run.

"My God! What was that?" yelled the reeve.

"We are lucky we aren't all roasted in our beds," said the excitable Stephen Meadow.

"Some sort of dragon I think," said Mabel. "It disappeared when it saw me."

"You—er—chased it?" said the reeve, wide eyed.

"Yes, it's quite shy. It doesn't like people very much, I think."

"Ha!" said Stephen, "Only for dinner!"

"It's not attempted to do anyone or anything any harm," said Mabel, perfectly calm.

"Mistress Wetherspring, how can you say such a thing?" said Matilda Peabody.

"Is anyone hurt? Did the beast set fire to anything? Are any animals hurt?"

Master Farmer piped up. "It tried to take one of my cows."

"Nonsense!" said Mabel.

She looked around the faces in front of her. More folk who had not seen the beast were now arriving. "It's gone now anyway."

"Gone to return whenever it wishes!" said Corngold, grimacing.

The reeve stood up straight. "Are we all agreed, we had better tell Master Steward what we have seen? And he can let Lord Stokke know. After all, it's his village."

"Oh I don't think…" began Mabel. And then she stopped.

If they told their lord, who was spending Christmas at Chalfield, in the north of the county, at one of his friend's manors, then he might send someone to investigate.

And that someone might—just *might*—be Sir Gabriel Warrener, Mabel's beloved.

She smiled.

"Well he has a proven record with mysteries, hasn't he?"

"Eh,' said a few voices.

"Oh, nothing."

"Then, young Adam... first thing, get your pony. Off to Chalfield with you. And you too Miller. The steward will write a letter."

Mabel smiled a secret smile.

Things had turned out quite well, after all.

*****

"A dragon?"

"Well the letter says it had the body and feet of a bird of prey, the head of a lion and wings like a dragon," said the Lord Stokke.

"Aw... sir, you don't really think...?"

"Several people saw it, Gabriel. I would not be worried but for the fact that several very sensible people saw it."

"Did Mistress Mabel see it, sir?"

Sir Robert Stokke consulted his letter, "No, her name is not on here."

"Hmmm." Gabriel Warrener paced up and down. "A body like a bird and the head of a lion, with large wings? That sounds to me as if it's a gryphon, sir."

"But I thought that it was the other way around..."

"Pardon?"

"A gryphon. The back half is lion-like, the front is a gigantic eagle."

"Well maybe it's... a bit of a...mistake, sir."

"It certainly is. I'll not have it terrorising my villages, Sir Gabriel. The creature has made a definite mistake there!"

"Are you going to go home to Bedwyn and...?"

"No, Sir Gabriel, *you are*. Find this thing, if it's real, and deal with it."

"You want me to go to Bedwyn, sir?"

"It's Christmas, young man, in a few days. *I'm* not going anywhere."

"Yes sir."

Gabriel walked down the stairs and out into the courtyard of Great Chalfield Manor. With a huge grin on his face, he took a quick step to the side, lifted off and clicked his heels together.

"Yes!" He was going back to Bedwyn. Back to Mabel.

Things had turned out well after all.

CHAPTER TWO
~ HUNTING THE GRYPHON ~

All the tedious journey to Bedwyn, Gabriel mused upon the beast which he was supposed to locate and which it was his task to despatch. He felt like St. George in the mummer's plays he'd seen.

How do you catch a gryphon?

He knew that in order to trap a unicorn one had to have a virgin sit and wait for them. The beast would then come and lay his head in her lap and you could either kill him or bind him with ropes. That a dragon might be tempted into capture with a pile of gold, was well known. And everyone knew that a basilisk would do your will if you gave them eggs. Yes, they were very fond of eggs. And then you'd need a weasel. A basilisk was really afraid of weasels!

But a gryphon? How do you even get near a fire breathing gryphon? As far as Gabriel knew, the gryphon didn't breathe fire. This was an odd detail supplied apparently, in the letter to Lord Stokke, by the steward and the reeve of Bedwyn village. They had definitely seen it breathing fire.

"What did its ears look like?" asked Gabriel when he reached Bedwyn and managed to find the reeve, Master Head.

"Oh the ears, Sir Gabriel? Erm... well, they were like a falcon's ears I suppose, sir."

"You're sure?"

"Well I wasn't... none of us were really looking at its ears. Why do you ask, sir?"

"I need to know what sort of beast I'm dealing with. The gryphon usually has the head of a falcon but you all say that it sported the head of a lion."

"A lion head, with large falcon ears and the body of a bird of prey— sir," said Master Corngold, coming up.

"With large talons," said Mistress Peabody.

Gabriel knew that Matilda Peabody was as blind as a mouldwarp in a mist. It had been proven in his previous visits. *She* could not be relied upon.

Gabriel fingered his shaven chin. "Hmmm." He needed to find Mabel. She would have a much better idea than these clod heads.

He located her in the linen store of the manor. He peered around the open door.

"I thought I'd find you here."

Mabel jumped. "Sir Gabriel! What brings you here?"

"Ah well!"

"Oh, I know. Our beast, I suppose?"

"Did you see it?"

"The head of a lion, the body of a falcon and the wings of a dragon?"

"You did see it!"

"Look Gabriel, there's something I have to tell you."

"Yeeeesss"

"The villagers are not lying."

"Good Lord! There really was such a beast?"

Gabriel swallowed. He was hoping that he'd be able to report to Lord Stokke that the thing was a figment of many imaginations. He really hadn't fancied tackling a gryphon.

"Yes, there was such a beast."

"Has it been back?"

Mabel folded a tablecloth. "Er no... no, it hasn't. It flew off over the forest."

"YOU saw it then?"

"Erm... Look I am a bit busy at the moment. If you come to my cottage later, I'll tell you all about it."

Gabriel looked at Mabel under his eyebrows. She looked back at him, carefully studying his face with its pale pink scar which travelled from the corner of his eye to the edge of his mouth.

She'd done a good job, she thought, of tidying him up after a rogue shape shifting wolf had attacked him and ruined his good looks. But to Mabel, he was still the handsome knight he had been when she'd first met him. The scar on his face did not diminish him in any way in her eyes.

There was a little puckering around the edge of the top lip and you could hardly see the marks where the stitches had gone in.

Gabriel saw a woman of diminutive stature with light brown to blonde hair tied up in a cap. Little tendrils of it escaped at her neck and the knight longed to touch them and fold them back into her head cloth. Mabel was twenty two; not particularly beautiful but she had an interesting face and pretty eyes and the sweetest snub nose he'd ever seen. Looking at her face made his heart constrict. He'd never felt this with anyone else he'd ever known.

She took up another piece of linen to fold. "I'll see you later."

"Mabel," Gabriel cleared his throat. "Does this thing really exist?"

She smiled at him and his heart gave another lurch. "Oh yes—it's real."

He narrowed his eyes. There was something about the way she'd said that.

"And you have to find it don't you?"

"Well. The Lord Stokke has tasked me with finding it and—with—disposing of it."

"Oh, that's very dangerous. Did they tell you it breathes fire?"

"Erm yes—they did," he said in worried tones.

"It might take you quite a time to find it…"

"I don't have any idea where to look."

Mabel pursed her lips. "I can probably help you there," she said.

"Look it's going to be dark soon..." said Sir Gabriel, "I've ridden thirty miles on potholed roads without food..."

"Then go into the hall and eat with the steward. I'll see you afterwards and then I'll tell you all about it."

*****

Half a furlong, half a cubit and half an inch away from the manor, Mabel was worrying.

They had not embraced. Gabriel had given her no peck on the cheek as he'd done before. He hadn't taken her hand. Not a crumb of affection had he shown her. Oh, perhaps he was having second thoughts about her.

All through her meagre supper, sitting in her house, she worried that he no longer cared about her. The last time he'd seen her, he'd kissed her. Properly. She really had thought that he loved her and now, just under three months later, he was behaving like a stranger.

She *so* wanted to keep him in Bedwyn.

She so wanted to find out if he still felt the same way about her.

The same way she felt about him.

'Oh you are an idiot, Mabel. He's a knight and you're a manor employee. —as different as wind from water—of course he doesn't love you.'

There was a scratch on her door and Gabriel called out. "Mistress Wetherspring?"

Oh how formal he was being. Her poor heart wobbled and she almost cried out. But at last she said, "Yes, Sir Gabriel." Well, two could play at that game.

He came in unbuckling and folding his sword belt, "I thought you might be dining in hall tonight."

"No, no I wanted to be here alone for a while," she said.

Gabriel lowered himself to the fireside stool with a huge sigh. "Aw... I am so tired."

"It's a long way to ride in one day."

"I stopped off at Cherhill for something to drink and to let my Bertran drink too and rest. I didn't push him."

"The road, I'm told, isn't good at the moment—lots of potholes and obstructions."

Bertran was Gabriel's beautiful pale buff, Flemish horse. He wasn't particularly built for speed but was good over many miles without rest.

"It was hard going over the Avebury downs but not too bad, all in all."

Mabel got up and poured ale for Sir Gabriel. She handed him a pottery mug and their hands brushed.

"You... you have been sent by the Lord Stokke?" said Mabel, pushing her hair behind her ears. In her own home, she wore no head cloth.

"You know I have."

"Are you really going to stay and look for it?"

"You say it's real. I must see if I can find out if it's been terrorising any other places locally. It can't just have been seen here, surely."

"Erm... Sir Gabriel?"

"Yes Mabel?"

Mabel had turned over in her mind the fact that she was desperate to keep Sir Gabriel here in Bedwyn. The longer he looked for the beast, the longer he would stay and she could have his company—at least at some part of the day. It was coming up to Christmas. How nice it would be to celebrate the season with him. She had thought that she could lead him astray a bit; make him search hither and thither for the gryphon but once she had him sitting in front of her, in her own home, she found she couldn't lie to him.

Then she realised he had not used her title—mistress. He'd just called her Mabel and she felt much better.

"Gabriel. The beast *was* real."

"Was...?"

"It was me."

Gabriel suddenly slapped his knee and made her jump. "I knew it!"

"What d'you mean—you knew it?"

He was chuckling loudly.

"How did you know it?"

"The body of a falcon, the head of a lion."

"What?"

"The gryphon is a creature with the body of a lion and the head of a falcon. You got it the wrong way round."

"Well, I had no idea the beast actually exists. I just... wanted to make up something interesting."

"Oh, Mabel!"

"I had no idea I was going to be seen and that they'd make such a fuss about it." And so she told him how she had come to be a gryphon.

"A flying pig! Hahaha. What a thing!"

"And then I thought, what if I tried something a bit more interesting. I had no notion at the time if it would work."

"Oh it worked—better than you ever thought it would," said Gabriel with a snigger.

"It was such fun but I didn't mean to terrify people or make the lord send you..." (Oh yes she did!)

"Well, I have never been so glad that I don't have to fight what amounts to a fire breathing dragon!" said Gabriel. "Part of me was hoping that it would all be a misunderstanding."

"Oh no. It was real. I really *was* the beast and I just couldn't help flying about a bit... and breathing fire."

Gabriel's mouth drew into a grin and he laughed again. "The gryphon doesn't breathe fire as far as I know, Mabel. What made you do that?"

"I have no idea—it was an accident."

"Oh, Mabel." He leapt up and embraced her. "It's good to be back."

"But now you won't stay. You'll go back to Chalfield."

"I'll stay a couple of days and maybe I'll pretend to go about looking for the creature."

"What will you tell Lord Stokke?"

"I'll have to tell him that it's moved on elsewhere and that I was unable to locate it."

"It's Christmas Eve tomorrow. You can't go back until Christmas is over—surely?"

Gabriel rubbed his tired face. "I'll think about it," he said, smiling sweetly at her.

*****

Christmas Eve dawned dull and windy. Mabel ran from her cottage to the manor hall to make sure all was well there for the Christmas celebrations. The lord was not in residence but the steward insisted that they still observe as much of the Christmastide as was possible.

The yule log was stored by the large central fire ready to be hoisted onto the embers of the last fire, by two hefty lads. The napery for the tables was clean, bright white and starched stiff as a spear—Mabel's job. Holly and ivy had been twined around every available post and beam early that morning. Mabel had supervised that too. And food would be plentiful for everyone. Mabel and the cooks had seen to that, for Mabel was housekeeper at Bedwyn Manor.

One thing they could not do, though, was go to church, for no religious Christmas celebration was allowed during the Interdict. It seemed a dereliction of duty somehow, to Mabel.

Sir Gabriel Warrener was in conversation with the cook and she approached the knight quietly. "Forgive me sir, but you asked me to come and show you where the fiery beast disappeared into the forest," she said, her eyes cast down demurely .

Gabriel cleared his throat. "Ah, Mistress Wetherspring. Yes. That would be most kind. Let us go—erm—monster hunting."

Gabriel took up his spear, had Bertran saddled and they walked off along the lane into the trees to the far side of Mabel's garth, towing his horse. If anyone had been listening they would have heard her say, "Here is where the beast disappeared into the forest, sir. I tracked it a further half a mile or so."

"Good, then we shall take the same path and see if it has left us any clues as to its whereabouts."

When they were a few more hundred yards into the trees, they fell about laughing.

"This is the strangest thing I have ever hunted. A gryphon which isn't a gryphon..."

"...Which isn't a gryphon but a woman."

"No one can ever say you are not extraordinary, Mabel," said Gabriel with a chuckle. "I have never been out hunting a gryphon with a girl before now!"

"Oh—and what have you been doing when you are out with a girl, pray, Sir Gabriel?"

He gave her a sidelong look. "You know full well that the sorts of girls I get to be involved with, never get the chance to go out into the forest—with anyone."

"Oh what a sheltered life they lead."

"Let alone be on their own with a man."

Mabel found a mossy log and sat down.

"Has your father said anything further about you marrying, Sir Gabriel?" she said suddenly. It was something which had been bothering her ever since she'd seen him again.

"I haven't seen him since you and I last met."

"Oh."

"Maybe it's for the best."

"Ah."

"That I haven't seen him."

An unseen fist seemed to tighten around the place where Mabel supposed her heart lay and that organ began to beat more rapidly. "Why is that?"

Gabriel plonked himself down beside her and laid down what passed for his gryphon hunting spear.

What Gabriel really wanted to say was, "Mabel, I cannot marry anyone else when I am so in love with you. If I marry, you will be my bride."

What he actually said was, "I have decided that I will not marry."

"Oh…" The fist let go of her heart and the blood rushed to her face. She looked away so that he might not see her flushing. "Not marry Agnes...de…The lady you are contracted to marry...?"

"de Gers. No, not marry anyone."

Mabel couldn't believe her ears. "But he will be angry, very angry," she said. "Your father…"

"Then let him be angry. And pass the estate to my little brother, if he will. I don't care."

"But, but... how will you…?"

"My father is in the pink of health. He will endure, I'm sure, for many more years. Things can change. We shall see what happens. But in the meantime, I will not marry."

Now the hand had hold of her heart again.

"Not marry anyone?"

"Not marry anyone."

"Oh."

"Unless…"

"Unless?"

Jumping up he caught her hand and pulled her up to stand before him. "Unless I can achieve fame and fortune by killing a gryphon and become feted throughout the land and rich to boot."

"Then you would have to kill me," she said laughing.

"That, Mabel Wetherspring, I shall never do."

He stooped and kissed her on the lips. "I would defend you to the last drop of my blood."

She looked up at him. "Oh Gabriel."

"I think pigs will be seen flying should I ever hurt you." They laughed together, standing in the forest with the wind roaring above them in the treetops. It sounded like a storm at the sea strand, the angry waves pulling the pebbles of the beach to and fro.

"Come, let's walk around a bit. Where does that lead?"

"That goes towards Chisbury. It's an old fortress. There was a small village there until recently. But now it's deserted. The folk were all killed."

"Killed?"

Mabel giggled. "Oh no! Not by a monster, although they *were* monsters. Men monsters. Some of the routiers from the castle at Marlborough, I heard—the King's men—they are devils in disguise. The King hanged them all. And now, of course, the place is haunted. Isn't it?"

"Ghosts don't worry me," said Gabriel, taking up his trusty spear again, "It's the living we should fear. Shall we ride to Chisbury to look for our gryphon?"

He pulled her up onto Bertran to ride pillion and they clopped gently along the narrow lane, the horse's hooves ringing on the hard ground. Not once did they see any evidence of the passage of the gryphon.

After almost an hour, they reached a rampart, obviously a remnant of a high wall made from earth and turf. They walked around the fortress and found an entrance which had once, no doubt, been a gateway. A steep approach road led them up into the round enclosure.

"That will have been a large gate once. And here and here, there would have been palings sunk into the ground to form an impenetrable fence." Gabriel pointed.

"Not a castle then?"

"Not as we know it.

"I have heard that the Saxons used it as a burgh and it fell out of use after that," said Mabel.

Gabriel walked around the flat enclosure. Bertran began to sidle and be nervous. "It's alright boy—there's nothing here to hurt you."

Mabel looked around and scanned the trees to the edge of the rampart. "Do you feel we are being watched?"

"No. But you do?"

"I do. And so does Bertran, I think."

"His ears are much more sensitive than ours. He hears voices on the wind."

"Perhaps it's the voices of those poor people hacked down here a few years ago," whispered Mabel.

"Do you hear anything?"

Mabel closed her eyes. "No. But just wait here." She made for a stand of ash clinging tenaciously to the edge of the ramparts and lifting her arms, spun three times to withershynnes. "I wish to be a sparrowhawk."

Gabriel watched as the bird came out of the trees and gained height, circling the ramparts and piercing the place with the stare of its all-seeing yellow eyes.

It took but a matter of moments. And then Mabel was back again, striding across the open space in the middle of the ramparts.

"Someone—I cannot tell who but it was most definitely human. It ran in and out of the trees and I could not follow too closely, for the branches were too close together for safe flying."

"So someone has followed us?"

"Perhaps they have, or maybe they were already here," said Mabel.

"I hope they didn't see you."

"Even if they did, by the way they moved, they did not want it known they'd been here. They won't say anything, I'm sure or they'd have to admit their own presence here."

"Could you tell if it was a man or woman?" asked Gabriel.

"Woman. With brown hair flying free."

"That means she is unmarried."

"Or a *young* woman."

"What can be the draw of this place to a lone woman?"

"Most people I know would avoid the place even if it meant going a further distance to get round it. It has a bad reputation."

"But where would they be going?"

"Stype, perhaps?"

"Where is that?"

"It's a village that way, about two miles. Only a few folk live there now."

Gabriel laughed and his voice echoed around the natural amphitheatre of the enclosure, "Is everywhere around here deserted?"

"Or they might be going to Bedwyn, of course. There are very few places close by."

They walked to the northern edge of the ramparts and looked out over downland as far as they could see.

"This is almost as far as the trees go. Over there is the road to Ramsbury," said Mabel, pointing. Then we are out of Wiltshire and into Berkshire."

"What's that?"

"Ah, that's the remains of the manor which used to lie here. It was burned down with the raiders—what was left of it."

A shiver went through her as she said this. Could she see the shadow of a man upon the manor wall or was it merely a plant clinging to the stones?

Gabriel was off down the vertiginous slope. "Mind how you go, it's steep here and if you fall you'll hurt yourself badly on the stones," he said.

He picked his way down the scree laden slope, sliding now and again and laughed as a fox nimbly passed him and landed safely at the bottom.

"Mabel Wetherspring, that's cheating!"

"Four legs are better than—oh!"

Gabriel reached her and followed her gaze. "What were you saying about legs?"

Mabel stared with horrified round eyes.

Just inside the ruined walls of the manor, what must once have been the main hall, was a body.

The legs were visible just outside the masonry and they were shapely and smooth, the kirtle being drawn up. But the head was not shapely or smooth.

Someone had taken a large stone, which had fallen from the walls, and had repeatedly hit the woman, so that it was hardly possible to see who she'd been. And strangely, very strangely, someone had covered her face with leaves. Large plantain leaves. There were a few leaves on plants growing in the location even in December.

"Someone did a good job of trying to disguise who she was by beating her features to a pulp," said Gabriel leaning over the corpse.

Mabel turned her face into his chest as he righted himself.

"*I* know who she is," she said, "but I haven't seen her for about six years! She was beautiful with perfect skin and an elegant long neck but I have to say, she isn't beautiful any longer."

CHAPTER THREE

~ GELLE ~

Master Lovegrove sat in his cottage and watched his only girl stirring the pottage pot.

Godyth looked up and smiled. Oh my! How like her mother she is, he thought.

Phillip Lovegrove had once had a wife. But she had run away years ago leaving him with five children to care for.

The eldest had been a boy, William, but he had died shortly after his mother left. They found the eight year old floating in the river one day. Then six months later Agnes, his daughter, four, was found in the barn having eaten deadly nightshade berries. She didn't survive. This left his third daughter Nalle who was bitten by a dog and died of a fever a while later, Henry aged three and Godyth who at the time had been five. Henry was now a strapping lad of nine and Godyth was a very useful and capable eleven.

How had he managed all those years? Through all the heartbreak. The shock of knowing that your beautiful wife had gone off to live with another man had been devastating. By all accounts she'd gone to live with a potter from Froxfield but rumours grew that she soon tired of him and was living on the edge of Ramsbury, alone in a rather ramshackle house to which men were invited for money. Oh the shame of it! His beautiful wife, Gelle, a woman of ill repute, living off immoral earnings.

Even though as a tied villein he was forbidden to leave the area, early on he'd tried to find her; indeed he had located and visited her but she just spat at him, told him to leave her alone and had thrown him out. She was happy with her new life. How was it possible to be happy with such a life?

He'd given his remaining children the best he could but life was hard and his children were forced to be old before their time. They'd had no real childhood, as much as a peasant's offspring might have a childhood. They all had to grow up quickly and help with the family plot and animals. All peasant children did but his children had to do so without a mother.

Phillip Lovegrove rose from his seat, downed his ale and went out into the open to tend his master's fields as he was duty bound to do.

Coming towards him he saw, in the distance, Mistress Wetherspring, the manor housekeeper and a man in a light blue surcoat with some pattern on it. He screwed up his eyes. Ah yes, it was that knight fellow, come to the village to investigate the sighting of the Beast of Bedwyn, (as it was becoming known). He looked up at the sky. Master Lovegrove hadn't seen it but he had no doubt it had been real. Life was like that, full of horrible things.

"Master Phillip!" called out Mabel. "Might we have a word?"

"Aye—a word if you must," said the man who was not known for his verbosity. Nor his friendliness.

"When did you last see your wife?" asked the knight.

Phillip Lovegrove's face creased into perplexity. "My wife—Gelle? Several years ago, sir—why?"

"We have some sad news," said Mabel.

"Her body was found today at Chisbury manor. She has been murdered," said Gabriel. "I am so sorry to be the bearer of such awful information."

The man looked from one face to another. His surroundings faded, the light of the day grew dark and he measured his length upon the dusty earth of the field, in a faint.

*****

It didn't take long to get all around the village that Gelle Lovegrove had been murdered. People speculated, as people are bound to do. An irate customer had killed her? A jealous wife, perhaps? All the old enmities were dragged up out of the dim and distant past. Oh yes. Master Stock of Stock Farm had had a thing for her, hadn't he? She had rebuffed him and he'd been very angry; given her a wallop or two. But that hadn't killed her, just blacked her eye. Mabel had heard he was a nasty bugger, though she didn't know him, indeed had never met him.

Then their close neighbour, Master Fulltooth had also had a fling with her, hadn't he? His wife had put a stop to that. They all knew that Master Fulltooth was a battered husband. Marian Fulltooth was very handy with her distaff. She could often be heard laying into him, yelling at him and him begging her for mercy, cottage walls and doors being thin.

The body of Gelle Lovegrove was viewed by the coroner. Gabriel and Mabel gave their version of finding the corpse and made a statement to Sir Aumary Belvoir, the local constable. What a thing to happen on a Christmas Eve. It was a Christmas eve no one would forget in a hurry.

The husband, no doubt, would be spoken to. The children too. And her mother, the dead woman's mother who also lived in Bedwyn and who often helped out in the home with the children, she would be questioned. But the authorities couldn't do anything immediately, for it was Christmas and a holiday. For twelve days. And after all, the woman was an unfree peasant. And a runaway. She had no rights.

Mabel and Gabriel sat in her cottage and mulled over the day. Mabel turned her face up to Gabriel. "I knew it was her as soon as I saw her hair. Her hair was very curly, dark and long. Very distinctive."

"What was she doing out there?"

"Living there apparently. She'd been evicted from her home in Ramsbury."

"So someone paid her a visit there at the derelict manor and…"

"That was the end of her," said Mabel mournfully.

They sat in silence for a moment. "Of course, people will say that the place did not want her there and took its revenge."

"What? How can a place…?" said Gabriel in amusement.

"You know what people are like. They love tales of ghosts and demons and…"

"Fabulous beasts…?" said Gabriel with a chuckle. "They are bound to want to think that there's some otherworldly cause to her death. But it was someone with a rock so—altogether human."

"She was a strange woman. Even when she lived here in Bedwyn, she was—strange."

"In what way?"

"She would make eyes at any man she could. She wasn't fussy. Though, I'm told, she really seemed to hate Master Stock out at Stock Farm. She was unfocussed and wild. It seemed she had no affection for her children, none of them. She would leave them to her mother—and her brother. And she was very… far away, as if she didn't belong. Like she was riding the wind."

"She had a brother?"

"Still has. He's a little bit… odd too."

"In what way?" asked Gabriel, lifting his ale pot to his lips.

"Not very bright. He is still in the village, perhaps we should go and speak to him. He lives with their mother close by the large barn. You can see him for yourself."

"I'll have to write to Lord Stokke to tell him that I'm staying. And that I haven't found the fiery beast and I need to tell him about the murder."

"It's not going to be our job to…"

"I know what you're about to say—not our job to look into this woman's death. It's never our job—but we do it," he grinned.

"Well, she was one of the lord's villeins, albeit one who absconded. He did try to bring her back but she just kept moving. In the end he gave up. She was almost feral."

Mabel threw another few twigs on the fire. "Should we be investigating murder, at Christmas?"

"You don't think it's a good time to do it? When everyone is at home for the holiday?" said Gabriel.

"I suppose so."

"Tomorrow we shall speak to all the family. See what they know." He stood up to leave.

"Oh—you're going—so early?" said Mabel.

"It's supper time. I don't want to miss the manor Christmas Eve supper. It's usually a good spread."

"I'll come with you," said Mabel, thinking, 'Don't thank me. It's only because of me you can eat so well!'

Men and their stomachs!.

*****

Meanwhile, twelve furlongs, twelve feet and twelve inches away in a deserted part of the forest a man was pacing back and forth between his inadequate fire and his ill-fitting door.

He slammed his fist onto the table top.

'She wasn't meant to be found. Her body was supposed to lie there and be pecked clean by kites and foxes. No one was supposed to find her, let alone recognise her.'

He screamed up to the heavens in rage but no one heard him. Certainly not Heaven.

He ground his teeth. He blasphemed.

'Well, that was how it was. So now he'd have to change his plans. That stupid girl. Why did she have to fiddle with her body? He'd get even and then he'd go away again. And no one would ever find him.'

*****

The body of Gelle Lovegrove was brought into Bedwyn late on Christmas Eve. It was sad to watch the procession by torchlight slowly winding its way along the main street.

Where would they take the body? Her husband had told them he would not have it in his house. The mother in shocked and whispered tones had told the steward that neither would it defile her house.

They had to put Gelle Lovegrove into an outhouse and there she had to stay until she could be buried.

Gabriel and Mabel wandered along the road on Christmas Day and coming towards them at a fast pace was a large man with a short, mucky, golden beard and a grimacing mouth.

"I want to see her!" he yelled at them with a sob.

"The brother," mouthed Mabel silently.

"I want to see her—she's my little sister."

"Ah, Master…" began Gabriel.

"Eadric—Eadric Ceorlson," said Mabel. "They are an old Saxon family. They've been here for centuries."

"Well at least someone cares for her," said Gabriel from the corner of his mouth before the man reached them.

Ceorlson was strong and tried to throw off Gabriel's grip.

"Ah Master Ceorlson, we are just coming to see you." Gabriel turned him back the way he'd come.

"Eadric—you know me. Mabel Wetherspring."

"Aye. Aye…"

"Come let's go back to your house and we can talk."

"I want to see her!"

"Believe me, Eadric, you don't. I was the one to discover her, we both were and you don't want to see her until the women have laid her out for her grave."

Mabel put a friendly hand on his arm and he nodded, his eyes red and puffy.

"Come, let's go back to your mother's."

*****

"Have you any idea who might have done this to your daughter, to your sister?"

The two relations sat immovable by the fire and said nothing.

"People are saying that—that Gelle had many men friends."

"She was a whore!" The mother suddenly burst out. "She ate men like some people eat cherries, and spat out their souls like cherry stones."

"Aw ma..." said Eadric, tears in his eyes.

"It's the truth."

"She has... had children, didn't she?"

"Two left. Godyth and Henry," said the mother with a sudden softness to her voice. "They both wanted to be here with me last evening and night," she said. "Henry has gone back to his father now but Godyth is still here. She's asleep in the loft. She s been here all last evening and night."

"Can you call her down?"

The woman looked at Gabriel as if his request had asked her to call down the moon.

"She doesn't know what has happened. Neither of them do. We just said—that something was wrong with their mother."

"Did they ever see her?"

"No—of course not."

Eadric had risen and went to the end of the cottage where a small ladder gave access to a loft.

He climbed it slowly.

There was a mumbled conversation and then a scream, an agonised scream and sobbing. A child came tumbling down the ladder and threw herself at her grandmother.

Mabel and Gabriel waited until the girl had stopped crying. Mabel found it hard not to intervene and take the poor child in her arms. Eadric hovered around, stepping from foot to foot, not knowing what to do.

"Godyth, you know me..." said Mabel quietly at last. "You remember, I live up by the big oak, on the other side of the river?"

The girl's face came up and her grandmother pushed away her hair. The same long dark curly hair that her mother had.

"I want me ma."

"What do you want *her* for?" said Mistress Ceorlson sharply. "She's never been any good to you."

"I want me ma."

Gabriel cleared his throat. "Godyth, my name is Sir Gabriel Warrener. I work for our lord Stokke..."

Suddenly the girl jumped up dry eyed. "I don't want to speak to you!"

Mabel stood up straight. "We know that this has been a shock, Godyth but that is no reason to be rude to Sir Gabriel."

"I don't want to speak to you either," said the girl with venom in her voice.

Her grandmother wound her arms around the child. "Come, let's take you back to your father. Henry will be there." She nodded to Gabriel and Mabel and exited the cottage.

"We shall get nothing from her for a while I suppose," said Gabriel, turning to Master Ceorlson. "It's been such a shock to her," he added,

"Did you know if your sister had any particular men friends?" asked Mabel.

"No."

"Had she any enemies, do you think?"

"Everyone loves her."

"Ah—don't think that is entirely true, Master Ceorlson," said Gabriel.

"Oh I know what you think of her because of the way she lived her life."

"No…"

"Everyone who knew her loved her."

"I know that you were once very close to her, Eadric," said Mabel. "Did you see her at all nowadays?"

"Now and again."

"When was the last time?" asked Gabriel.

The man cast his eyes up to the rafters. "Three days ago."

"Did she seem worried or upset?"

"No."

"Did her husband, Master Lovegrove, see her at all?"

"No, not him. Not usually."

"You seem very sure."

"She called Godyth's father a—a devil."

"Master Lovegrove? A devil?" said Mabel. "That's hard to believe."

"Aye—she called Godyth's father a devil."

Gabriel and Mabel looked at each other.

"Eadric, did Gelle think that her husband—was a wicked man, then?"

"No—he's a good man. He loved her—he loved her so much. Even when she left him, he was kind to her."

"Ah."

"It'll kill him this…"

"I am sure it will," said Mabel.

"My sister was—lovely…"

"Yes, I remember her. She was very beautiful," said Mabel. "But I do remember that she was—a little unreliable. She was, wasn't she, if you are honest?"

"Her mind was fragile—she couldn't live—live…"

"I know. I do remember. The priest tried to help her, didn't he?"

"They had to lock her up a couple of times."

Gabriel looked strangely at Eadric. "Lock her up—why? What had she done?"

"She used to cut herself and burn herself," said Eadric. "She couldn't help it."

Mabel turned Gabriel to face her and whispered. "If you look at the body, you'll find evidence of the harm she did to herself over the years, I'm sure."

"Well, yes—but she can't have hit herself on the head, can she?" he whispered.

"She was only a threat to herself," said Eadric as a tear rolled down his cheek.

"Never to her children?"

"No, never!"

Mabel sat down on a stool again. She felt more in control if she was seated. "Where was she living? Was it out at Chisbury, where we found her?"

"She'd only been there a few days. I don't know where she'd been before that." Eadric's voice was getting fainter and fainter.

"How did you know where she was?"

"She came to Bedwyn."

"Why did she come home, Eadric?" said Mabel.

"To—to—to tell Master Lovegrove to stop letting Godyth come to see her. She didn't want to see her. She pestered her."

"Master Lovegrove told us that he hadn't seen Gelle for years."

"Well, that—that—that wasn't exactly true."

"And what did little Godyth think about that? That her mother had told her she wasn't wanted."

The man screwed up his face in sadness. "I don't know—I don't know."

"Did she ever see her son, Henry?"

"Henry didn't want to see her. Only Godyth."

"And your mother didn't know, did she, that Godyth visited Gelle."

"No—no we kept that from her."

Gabriel was making his way to the door. "Well if there's anything else you remember, come to the manor and…"

"Eadric. Did you kill your sister?" said Mabel suddenly.

The man burst out crying. "I loved her...!" was all they could hear amongst the wails and gulps.

"Well, that told us very little," said Gabriel when they were at last out of the door.

"On the contrary, if Eadric is correct, we know Master Lovegrove lied to us. And why would he do that?"

"He saw his wife recently?"

"We need to speak to him again."

It was beginning to drizzle, as they made their way from the house by the barn to Master Lovegrove's house on the lane by the river.

"I think it would be a good idea if I went and listened in to a few family conversations later. You never know what I might pick up," said Mabel.

"Which houses?"

"The Lovegroves, the Fulltooths, anyone else with a connection to Gelle Lovegrove."

"I'd like to go back to Chisbury and poke around the place where we found her."

"The coroner will have done that," said Mabel. "I suspect any evidence we might have been able to gather will have been ruined by the presence of the coroner's men or the constable."

"With your hawk eyes—we might find something that they've missed."

"Oh—so you want me to be a hawk, do you?"

"As long as you don't have the head of a lion and breathe fire—you can be whatever bird you like," said Gabriel with a sarcastic smile.

*****

Godyth was sitting with Master Lovegrove at the family table. Her grandma was close by and Henry was feeding the fire with twigs.

Lovegrove immediately jumped up and put his hand out for

Godyth. She came to him willingly and nestled into his side.

"Why do we have to speak to these people?" she said roughly. "I don't want to speak to these people."

"I would say the same thing." Lovegrove stepped forward and jutted his chin pugnaciously. "What gives you the right, Mistress Wetherspring, to come into our home at Christmas—the sacred time of Christmas—and question us?"

Gabriel put his hand onto the pommel of his sword. "By the authority invested in us by our lord and master, Lord Robert Stokke, Lovegrove. I'm sure I don't have to remind you that he is master of us all here—free man or serf."

Lovegrove subsided.

"He has tasked Mistress Wetherspring and me with trying to find out what happened to your wife." It wasn't entirely true but Lovegrove wasn't to know. "You want to know that—don't you?"

The man was silent.

"Right. Can you tell us when you last saw your mother, Godyth?"

The girl's head came up quickly as if she had been startled by the question. Mabel was certain she *had* been startled. She had not expected to be questioned.

"I…"

"Just answer the knight, Godyth," said her father in a surly tone.

"I saw her yesterday."

Master Lovegrove flinched but remained silent.

"And what happened when you saw her?" said Mabel gently.

"I—tore my kirtle—I don't know how…"

"It's a difficult climb isn't it, up into the Chisbury ring and hard going down again to the old manor house?" said Mabel, trying to encourage the child to speak.

"I tore it and got muddy. So I had to wash it in the brook."

'Hmm' thought Mabel, 'there was no mud when we were there.'

"Did you see her?"

"Aye I did."

"What did she say?" asked Gabriel.

Godyth looked towards her father.

"Answer the man, girl," he said gruffly.

"She clipped me round me ear fer getting messy then told me to go away. She was busy. She didn't want to see me."

Mabel flashed a look at Gabriel. He'd got a surprised look on his face.

"And did that make you feel bad, Godyth?" he asked.

The girl shrugged. "She told me to go home to my grannie or find uncle Ed."

"And so you did?"

"I did." Brown eyes looked defiantly into Mabel's.

"Did anyone know you'd been missing?"

"I came back here. There was no one here then."

"So no one, not even your father knew you'd been to see your mother?"

Once more the brown eyes didn't waver.

"I went to grannie's and only uncle Ed was there. He was drunk. He's always drunk. He was telling me how he loved my mother. He's daft."

Swiftly, Mabel touched Gabriel's knee under the table.

"Sir—might I have a word—outside?"

"What?"

"A word."

"Ah yes—alright.

They stood a few yards away from the door and Mabel whispered.

"I saw her, Gabriel."

"What?"

"It was her—she was running away."

"No, she was at her grandma's. She was asleep in the loft. We know that."

"It was her. I saw her, remember? I just couldn't identify her at the time. But now I can. She was at Chisbury."

Gabriel paced around a little. He seemed angry but Mabel knew it was worry. Worry and uncertainty of a sort.

"Right. Let's take her out right away and speak to her alone," he said finally.

"Do you think her father will let us?"

"I'm telling you, Mabel—he has no choice."

They went back into the cottage.

"I'd like Godyth to come with us outside, Master Lovegrove," said Mabel. "We need a word with her on her own."

Mabel took hold of Godyth's sleeve. She saw where it had been torn and muddied and had been washed.

Lovegrove suddenly leapt up. "You say nothing to them, Goddy, do you hear me—nothing."

Mistress Ceorlson put a hand on his arm.

Gabriel held him back and stood at the door. "Speak to her alone," he said to Mabel.

"Say nothing? What does your father mean 'say nothing', Godyth?" asked Mabel as she walked the girl across the road to the river. With her back to the stream and Mabel in front of her, she felt that the child was unlikely to try and escape. But for good measure she held onto the sleeve of her threadbare yellow brown kirtle.

"What must you say nothing about?"

The large brown eyes slid from Mabel's face. "I—don't know."

"Oh I think you do."

"No, I don't!" She lurched forward and pushed Mabel sharply in her middle. Mabel wasn't expecting this and she staggered back. She was only a small woman and Godyth, even though she was only eleven, was actually taller and bigger than Mabel. The child ran down the river bank lane and disappeared by Master Stephen Meadow's house. From there she could easily be away over the fields.

"She's gone," said Mabel when she re-entered the house.

Lovegrove breathed out. "She'll be back when she gets hungry, I suppose," he said.

'That was definitely relief, that sigh,' thought Mabel.

"We have just been talking about the day Gelle came to see Master Lovegrove, haven't we, Phillip?"

The man gave Gabriel an angry stare. "I don't remember."

"She came to see you to tell you to make Godyth—little Godyth—stop visiting her. Why would she do that? Eh?"

"She was a wicked and unnatural mother," said Lovegrove. "She never loved any of our children."

"That's true, sir," said Mistress Ceorlson, speaking for the first time.

"Is that why she ran away? Because she felt she couldn't be a good mother to your five children? There were five at the time she left, weren't there?" said Gabriel.

"She left me with five small children, the youngest was only three. She never wanted to see any of them again."

"And now there are only two left."

Henry came to stand at his father's side. "Father loves us both," he said defiantly.

"I am sure he does, Henry," said Mabel, smiling. "He only has you and your sister left now. He's looked after you well."

The boy nodded exaggeratedly.

"You never saw your mother once she'd gone, did you?"

"I was out workin' when she came that time. Only da saw her. And Godyth."

"Ah—so she *did* come to see you, Master Lovegrove? When was that then?" asked Gabriel.

Phillip Lovegrove gave a despairing look at his son. It basically said. 'You and your big mouth!'

"When was this, Master Lovegrove?" asked Mabel, sitting at the table and putting out her hands to within an inch of Phillip Lovegrove's.

She hoped the gesture would calm him. Maybe make him think that she was on his side. He snatched his hands away.

"The last time I saw her was—Samhain. She came, the witch, to torment me. On the evening of the rising of the dead, she came to torment me."

"What did she want?"

"She said she was going away—further away—and that I wasn't to try to find her and I wasn't to let Godyth find her. And she wanted money."

"What happened?" said Gabriel.

"I threw her out and barred the door."

"And you weren't here, Henry?"

He shook his head.

"Can I go now? I have things to do." Without a look at his father and no word spoken, but a face like thunder, he left.

"Six years—six years and suddenly she turns up on my doorstep."

"How did that make you feel?" asked Mabel.

"Angry."

Gabriel stood up taller. "Angry?"

"The woman had made me a cuckold over and over. How do you think it made me feel? Laughed at, for six years whilst she went about like a wanton..."

"Oh I don't think your friends here in the village thought ill of you because of Gelle's behaviour," began Mabel. "But..."

"What would *you* know?"

After this Master Lovegrove would say nothing further. He folded his arms and sat silently staring at the wall.

Gabriel and Mabel walked slowly towards her cottage.

"I might learn more, simply by eavesdropping."

"Tonight, when they are all together, see what they talk about," said Gabriel.

Suddenly there was a shout. A panicked shout. It echoed over the meadow at the back of Stephen's cottage and close by the church.

"That sounded like a child," said Gabriel.

"When she left me, Godyth ran that way." Mabel picked up her skirts and ran.

It took them both a mere heartbeat or two to reach the churchyard.

"Godyth!" shouted Mabel searching the ground about. "She can't be in the church, it's locked."

"It might not be her."

But Mabel knew there were no other children at this end of the village and there were certainly none playing out in the road or round and about.

The two of them dashed frantically about, trying to locate Godyth, calling her name over and over.

They ran into the meadow but could see nothing. At last, as they back tracked and crossed the road, they came to the river bank where it forked and formed a small pool.

Mabel remembered this pool well. It was where she had found Mistress Peabody that time; the time the woman had been trying to drown herself and Mabel had saved her life by changing into a swan.

No one was about. They were all celebrating Christmas in their own homes or at the manor.

Mabel and Gabriel looked across to the other side where the pool touched the road to the village green and saw a dark blob floating in the reed pierced water.

"No! It's Godyth!" cried Mabel.

Gabriel outpaced her and was the first to reach the water's edge.

Tendrils of dark hair floated out on the lazy ripple of the pond. Arms were wide flung and dipping and rising as the stiff breeze blew little wavelets around them. Blood oozed from the head and floated from the hair in strings. The face was submerged.

But as Gabriel waded in, Mabel realised that it wasn't Godyth.

It was her brother Henry.

And he was dead.

CHAPTER FOUR
~ COCKS AND HENS ~

A little brown owl skirted the trees to the edge of the Barr Field Copse. It swooped over Master Farmer's house and flew over the thatch of Mistress Peabody's cottage alighting on the roof of the Lovegrove dwelling.

It had been dark for a short while but on Christmas day, folk had not retired to their beds but were sitting by the light of an oil lamp or a tallow candle or simply the fire, to tell tales and sing songs. One such song had been lifted to the thatch of Mistress Peabody's house and Mabel had heard the bass tones of Tom, her son, as she passed overhead.

There was no such frivolity in the Lovegrove house for the only son had just been found dead in the river, his head caved in on a rock. Mabel owl had thought that she might hear crying. Either from Master Lovegrove himself or his mother-in-law or from Godyth but the house was almost silent. That was eerie.

She had left Gabriel tucking into a hearty Christmas day supper at the hall. She'd join him when she'd learned anything she could.

Mabel flew down to the edge of the thatch. She could hear quiet conversation coming from the house. Almost whispers.

"Damn, I can't hear what they're saying."

She turned three times to withershynnes, her wings outspread. "I wish to be a tiny mouse."

As her nose turned into a quivering little pink blob, she could smell all sorts of things she'd never realised had odours. She grew tiny pink claws where her sharp owl claws had been and a long tail emerged from her spine which allowed her to balance so perfectly on the thatch.

Mabel mouse ran under the eaves and pushed her way under the thatch where, as it met the daub wall, there was a slight gap. She raced down the inner door catching hold of the wood with her sharp little claws.

Now she could hear.

To her surprise, Master Lovegrove was alone and he was talking to himself sitting by the fire poking the pitiful flames.

"My wife—Gelle, oh Gelle—why did you go off? What was I to do? Left me with five children. To go and lead a debauched life. I got no alibi—no alibi..." Mabel could see the tears which wet his cheeks.

It seemed as if somehow, Lovegrove was running over in his mind how he felt about his predicament.

"The court will see that as a motive—won't they, but why—why all these years later? I put up with it for years—why?"

Mabel watched as he rose and kicked a small twig which had fallen from the fire bed.

"They've got Godyth—they've got her," he said. "She'll tell—she will."

When Mabel and Gabriel had at last found Godyth after her brother's death and had taken her to her grandmother's house, Mabel had finally been able to question her.

"Godyth, did you see what happened to your brother?"

"No. I never."

"What do you think happened to him?"

"I dunno. He fell, slipped I suppose."

Mabel had sighed. "What did your father mean when he said, say nothing?"

"I...I..." the girl had stammered and had looked down at the ground.

"Say nothing, nothing about me ma."

Mabel had suddenly had a thought. It was a horrible thought but she had to have an answer.

"Godyth, when you last saw your mother, was she still alive?"

The brown eyes had searched everyone's face; first her grandam's and then Gabriel's, lastly Mabel's. Slowly she'd shaken her head.

So, Godyth had seen her mother dead. Had she been there when Master Lovegrove killed her?

And now, sitting alone, Lovegrove was burbling on. "Now Henry... ooooh now Henry. I'm cursed... cursed!" His voice rose from a whisper.

"They'll question Godyth... I know they'll question Godyth. And she's only a girl."

He ran his hand through his hair.

"They'll accuse me... I know they'll accuse me."

He sat down and sobbed for a short while.

"They'll know what I did—they have to know—I did it."

Mabel was so surprised that she almost fell from her place on the stones of the cottage base. She had to become herself again and see if she could get Lovegrove to admit his guilt to her. Strike now when he was in a confessing mood.

Once outside and Mabel Wetherspring once more, she called out at the door.

"Master Lovegrove, it's Mabel. Are you alright? Can I come in?"

The man was sitting staring at the earthen floor as she appeared in the door hole. The light was poor and came only from the scant flames.

"Master Lovegrove. Can I come in and speak to you? I have something to tell you."

The man wiped his nose on his sleeve.

"Your daughter Godyth admitted that she was at the place where your wife was found. She *had* visited her mother and she tells me that when she was there, her mother was already dead."

Mabel came further into the cott her hand still on the door.

SUSANNA M. NEWSTEAD

"I have a horrible feeling that maybe you killed your wife in front of Godyth."

"No! NO!" he cried out.

"She is a loyal daughter. She wants to protect you. But you realise that she will tell the truth in time. She's only young. If you killed Gelle, you know you will be found out."

The man sobbed into his hands.

"Leave Godyth out of this."

"I cannot promise that." Mabel came in and closed the door. She knew that it was a dangerous thing to do, if Lovegrove was indeed a man with his mind on murder.

"But if you tell us all you know I'm sure that the authorities will look kindly on you."

Lovegrove wiped away his tears with the flat of his hands.

"I couldn't have Godyth hanging around her. If Gelle was going to carry on living in such an immoral way. I told her time and again."

"So you saw her several times?"

"Aye—aye I did."

"Why did you lie, Phillip?"

"Why do you think,?"

"Because you killed her?"

His response was a sort of sobbing laugh.

"Why did she say that you were a wicked man? She did describe you as a wicked man to her brother and her mother."

Lovegrove stared at her with red rimmed eyes.

"My wife was—disturbed—possessed. You have to understand. She was her own worst enemy sometimes."

"So you went to see her and found that Godyth was there?"

"I lost my temper. I told my daughter to go home to her grannie's and she ran."

"And then what?"

"Then I tried one last time to reason with Gelle. She spat at me. She hit me and…"

"And..." He swallowed.

"I lost my temper."

The man threw his hands to his face.

"And I killed her."

"What did you kill her with?"

"A stone."

Mabel stepped nearer to him, her heart hammering in her chest. "Will you report that to the steward, Phillip? Will you confess to the killing of your wife?

"Aye I will."

*****

Mabel chewed her lip all the way to the manor house. She'd penned Master Lovegrove in his house by wedging some logs between the door jambs and went to report to Master Steward and to Gabriel, that Phillip had confessed.

"Well, that's that," said Gabriel glibly as he tucked into a mixture of fruits cooked in hippocras on the top table of the hall of the manor.

Mabel pulled a face.

"What's that for?"

"I'm not sure, Sir Gabriel. I asked Phillip Lovegrove about the leaves which covered his wife's face and he was very puzzled. He really was."

"He was feigning it."

"No, no, he meant it. He had no idea what I was talking about."

"Which means?"

Mabel pulled the dish nearer to her and dipped her spoon into the fruit mixture.

"It means that someone else put the leaves over her face."

"But why?"

"I want to talk to Godyth on her own again."

"What?

She repeated that request when she'd walked back to Mistress Ceorlson's house with Gabriel in tow.

Eadric jumped up. "Ah no—she's still upset. You can't talk to…"

"Eadric please, just go outside," said Mabel softly. "It will make no difference to what happens, I promise."

His eyes filled with tears and he left, dipping his head under the lintel and taking his reluctant mother with him.

"Godyth. Sir Gabriel and I want to ask you some questions. Is that alright?"

The cottage interior was as dark as the last house had been and it wasn't possible to see into the corners of the room. The girl gave the tiniest of nods in the gloom.

"When your father hit your mother, did you see him do it?"

She shook her dark curls. "No, I'd run away. He told me to go."

"And there was no one else there?"

"No. No one."

"So—did you go back in after Master Lovegrove left?"

Her eyes, those dark brown, shining pools, stared into Mabel's own and she gave just one nod.

"But Godyth—did you know that your mother…"

"Why did you go back ?" asked Gabriel, totally perplexed. It was obvious by his face he thought it odd that the girl would have gone back to the ruined house where her mother lay murdered.

"She was dead," said Godyth.

Mabel quickly looked at Sir Gabriel and got her question in swiftly before he led the child astray.

"What did she look like, Godyth?"

The girl's pale face framed by the curly hair was still and unreadable.

"I closed her eyes because they were still open," she said.

*****

"Of course, we have a problem," said Gabriel late the next morning. Both of them were watching the young men parade around the village on the wren hunt, a traditional festival held on St. Stephen's Day, the second of the twelve days of Christmas. The death of Henry Lovegrove had not prevented the long established and ever moving cycle of village festivities.

"Oh? What's that?"

"How did Henry die? Did he fall? Or did he slip. Was he pushed? And was the wound to his head inflicted intentionally?"

"You think it might be murder then?"

"But and it's a big but, if it was murder, Master Lovegrove cannot have killed his son. He was at home possibly with Godyth and his mother-in-law when the deed was done."

Gabriel folded his arms and looked down on Mabel. She'd plaited her hair that day and it hung down her back, almost to her bottom. A white head cloth framed her face and she wore her usual dark blanket cloak, for it was chilly.

"Have we two murderers, do you think?"

"No, surely not. But when you think about it…"

Mabel looked around the assembled villagers. "The corpse is in Mistress Ceorlson's house. She's standing over there with Godyth. Why don't we go and have a look at Henry's body, while the house is empty?"

They pushed to the back of the crowd and were soon standing looking down at young Henry Lovegrove. Master Phillip Lovegrove had been moved to the lockup by the steward and reeve and the house was empty.

It was such a sad sight. The child was lying on the trestle with a blanket over him. His clothes had been removed and he'd ceased to drip gently to the floor. The beaten earth was dark where the water had stained it.

"So young—he was only nine," said Gabriel sadly, leaning over with his greater height to look at the wound to the boy's head.

Mabel poked her head from the door. No one was around outside. "Quickly!" She scurried inside. "Help me move him."

"What? Why?"

"No time, just lift him onto his front."

"Mabel this is most irreverent."

"Gabriel, it will be even more irreverent if the boy was murdered and we don't work that out. It will be criminal of us not to investigate."

"How?"

"Just turn him on his front."

Gabriel rolled the child so that he was on his side, then pulled the arm until he was prone and the head was turned.

"No rigor."

"No."

"Well that's to be expected as rigor will have set in and passed at this hour."

Mabel took a deep breath and pushed on the torso. Quickly she ducked to look at the corpse's face.

"Aha!"

"What?"

Gabriel stooped to bring his face near to hers. He felt the warmth of her body close to him. He felt a jolt as if she'd struck him. 'Oh! So that's what it feels like to be so close to her,' he thought, inching even closer.

"No water is coming from his lungs." Mabel chewed her lip. "Can you press him harder than I could?"

"Mabel this is…?"

"Oh Gabriel, just do it, please."

He sighed and pressed down with two hands on the boy's back.

"Nothing."

"And that means?"

"He was dead when he went into the water. He took no water into his lungs. He wasn't alive when he hit the pond, not breathing. He fell forward and floated there and didn't drown."

They stared at each other and then at poor Henry.

Together they looked carefully at the back of his head.

"A large wound. It crushed the skull there, see?" said Mabel. "Now, what might have made a wound like that?"

Gabriel grimaced. "A large rock? A heavy branch?"

They replaced the body tidily as they'd found him and stepped back.

"Did you see anything like that close by when we found Henry floating in the pond?"

"No—I have to say—I didn't, though I wasn't *really* looking, " said Gabriel.

"Then we shall have to go and look," said Mabel, covering Henry's head with the blanket. She whispered to the young lad as his features disappeared. "I'll find out who did this, Henry. I will. I promise."

They crossed themselves and left.

*****

"What's that for?"

"You'll have to fish out whatever I find in the pond."

"You're going into the pond? You can't swim. You'll drown!"

Mabel looked up at him. Even though she had feelings for him and thought she loved him dearly, sometimes, she thought, he was a bit dense. Their investigation of the surroundings of the pond had turned up nothing which might be responsible for the wound on the boy's head and so the actual pond had to be investigated.

"I'll be a fish and I'll try to locate the 'weapon'. Then I'll try to get it to a point where you can net it and get it out—right?"

"Ah—right—yes—"

"Just make sure no one sees us."

"How am I supposed to do …?"

Mabel waded into the pond until the water reached her knees.

She turned withershynnes, (not easy with the weight of her kirtle), and said, "I'd like to be a large roach fish."

Gabriel watched as Mabel disappeared into the water.

"God! I hope there are no pike in this pond," he said to himself.

He waited and as he waited, he did some spear drill with the length of Mabel's net handle. Anyone who saw him might wonder what he was up to but knights were a strange bunch. Peasants would never understand them.

*****

Mabel's human body shrank and she lost her legs and arms. Her back and sides became a silver green and rust red fins grew where her appendages once lay. Her eyes turned red.

She scanned the water and dived to the bottom. There were other roach languidly swimming about but they never bothered her. How pretty they are, she thought, with their attractive silveriness and sleek shape.

Now, she had to locate where Henry had gone into the water. She swam a few feet to the base of the reeds. He'd been here, just a few feet out and so she began to swim about with her fish eyes fixed to the bed of the pool.

Hmm—it was amazing what had been thrown into the pond. She found a rusty old sword and not far from that, a part of a helmet, also rusted. Little minnows were sheltering there in the eye sockets and a few water snails were tracking up the nasal and along the brow. There were plenty of sunken windblown twigs but no large branches. That was no surprise, there were no major trees close by. She made another arc. Someone had lost a bucket and it was partially buried under the silt. It had been there a long time so no, that could not be the murder weapon.

She swam on. Suddenly, with a jolt, she realised that she'd swum into a fish trap. One of those conical wicker apparatus which was thrown into water, checked periodically and dragged out again with a haul for supper.

Other fish had made the same mistake.

Panic set in. She turned and turned in the water and then on her last turn, her human brain took over.

Mabel turned about and with a 'bubble... bubble... bubble,' she attempted to cry out, "Follow me!" but no fish heard her or for that matter followed. They were rather stupid, she thought.

Ah well if they wanted to end up in a fish pie that was their own lookout.

Mabel had no intention of ending up as someone's bony dinner.

Cleverly she slipped out of the trap again through the tiny entrance.

'Hmm—what have we got here?'

Sunk to the bottom of the pond was the remains of a little boat. A tiny boat. She thought she'd heard them called coracles. She hoped this one's sailor had escaped, for it was in a very poor way. An eel looked at her with a white eye from a gash in the boat's side. She was in no danger from him. He spent most of the day sleeping and was most active at night.

She swam on.

"Aha!" There on the pond's grimy bottom, lay a large rock. Quickly Mabel swam around to make sure that this was not just one of many but, no, it was a single rock and was totally out of place here.

As quickly as she could, she turned withershynnes and in the next instant became an otter.

She rose to the surface to see Gabriel lurching about with the handle of her net and making odd noises at—nothing.

'What the devil was he doing?'

She swam to the bank, chirruping for all she was worth "GabrielWarrenerpayattentionIhavefoundsomething!"

The knight saw the otter from the corner of his eye and stood up to attention.

"Ahem! Is that you, Mabel?" He glanced around. No one had heard him.

Mabel took a deep breath and dived again, coming up a few feet nearer to him.

"Ofcourseit'sme," she chunnered. "Followmetothereedsandthenleanover."

"Ah. Right." He hadn't a clue what she'd said but he was sure it was Mabel and that she wanted him to follow her.

Gabriel scanned the water's surface. The otter rose and dived a few times and each time it was a little nearer to the bank.

Under the water with every new breath, Mabel was moving the rock closer to the bank, with her little claws and her amazingly powerful tail.

Suddenly the little otter ran up the bank and dived for the cover of Master Mosspath's outhouse. Soon after that, Mabel came strolling out adjusting her head cloth.

"Now I've got the rock as close to the bank as I could, you'll have to fish for it. About—" She inspected the water's surface. "There." She pointed.

Gabriel scanned her up and down. She wasn't even wet. This magic of hers was absolutely amazing!

He leaned out over the weeds and swished the net to and fro.

"A little more that way…"

"Ah yes—" Something had caught on the net. He pulled hard.

"We need something less flimsy," he said, his teeth showing in a grimace. "This is going to break."

"Try again. I'll scout around for something to use."

Gabriel raked the bottom of the pond with his net and the water grew muddy. Slowly the rock tumbled into the shallows but it was still a few feet away.

Mabel came back with a length of wood.

"Try this."

Gabriel leaned sideways and dragged the wood through the water; slowly the rock reached him and he stooped to extend his hand for it, throwing his piece of wood behind him on the bank.

"Whatever are you doing, Sir Gabriel?" came a voice. It completely startled the knight so that with an 'ooer' he lost his foothold on the slippery bank, wheeled his arms around for a heartbeat and teetered on the brink of the pond. Sadly it was not enough to steady him and he tumbled into the shallows with a muddy splash.

*****

"So, Master Steward," said Gabriel, wringing out his wet, muddy cotte, "We think this is the rock which killed Henry Lovegrove.

"Oh my. Oh no." The steward had been on his way back to the manor house from the wren hunt when he'd seen Gabriel fishing in the pond.

"I think, if we look at it carefully, we'll see that it's been prised out of the top of the church wall," said Mabel. "It's one of the cocks—or the hens."

"Really, Mistress Wetherspring?" said Henry, the manor steward. "How do you come to that conclusion?"

"I don't know. It just looks like one of the church wall stones. It's the only dry stone wall around here apart from Master Farmer's wall and there's no mortar attaching to it. The only stone buildings are the church and the manor and it's not from the church."

"Are you sure that the lad just didn't fall in?"

"He fell forward, Henry," said Mabel. "And there's a huge wound to the *back* of his head. There are no other rocks in the pool, just this one and if you look at the boy's head, it's a jagged wound. If he'd just fallen in he would have been able to get out."

"He didn't fall *forward* and hit his head. He was encouraged into the water," said Gabriel. "By a blow to the *back* of his head."

"But..."

"You saw what happened when Sir Gabriel fell in the water, Master Steward? He fell forward. There was no rock there on which he might hit himself and if there had been a rock, he would have been injured on the front of his head. Luckily he fell in the muddy shallows. Henry Lovegrove, however, was struck from behind and pushed into the deeper water."

"Luckily?" muttered Gabriel squeezing more water from his cotte.

Mabel grimaced. "And the rock was thrown in after him."

They all walked up to the church wall. There were a few gaps in the enclosure and the stone they'd found was of exactly the same kind.

The steward shook his head. "How did you know where to look?"

"Oh—it was just a guess."

"I'll have to tell the coroner and the constable, of course."

"We'll explain what we found, Henry, don't worry."

He went off muttering, "Oh why does it have to be murder? Why does it have to be here on my manor? Why now?"

"It's spoiled his Christmas," said Sir Gabriel.

"Anything which makes him have to do some work, will spoil things for him, Gabriel."

Gabriel Warrener chuckled. "Whereas we revel in the excitement!"

"Oh, I must say it was very exciting when you fell in the pond! I will be laughing about that for weeks!"

Gabriel lifted his wet sleeves. "I had better get to my pack and change."

They walked side by side along the lane, turned into the High Street and were approaching the manor when Godyth came running up out of breath.

"Mistress Wetherspring!" she yelled. "I've seen it—I've seen it."

"What have you seen, Godyth?"

"The monster. The fire breathing beast."

"When?"

"Just now. Over the road." She pointed to the river. "It was like they said. Big and breathing fire!"

"Ah…"

"Are you sure?" said Gabriel, giving Mabel a quick wink.

"I saw it. I think that it's what made my brother fall into the pond! Yes, I'm sure it did! It attacked him and he fell in."

*****

"An over-excitable imagination," said Gabriel with a chuckle when they'd reached the privacy of Mabel's cottage.

"She's had two terrible shocks—first her mother and then her brother. She's bound to be trying to find reasons for it all."

"And her father taken up for the murder of her mother."

"Poor Godyth," said Mabel.

Mabel built up the fire and started to prepare some mulled ale whilst, once in clean, dry clothes, Gabriel took out his wax tablet and began to scribble some notes.

"I must write to Lord Stokke to tell him what's been going on. He's got two villeins dead now. There will be heriot to pay and the Lovegrove cottage will be unoccupied once..."

"Godyth still has a home there."

"She's only eleven. She won't be eligible to inherit will she? Her grannie might."

"I was twelve when I took possession of this house. Godyth will be twelve in March. It's not far off. She becomes a woman in the eyes of the law then. If she pays the heriot, then she'll be able to run her own home. She would have been subject to her brother's or her uncle's care but now..."

Gabriel shrugged.

"That's only if Master Lovegrove is convicted of the murder of his wife and... Of course if he IS then everything will be confiscated and become Crown property"

"Oh yes of course—but..."

"Aw c'mon, Mabel. He's admitted to it."

"Yes I know but something doesn't sit right, does it?"

He paused with the stylus over the wax. "What doesn't sit right?"

Mabel threw herself down on her stool and sighed. "Master Lovegrove. There has never been a scrap of trouble surrounding the family. All except with Gelle and she's been away for six years."

"What do you mean?"

"If Phillip Lovegrove had a temper, enough to kill his wife after six years, you'd think that it would manifest itself as a problem in the home, to Godyth and Henry. And there has never been as much as a squeak from either of them."

"You mean he didn't mistreat them?"

"In a village like this, Gabriel, every man knows his neighbour's business..."

"Except yours..." he chortled.

"That's because I am very careful."

"But not careful enough recently."

"Ah well—and it helps that I live alone."

Gabriel looked quickly at the floor. "Yes I suppose that's true." Into his mind came a little scene with Mabel and him happily standing arm in arm in the doorway of her cottage whilst two children, a boy and a girl, played in the garth. Suddenly one of them became a huge dragon and roared over the roof, setting fire to the thatch.

He came back to the present immediately.

"Ahem! What you mean is, if Master Lovegrove's temper was enough to kill Gelle, then someone would have known about it and that the children would..."

"Be black and blue from beatings. And they aren't. They never have been."

Gabriel threw his wax tablet on the table. "Aw no! Now you are saying that Lovegrove didn't kill Gelle. So if he didn't, who did?"

"I don't know. But it must be someone whom he will protect. Someone he cares for. It must be. Why else would he confess to a murder and put himself in danger of the noose?"

She handed him a warm pot of ale.

He looked at the fire and the pot suspended over it. Peeking into it he grimaced.

"Pottage again? Shall we go and eat in the manor tonight. All this murder has given me an appetite."

That, thought Mabel, was one of the major differences between men and women. Men were made hungry by death. Women completely lost their appetites.

*****

At the third hour past midnight on the third day of Christmas, Mabel Wetherspring crept out of her home and looked up at the sky. It would be dark roughly until the hour of terce. She had some investigating to do. She'd left Sir Gabriel Warrener snoring on his palliasse in her cottage.

She scurried around the back of her cott, the most private outside space she had and thought carefully. Lifting her arms, she spun withershynnes three times and said, "I wish to be a barn owl.

Her human face suddenly dished and her nose grew into a small but sharp beak. Her eyes became beads of polished black agate either side of a white soft feathered nose. Her body grew feathers, mottled white and buff with grey-black bandings. She stretched out her wings, lifted her feet and she was off over the village, silently weaving between the cottages. She could see everything in amazing detail. Things she never noticed as a human, were so obvious to a barn owl at night in the dark.

The little gap in Master Farmer's barn roof where a tired owl might rest and not be seen during daylight hours. A family of mice scurrying about Mistress Peabody's hen house after the grain she'd dropped for her fowl. They scattered as Mabel glided noiselessly overhead. She saw the swans on the river, asleep with their beaks tucked into their wings. She heard a badger rootling around in the verge on Brown's Lane and making a deal of noise and wheeled round to skim over Master Hartshorn's cherry orchard. Across the road, she approached the house of Mistress Ceorlson and her son then landed on the roof to listen.

There was no noise. How could they be asleep when there was so much wrong in their lives? Perhaps it was the sleep of mental exhaustion—exhaustion with managing the grief and worry?

Mabel became a small mouse and with a quick look to the skies; she didn't want to become supper for a hungry owl, she scurried up the daub wall and pressed herself through a small hole between the shutters.

Her whiskers trembled. Godyth was on her bed curled up asleep on her side, by the back wall, a small night candle on its pricket, sitting in a bowl of water on the floor beside her.

There was no other light.

Her uncle Eadric was asleep and snoring on his back.

Mistress Ceorlson was sitting on a bench, her eyes open, staring at the fire which was damped down for the night. She obviously couldn't sleep.

She didn't see the tiny mouse scuttle across the floor to disappear amongst the shoes which had been laid by the bottom of Eadric's bed. Two pairs. Eadric's large ones and Godyth's smaller pair.

Mabel's mouse whiskers twitched and she sniffed.

How wonderful was a mouse's nose? She could immediately identify where the wearer had been.

Eadric's brown shoe soles were pink and sour with the juices of the crab apple. There was only one place in the village where crab apples grew in profusion and ripened later in October and November and fell to the ground in December. Most fruit in other places were well over by November.

Godyth's shoes were wet. Mabel hadn't noticed it before. Hadn't seen it when she spoke to the girl earlier. But now, as a mouse, she smelled the muddy water of the pond.

Quietly so as not to startle the older woman, Mabel scampered across the floor and slowly came up to the woman's feet which were crossed at the ankles.

Mistress Ceorlson yawned and closed her eyes momentarily.

Mabel reared up on her hind legs and sniffed the woman's shoes.

Nothing in particular.

The little mouse ran around the edge of the room and up through the gap in the shutter.

She didn't like what she had discovered but she'd keep it to herself for a while.

CHAPTER FIVE
~ TWELFTH NIGHT ~

"**M**istress Wetherspring?"
"Yes Mistress Chatterwell?"

"Have you seen little Johnny?"

"No—no I haven't. Why, where did he go?"

He went to watch the wren hunt yesterday with his brother and Alfred was busy as he was part of the hunt and he lost sight of Johnny and..."

"Now he's missing?"

"Aye, now he is. He didn't come home last night."

"Oh Mistress Chatterwell, you should have reported him missing before this."

"Well, he does go to his friends' houses. Quite often."

"And stays the night?"

His mother shrugged.

"Where might he go?"

"I don't know. We've looked everywhere."

"You have no other relations here in Bedwyn have you?"

"No. And I know he wouldn't go into the forest."

Mabel grimaced. "Ah—but since he saw the flying pig..."

"He saw nothing of the kind—it was sheer foolery."

"Since he *said* he'd seen the flying pig..."

"Pah!"

"He's been fascinated by the thing and I've seen him standing outside my garden, looking up at my oak tree."

"It's very silly behaviour."

"He wouldn't go too far, I'm sure."

"I thought he'd come back. I know he will when he gets hungry."

But he didn't.

*****

"Gabriel, wake up.. quickly."

"What?"

"It's little Johnny, he's missing."

"What?"

"My neighbour across the road has a boy. You know him—Johnny."

"Chatterwell—yes? He's missing?"

Gabriel was all ready to turn over and go back to sleep. "He'll turn up."

"They've searched the village houses. They need more people to help. The barns and pig pens and the cattle sheds need to be looked into."

"There are plenty of folk in the village." Gabriel closed his eyes.

"I'm worried about him, Gabriel."

He opened one eye. "Why are you especially worried about him?"

He sat up and combed his blond hair with his fingers.

Suddenly he was scratching his side. "Have you got fleas in the house, Mabel?"

Mabel tutted, "Of course I haven't. You will have been bitten yesterday by the gnats which frequent the pond. I'll find you something to put on the bites."

In a short while, Gabriel was up and dressed and taking deep breaths of morning air outside the cottage.

"The pond. We need to check the pond," said Mabel.

"No! You don't think...?"

"I don't know but we do need to check."

"What about the river?"

"Master Steward has people looking the length of it now."

They approached the pond.

Johnny's mother came running up. "Arnulf is taking a party out to comb the nearer woods now." This was Johnny's father.

"We'll take a boat and look in the pond," said Gabriel, not stopping to think how his words would be received.

"Ahhhh!" said Mistress Chatterwell, tying her head cloth tighter and nearly strangling herself in her anguish. "Nooo..."

"Can Johnny swim?" asked Mabel?

"No—no, of course he can't swim," said his mother. "If God had wanted people to swim, then He would have given them fins or webbed feet." She looked out over the small pond and swallowed down tears. "You don't think...?"

"No—we don't but we shall still have a look."

Mabel turned the woman around. "You go with Sir Gabriel and join the searches in the woods."

Once they'd gone. Mabel looked carefully over her shoulder.

Quickly she turned withershynnes. "I wish to be an otter."

Mabel felt her eyes shift to the side of her face. Her head became smooth, hairy and brown. Tiny dish shaped ears grew from the top of her head. Her body shrank but became long and sleek and didn't stop changing until she'd developed a long powerful tail. She dashed into the water and dived in a wave and a plume of white spray.

Firstly she quartered the bank side, weaving her way through the rushes, reedmace and the dead stalks of underwater plants. She swam up to the river and searched where the pool widened out in shallows of the remains of loosestrife and willowherb. She found nothing.

Back into the pool she circled the depths, rising to the surface to breathe when necessary. She had been amazed on the occasions she had turned into an otter, to discover that they could hold their breath underwater for many heartbeats.

She saw the sword and helmet, the bucket and the little boat she'd seen before, but thankfully no sign of Johnny Chatterwell. She knew that a dead body would sink and after a while, reemerge on the surface.

Just to make sure, she dived again into the deepest part of the pond. Something glinted on the mud of the pool's bed. Ah, the sun must have made an appearance or there would be no light by which to see so well.

Mabel picked the little thing up in her otterine fingers. It was a small brooch and she clutched it in her claws.

Time to regain her human shape again.

Master Mosspath's outhouse came into use once more and Mabel walked down the lane with the tiny brooch in her hand.

It had not been in the water very long. It was base metal but had been quite well silvered and was not rusty and the little pin to the back was nevertheless sharp for its sojourn in water. It bore a tiny inscription all around the circular edge. *'Ave Maria Gracia Plena Invan'.* 'Hail Mary full of grace.'

Was this part of the river where people would offer to the old gods; things of value and worth to the people of Bedwyn? Mabel knew that this sort of thing went on out in the pools of the forest where there were no prying eyes of the church. But she didn't think that this brooch had been a votive offering. Someone had lost it, and recently. To whom had it belonged?

They still hadn't found little Johnny and were now widening the search to the further forest.

The watery sun was poking through the clouds as Mabel and Gabriel walked into the forest edge by her cottage.

"I've seen Johnny standing here several times. He was obviously fascinated by the flying pig and the monster and was waiting for them to reappear.

"Only they didn't," said Gabriel. "And wouldn't."

'That's right—try to make me feel bad,' thought Mabel to herself.

"I'll become a forest falcon. That'll give me good eyesight and I'll quarter the forest up to the common. I can cover more ground that way."

Gabriel nodded. "You don't think something has happened to him do you?"

She shrugged. "In the light of everything that's been going on, I…"

Suddenly there was a screech and Mistress Chatterwell came running out of the forest trees which bordered the village green, pointing.

Mabel turned her head to the trees behind her.

"Johnny!"

Little Johnny came slowly out of the wall of green holly, behind Mabel's house, a rather sheepish look on his face.

"Oh thank the Heavens!" said Mabel.

Mistress Mosspath ran up to the young lad and gave him a shake. "Oh young Johnny, you don't know what you done to yer ma—to all of us."

Johnny wiped a grimy hand over a grimy face, quite teary.

"Sorry. I got lost." He looked back into the trees. "Master Ceorlson found me."

Dragging his feet, Eadric Ceorlson came out of the woods behind Johnny. It was obvious he'd given the boy a shove to propel him out of the greenery. Mabel got the feeling that if Johnny had not said anything, Eadric would have stayed hanging back and they wouldn't have seen him. He would have melted away into the trees.

"Well done, Master Ceorlson!" said a beaming Gabriel.

"Where did you find him? asked Johnny's mother, enveloping her son in a huge embrace and clipping his ear at the same time.

"He… he was sitting on the common. He'd been looking for the river, he said."

"Aye—I was mortal thirsty."

"That will teach you to go off on yer own," said Mistress Chatterwell now reduced to crying tears of relief.

"I wa'n't on me own."

"Who was with you...?" asked Gabriel.

"There was no one with him," said Eadric.

"I was looking for the flying pig."

"Yes, I know you were," said Mabel.

"Did you find it?" asked Gabriel, hunkering down in front of the lad.

"No, I didn't," said a very disappointed Johnny Chatterwell. "But I'll keep looking."

"You take care—eh?" said Eadric as he backed away and disappeared around the nearest building.

"Thank you Eadric," said Mistress Chatterwell, happily.

"Johnny, you mustn't keep looking for the pig. I happen to know that it's gone far away now," said Mabel with authority.

Johnny peered at her with disbelieving eyes. "You said it didn't exist..."

"Well, yes I did and because *I've* never seen it, I can't surely say that it does. But I have heard from those who *have* seen it that—that it's been seen out near—near—Cadley."

"Aw—that's a long way away." Johnny looked as if he'd burst into tears.

"So—no more searching eh? Not for the pig or for the Beast of Bedwyn."

Johnny kicked his foot against a tussock of grass and his loose shoe flew off.

"Aw—bother!" he said.

*****

It was Twelfth Night. The last of the Christmas celebrations; a night when everyone feasted, drank and danced at the lord's expense. Of course Lord Robert Stokke was still visiting his friend at Chalfield Manor in the north of the county but his village of Bedwyn ate, drank and made merry without him. A bonfire had been lit on the village green and one of Master Hogg's pigs was roasted and everyone became slowly tipsy on the ale and mead provided by the manor.

Gabriel and Mabel were sitting outside her cott on the log which served as an outdoor bench. They were, both of them, just a little drunk on mead.

"Do you think Johnny'll stop looking?"

"I think he'll forget in time."

They had been talking about little Johnny Chatterwell and his insistence that he had seen a flying pig.

"What about his sister?"

"She was easier to convince. She saw me just once fleetingly and so it was easier to make her believe it was something else."

"And all those in the village who saw the groffun? I mean gruffin..."

Mabel gave Gabriel a sidelong look. "It's moved on hasn't it?"

"Oh?"

"It's gone on to terrorsise... terriferise—frighten other villages. It won't be back here."

Gabriel chuckled and drained his mead pot. "How are you going to convince them of that?"

"I shall write a letter to the steward..."

"Master Bitterfear?"

"Henry, yes. In it I'll explain that it's gone up north and that it has been slain by a harty of punters."

"Ah—that should do it," said Gabriel with an unconvinced chuckle and a hiccough.

Mabel rose unsteadily. "In fact I'll go there now. While everyone is busy here dancing and..."

"What—go to the manor...?"

"Yeah and get into my office and write a letter."

"Well then, let's go."

Holding each other up as best they could, they staggered down the lane, wove down the High Street and entered the manor. Mabel lit a candle from the box by the door.

Few people were about here and they were all enjoying themselves too much to take any notice of Gabriel and Mabel.

Mabel took some time to unlock her office door, not being able to see her key in a lock which, strangely, kept moving about. This was the buttery where the manor wine and other liquids were stored and where she had a corner in which to keep her records.

She stumbled to the table. Things were going round and round and her vision was a little blurred.

"Won't he know it's you who has wretten the litter?"

"Henry?" Mabel chuckled, "Ach no. He'll have no idea."

She took out parchment and loaded her pen with ink.

"Bring the candle closer," she said.

'To whom it may concern. Let it be known that the monster which has been terrorising the forest and its inhabitants was today hunted down and slain by a party of huntsmen from the villages of Cadley, Clench and Manton. The body was burned upon a pyre. It will no longer be of any trouble to the forest dwellers.'

Gabriel hiccoughed. "You think that'll do it?"

"Let's go and put it into Enry's hoffice."

They crept along the screens passage and entered Henry's domain. They had seen him dancing with the elderly Widow Tapscott on the village green and knew he wouldn't be there.

Tip toeing to the table Mabel laid the missive upon the wooden surface and as she turned abruptly to leave, Gabriel came too close behind her. *Far too close.*

"Oooh!" He stood on her foot, lost his balance and lurched

towards her.

"Shhhh!" said Mabel loudly, her finger to her lips—or the vicinity of her lips, "We don't want anyone..."

It was no good, he collided with Mabel and to save her from falling he wrapped his arms around her.

"Oooh. We are more than a little drunk you know!" giggled Mabel.

His head came closer to her own.

"But that doesn't excuse us..."

Gabriel's mead soaked lips met her own and his two hands came up to cradle her head as he kissed her.

"Ooh!"

Then there was nothing but the slurping of the kiss and the breath from both their noses.

"Gavrribul... I beed to breave."

"Sorry... sorry."

He lifted his head and then, as if she had not pulled away, he came close again.

"Oh Mabel—I wish..."

Mabel ended up on her back on the surface of the table.

Gabriel wriggled closer to her.

Their lips met again.

"Oh Gabriel..."

Never in her wildest dreams had Mabel thought she could ever feel this way about anyone.

Even if she *was* a bit tipsy. This was sheer Heaven. Choirs of angels were singing in her head. Her body was floating. Petals of sweet smelling flowers were raining down on her.

They both wriggled a little flatter on the table.

"Oh—oh," said Mabel, her innards going quite mushy.

Master Buttermere's pens and styli went skidding along the table's surface.

The parchments which had been laid tidily upon the table top rolled up and fell to the floor. His account tallies went tumbling off the edge.

Mabel grabbed Gabriel by his long blond locks and pulled his lips to hers again. She simply couldn't help herself. This kiss was longer and sloppier.

And then, inevitably, the table groaned and creaked.

Both Mabel and Sir Gabriel were off the ground and their whole weight was on the old piece of furniture.

It buckled and the top came away from two legs, the cross bar gave a crunch and split and, as the table toppled, the lovers were propelled into the gap in the middle and pinned to the floor by the creaking wood.

"Oh for Heaven's sake!" yelled Gabriel as he landed on top of Mabel with an "Oomph!"

Then they both dissolved into a fit of impossibly hysterical laughter.

*****

They lay there for a while, arms wrapped around each other and sobered up a little.

At last Gabriel gave Mabel a peck on her nose and said, "Mabel, are you a virgin?"

"What kind of question is that?" She wriggled away from him.

"A simple one?"

"Of course I am. I'm not married—am I?"

"Well—that doesn't always mean..." he said.

"Are you?"

"How does that...?"

"Well?"

"As it happens—no."

"Hmmmph."

Gabriel took a deep breath. Best leave that subject alone.

"I suppose we had better get up and try to mend the table."

"What's wrong with it?"

Gabriel picked up a leg and looked under the table top.

"Oh dear! The back legs have come away from the top. We need to put them back on. And the cross bar is split."

Whilst Mabel ran (or rather staggered), to get some glue from the manor woodworker's workshop, Gabriel propped the table against the wall, made good the split bar by pushing it back in place and collected together all the paraphernalia which had been stored on the table in the steward's office. He had no idea how it had been arranged but he thought Mabel probably did. It was just like her to know everything about the steward's office.

A warm glow suffused his body as he thought of her. Quite apart from being a shapeshifter, she was a remarkable woman. The most remarkable woman he'd ever met. He remembered the kisses and embraces and his mind went off to a warm, sunny meadow where Mabel and he, dressed only in their under garments, were walking hand in hand. They fell down in the soft grass and... A smile came to his face as he imagined the rest.

"This is all I could find." Mabel's voice broke into his reverie. Damn! In his daydream they'd just been getting down to—business! Her thigh was so soft; she was inching her hand along his naked breast... Ah no—in reality it was a dribble of ink!

"Glue?"

"It must be for wood, it smells revolting. Master Buttermere won't come in here early tomorrow. It'll have time to mend."

Gabriel watched as, with a brush, she liberally coated the top of the bulky leg with glue and pinned back what was left of the peg in the join. He jammed the top back on and steadied the table.

"There, that'll do."

They looked at each other carefully and with a degree of embarrassment.

"You have a smut of something on your cheek."

"Oh—have I?"

He dragged his thumb across her face. "There."

"And you are full of bits from the floor." She ran her hands along his cotte picking off bits of rush and straw.

Gabriel thought it was exquisite torment.

"Right perhaps we'd better make ourselves scarce," he said, backing off.

"Yes—right."

"Where's the letter you wrote?"

She pulled it to the top of the table and held it with her forefinger so it didn't move.

"Good as new!" she said throatily.

"Ahem."

*****

The next morning, Mabel took herself off to fly above the forest as she'd wanted to do on the day she'd made a mistake and turned into a flying pig.

The day was cold and there was a north east wind blowing, but Mabel rose higher and higher, wheeling about on strong russet wings. Her nose itched. She knew it was an incredibly sensitive part of a kite. She'd heard from the Lord Stokke's falconer that a kite could smell carrion miles away. Was this what she was smelling?

She wasn't hungry and she'd not be tempted to eat a dead body anyway.

She flapped once and rose higher. She felt as if she could fly up to Heaven.

Gabriel had kissed her last night. Had kissed her passionately. And if the table had not buckled under their weight then who knows what might have happened. A gust of wind blew up her feathers and she turned side onto it and floated with the flurry as far as she could go. She was now over the trees at Chisbury copse and she recognised the ruined manor where Gabriel and she had found the body of Gelle

76

Lovegrove.

The woman had been buried this morning beside her young son Henry. The sexton had dug holes in the ground at the back of the church wall outside the churchyard and dropped them both in there with little ceremony and no religious rites. How sad that had been. She also felt sad that neither she nor Gabriel had been able to make any headway with the murders.

Wheeling around in the wind, high above the forest, Mabel thought about her relationship with Sir Gabriel Warrener. He hadn't *actually* said he loved her. But it certainly felt that way when he'd kissed her. But she was not so naive as not to understand what men were like. Yes, even men like Gabriel. He'd admitted he'd had other women. She wasn't going to be another in a long line of conquests, of that she was sure.

Or was she? She sighed longingly. She knew he was far above her in the hierarchy.

She didn't know what to do.

Descending in order to have a look at the place where they'd found the body of Gelle Lovegrove, her eye was caught by a piece of blue material waving about in the wind, at the base of the scree slope which Gabriel and she had negotiated that fateful day. She was sure it hadn't been there when they'd discovered Gelle's body.

She circled, unaffected by the buffeting of the wind, turning her powerful body and steering with her tail. The fabric was at the bottom of the scree slope. And there was a delicious smell of ham soup.

Nearer and nearer she flew and landed on the grass outside the old manor.

"I wish to be Mabel Wetherspring again." She turned deosil.

She pulled her wind-blown hair into her keeping once more and re-tied her head cloth. Now she was ready to investigate.

She lifted the blue material from the rocks which pinned it down.

Shockingly, out rolled a little body.

Mabel screeched. She really hadn't expected that.

The tiny body was black and blue and full of cuts and abrasions. The smell of ham soup had been replaced by the sweet smell of cooked pears. Mabel looked up the slope. 'Oh no, it looks as if he's fallen down the scree.' His injuries were consistent with a fall amongst jagged rocks. The small body's clothes were torn. Gently she teased back the hair.

It was Archard Tapscott. The youngest child of Master Edwin. She was in no doubt that the boy was dead.

He had only been three years old!

Strangely stuck to his forehead were the remnants of what looked like a plantain leaf which, Mabel thought, had originally been placed over his eyes.

CHAPTER SIX
~ THE CLIFF ~

"Oh the wailing and crying! Mabel couldn't stand it. She took herself off into the forest to sit and brood in the quiet.

She really must stop finding bodies. They'd begin to think she was cursed. A Jonah. Someone who might, inevitably, be a scapegoat. She really didn't want that!

Who would wish poor little Archard dead? He can't have done anything to anyone. Mabel would believe it was an accident but for the little plantain leaf. That had been suspicious. And the fact that the body had been covered over with stones. She remembered Archard as she'd last seen him, half asleep under a tree by the green at Master Hartshorn's orchard with a piece of crackling in his mouth on Twelfth Night. Oh! It wasn't fair. Why could the body not have been stupid Stephen Meadow's? He'd be no loss. She mentally slapped herself as she said this. 'Really Mabel. BEHAVE!'

But little Archie? He'd been a sweet child. She shed a tear or two, or she would have done if she'd been able. Sadly robins were unable to cry. She let out a mournful trill or three in compensation.

She'd managed to explain away her finding of the body. She had been back to look at the old manor again to look for clues into the death of Mistress Lovegrove and there he was. Archard. Apparently no one had yet missed him. His grannie was supposed to be looking after him but she'd been sleeping away the morning hours following her over indulgence of the night before. No one had known he'd gone.

"Mistress Wetherspring—are you there?"

'Damn! It's Henry Buttermere, the steward,' said Mabel to herself. 'What does he want?'

She flew down to the ground and, after a while negotiated the forest floor, and came ambling out of the trees as herself, rounding the back of her cott.

"Master Henry, what can I do for you?"

"I've had a—letter—well a note…"

"Oh?" she said, trying to keep her voice neutral.

"About the flying beast we have had here in Bedwyn."

"Yes?"

"It says that it's been—er—apprehended and killed."

"Oh that's good."

Henry had the piece of parchment in his hand. "It's written on one of your palimpsests…there's a list of laundry to be repaired on the back. It looks like your handwriting."

"No?" said Mabel, trying to look surprised. In fact she *was* surprised. Idiot! She'd not have made a mistake like that if she'd been sober!

"Well someone must have found it and re-used it."

"But why?"

"Master Buttermere, I have no idea. Have you asked Sir Gabriel Warrener? He is more likely to know about killings and beasts than I am."

"Yes, I suppose so. It *does* look like your hand though."

She took the parchment from him.

"Ah no— it's nothing like. It's all wavering. I write a better hand than that and I don't know anything about a beast. I never saw it."

He took back the parchment and stared at her.

"I have work to do—so sorry, can't stand chatting," said Mabel and with a nod, she ran off.

"Damn!"

Master Henry followed her muttering. "I can't see why you'd write such a note, I'm sure. But I am convinced it's your hand..."

"Ah, Sir Gabriel," said Mabel as she reached the manor screens passage and found the knight just inside the door.

"Sir, Master Buttermere has had a note about the monster seen in the forest. Do you know anything about that?"

"The monster? Or the note?"

"The flying beast."

"Ah no—I'm afraid I don't. I didn't see it of course and although I have been searching for it, I have managed to see nothing of it. Yet." He smiled.

"Well it's been found and dealt with apparently."

"Oh—good. That means I don't have to search for it any longer with a view to—getting intimate with it—er—killing it."

A shadow of a smile passed Mabel's lips.

"Master Buttermere seems to believe that I wrote the note. Can you imagine?"

"No...?" Gabriel gave a forced laugh. "Indeed, why would that be?"

"It is in Mistress Wetherspring's hand, I'm sure of it and on a piece of her parchment."

"Any one who can write, sir, will have been able to..."

"But so few here *can* write, Sir Gabriel."

"Well. As long as the beast will bother us no longer, does it really matter who reported its demise?"

Henry opened his office door. "I am still not entirely satisfied."

What Gabriel wanted to say was... 'I'm not at all surprised. That's because you are so ugly and stupid.'

But what he actually said was, "Oh erm—why is that then?"

"Please come in."

Gabriel and Mabel exchanged worried looks whilst Henry searched the parchments on his table.

"Ah here. Here we have a further sample of your writing, Mistress Wetherspring. It is the list which you…"

"I'm sure you have better things to do than to—than to—" began Mabel.

Henry Buttermere held the parchment at arms length and narrowed his eyes. He inched his posterior onto his table to lean against it.

"Your eyes don't seem to be what they were, Master Henry," said Mabel.

"They are perfectly alright, thank you."

Staring, he soaked in the appearance of Sir Gabriel and Mabel ranged in front of him and his face took on a stern look.

"You seem to be spending a lot of time in Mistress Wetherspring's company, Sir Gabriel? Lately."

"That's because the Lord Stokke has asked both of us to look into the flying beast which has been seen."

"Which is now deceased, I'm told."

"And into the murder of Gelle Lovegrove and her son."

"For which we have a culprit. And young Henry, no doubt fell in the pond and hit his head. *That* was no murder."

"The little lad Archard Tapscott, Henry?" said Mabel.

"We are unsure about any of it," said Gabriel quickly. "It's all suspicious."

"And these investigations require you, Sir Gabriel, to stay in Mistress Wetherspring's cottage, all night, hmmm?"

Gabriel didn't miss a beat.

"Lord Robert asked me to look after Mistress Wetherspring. We know that sometimes investigations of the sort we are forced to make, lead us into danger, Master Buttermere. This has been the case in the past. Would you have Mistress Mabel unguarded?"

"Unguarded? Ah—I see."

They could tell he wasn't quite convinced.

"Are you following us, Master Buttermere?" said Mabel.

"Following you?"

"That you know what Sir Gabriel is doing during his private time here in Bedwyn?"

"Certainly not—but I..." Master Henry leaned his whole weight on the table edge. "Have noticed..."

There was a strange creaking, a loud crack, the table buckled, broke and tipped the steward onto the floor. He fell with a long drawn out 'Argh!' of surprise.

Gabriel and Mabel beat a hasty retreat and swiftly closed the door.

*****

They had just about stopped laughing when they'd reached Mabel's cott.

"We shouldn't be laughing. It's no laughing matter that a little lad has had his brains knocked out or that another has been pushed down a cliff," said Mabel suddenly serious. "We need to find out more about how Little Archard managed to get almost a mile to Chisbury."

"I suppose he was playing, wandered into the woods and just kept walking."

Gabriel grimaced.

"He was only three. I don't believe it. He was taken there, I'm sure."

"Are his family able to answer some questions or—are we a bit too early with the questioning?"

"The sooner the better. I think things might be forgotten if we leave it too long."

The Tapscott household consisted of father, mother, three children and grandmother, the Widow Tapscott, who had been looking after the child Archard on the morning of his death. She was now to be found weeping into her apron alone in the house. The remaining children were staying with a neighbour, Mistress Mosspath, and the parents of the unfortunate lad were away bringing his body home.

"He's never gone off before," said his grannie in a high pitched wail. "I only took my eye off him for a moment."

"Mistress Beatrice, your daughter-in-law said that you had been drinking and were not awake when he wandered off. Is this true?"

"Only an instant—just a heartbeat."

"That's all it takes, I'm afraid," said Mabel.

The woman wept louder and harder.

"When did you last see him?"

"In his bed at roughly about the third hour. Terce. We all slept late because of the celebrations."

"Where were his parents?"

"I don't know—I was—asleep."

"So Archard's parents went out and the children, the other children, where were they?"

"John went out with his father, I suppose and Edith with her mother."

"And you were alone with Archard?"

She nodded and wiped her nose on her sleeve. "Ohhh they are blaming *me*—will they arrest me—for his death?"

"No. I don't suppose they will," said Gabriel.

"But you will have to live with his death for the rest of your life. That is an immense punishment for a moment of inattention," added Mabel sadly.

The woman stared at her as if she hadn't thought of such a thing and then gave a huge screeching cry.

To stop her from wailing, Mabel asked,

"So you think he just wandered off and no one saw him go. He wasn't with anyone?"

"No," said Widow Tapscott. " No, no one saw him. It's just the same—the same as that other time."

"Just the same as which other time?"

"Just the same as the little lad who was killed a year ago." Suddenly the woman had stopped crying.

"I don't remember anyone being killed last year," said Mabel. "I've lived here all my life."

"Ah no—they weren't from Bedwyn. This was in Crofton. "

Gabriel's puzzled face turned to Mabel.

"A forest village a little way from here."

"A little lad went missing?"

"He wandered off and fell off the cliff where the river is," said the woman. "It was my cousin's girl's boy."

Mabel could only think how very unlucky this family was.

"Where exactly?" asked Gabriel.

"I dunno."

"Do you know who found him?"

"No, I'm not sure. It was some fella who was working on the river I think."

Gabriel's eye moved slowly to Mabel's face.

"Are you thinking what I'm thinking?"

"I think I might be."

*****

Four hundred feet, four inches and four heartbeats away from the Tapscott's house, a man was skulking behind the trees at the back of Mabel's cott. He couldn't afford to be seen, for he knew what would happen. The villagers would drive him away and then he'd never know what was going on. And he desperately wanted to know what was going on. He stretched his overlong and scrawny neck, running his fingers around the rough stuff of the neck of his knee length tunic.

Was his scrawny neck in danger of being stretched, or was he going to get away with it?

He spat. No one was home. He'd have to come back at night.

*****

Crofton was a village a little to the south of Bedwyn. The river ran through it and there were pools where some of the local inhabitants fished for brown trout and other fish to supply the towns round and about and the castle at Marlborough.

Mabel made inquiries of a few of the Bedwyn villagers. Master Wilfred Hartshorn had been the best informed about the incident.

The cliff at the river was quite steep, he'd said. Apparently some children had been playing there. "It was a young lad by the name of Dunstan Durwood. A few of them had been playing and Dunstan went over the edge."

"Did no one miss him?"

"The children had been told not to play there and they were rather afraid because they'd disobeyed. They didn't say anything until later by which time the lad was dead and someone else had found him."

"Oh who was that?" asked Gabriel.

Master Hartshorn took off his coif and scratched his head. "Some fella who'd been working the river. Erm—a fisherman I think."

"Nah, Master Hartshorn, it wasn't a fisherman, it was a boatman," said Mistress Hartshorn.

"Ah so the man found the body in the river?"

"Well—no—not immediately—and not in the river."

"Can you tell me what happened from the beginning, Joan?" said Mabel, a little short of patience.

The elder Hartshorn offspring, Thierry, who was about thirteen years of age, suddenly began the story again, riding over his mother's words.

"The lad went over and the children said they scattered, see. They were scared, see. Scared they'd get told off. So this fella was coming along the road at the top, see, and he sees the body and when he realises it's dead, runs off for the authorities, see."

"Thank you."

"But by the time they got there the body was definitely dead," added Thierry Hartshorn.

"Ah yes. Bodies *are* usually dead," said Gabriel, taking out his little waxed tablet. "Do we have a name for him? This man."

They all shook their heads.

"The children said that there was a man who had been seen holding onto a child and that made them a bit afraid," said the elder Hartshorn.

"Oh?"

"Where was the man who found the body?"

"Was it the same one who was holding onto a child?" asked Gabriel.

"I think they said at the top, on the lane."

"Could they see what he was like?"

Master Hartshorn sighed. "Just that he was tall with a beard and he wore a hood."

"Thank you, that's very useful information."

Gabriel and Mabel were walking back to her cottage when she suddenly stopped.

"Ah. —Gabriel…?"

"Yes?"

"If this happened where I think it did and I have only been there once, then it's not possible to see the river or the banks, from the road at the top of the cliff."

"So this man lied."

"It would appear so."

"We need to have a look," said Gabriel. "For ourselves."

*****

They set off for Crofton, in quite a gale, Mabel riding pillion on Bertran. They were silent for some while.

"I hope this isn't one of those clues which is no clue at all," said Gabriel at last, as he navigated the rough road south from Bedwyn to

Crofton.

"We need all the help we can get, Gabriel," said Mabel. "We aren't getting anywhere with this."

"And we have no idea who this new man is. Or where he comes from."

Mabel didn't answer.

"Mabel?"

"Yes."

"You are going to have to be very careful with Master Buttermere."

"I can handle Henry." She shifted her bottom in the saddle and drew away from Gabriel.

"He is a suspicious man. It only needs him to spy on you and—well—it could be disastrous for you."

"Master Henry Buttermere is too lazy to spy. He rarely comes out of the manor. And is too dense to know what's happening right in front of his nose."

"He obviously thinks there's something going on between—between *us* though, doesn't he?"

"Well—he's wrong."

"Is he?"

"He is—isn't he?"

Mabel drew closer to Sir Gabriel again and laid her cheek on his back, wrapping her arms around him. Simply for security, you understand.

"Well...?"

"Take the next road left. I think the place where it happened is just where the trees thin," said Mabel.

Into their view came a stand of old oaks and birches and beyond, some large, spiny gorse bushes many of which were just coming into flower.

"Is this the place?"

Mabel wriggled from Bertran's back. She didn't want to make

contact with Gabriel, the close contact was becoming emotionally painful and she knew that he'd want to help her down from the saddle.

"Be careful, from what I remember, it's quite a drop," she said.

They walked Bertran a few feet towards the gorse.

"You stay here, boy." Gabriel wound the reins around a spiky branch. The smell of the gorse flowers was lovely.

The wind buffeted their clothing as they reached the slope.

"So here's a path. There's the road."

"And you are absolutely right, the river and bank cannot be seen from there," said Gabriel leaning over. "Or here."

"So whoever found the young lad's body was not up here. He was down there."

"He cannot have seen the body from this road."

"But why would he say that he had?"

They walked a little further down the path.

"Wait here for me. I want to scout around, just to make sure that there isn't another path or a further steep bank."

Mabel turned withershynnes and lifting off into the wind, she dived from the edge of the cliff.

Gabriel watched her go, his heart in his mouth. How could she just dive off like that? What if she'd failed to fly? He watched the kite gain height and fly over the river valley with its ponds and pools.

She was so confident with this magic of hers. He shielded his eyes from the fitful sun and watched as Mabel took a turn over the gorse and swooped low over the water. He'd never get used to her being so reckless; it worried him.

No sooner had he lost sight of her than she was back and standing behind him.

"It was here. Without a doubt."

Gabriel looked around at the grass and the little lane, further off. He stared up at the sky.

"The children were playing here and one went over—about..." He leaned over the edge of the bank... "Here? I—oooh!"

89

A freak gust of wind took hold of his split cotte, and lifted him as if he weighed nothing. His feet went from under him and he toppled over the edge in a sliding movement.

"No—Gabriel!" cried Mabel, reaching out but she missed him.

She instantly dropped to her knees and could see Gabriel clinging to a tuft of rough grass at the edge of the bank a few feet below, his legs dangling in the air.

What could she do?

Lying flat she inched closer to the edge and extended her arm but it was no good. She couldn't reach and the edge just crumbled away in a trickle of earth and pebbles.

She yelled against the wind.

"Gabriel. I shall become a goat. Cling to me."

In the next instant she was almost moving over the edge as she was turning withershynnes and saying, "I wish to be a goat with long horns."

Gabriel was yelling something at her but the wind took his voice away.

Mabel's feet developed little cloven hooves. Her body doubled over and her arms became legs. Her nose lengthened and long horns grew from her forehead. Her skin became pale and rough coated. She dug in those cloven hooves and started over the edge of the grass strewn cliff.

She put down her head and puffed and she saw Gabriel's hand disengage from the tuft of grass which had saved him and which was gradually parting from the chalky soil of the bank. The wind continued to buffet them both.

She shouted loudly. This was meant to sound like, "Take hold of my horns," but it came out as a feeble bleating.

She felt him grasp her left horn.

She pulled back and dug in her rear hooves but she realised she was beginning to slide. She pulled harder.

Gabriel scrabbled up the pebbly bank and now both hands

reached for her horns.

She could see he now had a purchase on the plants of the drop with his booted feet. Slowly she drew backwards.

Suddenly the grass of the edge parted from the soil and Gabriel fell a foot or so down the cliff face.

Mabel could see the horror in his red face, red with the exertion of staying upright.

Gabriel climbed and Mabel pulled and at last he came over the top puffing heavily.

"I thought I was…"

"Naaaagh"

Gabriel rolled to safety down the slight slope of the grass, between the gorse bushes, at the top and lay there panting. After a while he got to his knees rather shakily.

"The wind was more powerful than I thought."

"Naaggh."

He ran his hands through his hair and wiped his sweating forehead. "Thank you Lord and thank you Mabel."

He looked around to make sure no one had been watching. That could have been very embarrassing.

"Maybe that's what happened to the little lad?"

"Master Hartshorn said that, when it happened, it was a still summer's evening. No wind," said Mabel, back to herself again.

"Ah… well."

Neither of them wanted to talk about what had just happened.

Gabriel looked over the lip of the small valley more carefully this time. His heart was ceasing to hammer.

"How do we get down there?"

"This way. Lead Bertran."

In no time at all they were at the side of the small river which wound its way through lush grasses and looking up at the hill which had nearly been the end of Sir Gabriel Warrener.

They both looked up at the slope.

"There are plenty of places where a small body might stop en route."

"You mean," said Mabel, "that even if you fell, you might not fall the whole way...?"

"Not if you weighed nothing."

"Not if you were a three year old child you mean."

"I, on the other hand, would have plummeted like a pebble tossed into water."

"And no doubt you'd have fallen foul of the nasty stones on the way down and just here."

They looked at those nasty stones and then at each other.

"Thank you, Mabel."

"I'm useful sometimes."

He wanted to take her in his arms and tell her how much he loved her. He wanted to kiss her. But the moment had passed.

She'd turned away.

"I think the child was probably pushed off. Or if he did fall, someone made sure that he didn't recover when he got to the bottom."

"Hmmm."

"Gabriel. There's something I haven't completely shared with you—yet."

"Ooh—what's that." His heart skipped a beat.

"Someone, not necessarily the killer, is covering the eyes of all the children, with leaves. Just like Mistress Gelle."

"What?"

"We saw nothing on Henry Lovegrove because he was in the water but Archard and this little lad..."

"Dunstan... Durwood?"

"They both had leaves on their faces. And so did Mistress Lovegrove. Gelle, you remember."

"And you didn't tell me this because...?"

"At first I thought it was pure coincidence and then I was unsure what it meant."

"And what does it mean?" he said with a slight irritation in his voice.

"Someone doesn't want to be seen by the dead. Someone covers the dead eyes, covers them with leaves."

"Why?"

"I have no idea."

She fiddled in her tight sleeve.

"And then there's this."

"A brooch?"

The little silver brooch lay on the palm of her hand.

"I found it in the river when I went to look for Johnny," said Mabel.

"It looks new."

Gabriel took it from her. His fingers grazed the palm of her hand and it sent a shiver through her.

"It might be nothing to do with our crimes but d'you know—I seem to know that I've seen it before but for the life of me, I can't remember where," he said.

CHAPTER SEVEN
~ THE SPARROW ~

As they trotted home they discussed the leaves which had been found on the faces of the bodies.

"How do you know about Dunstan?" asked Gabriel. "You didn't see the body."

"Master Hartshorn is part of a huge forest-wide family. There are Hartshorns in almost every village in Savernake. One of his relatives helped to bring in the body and noticed the plantain leaf. Of course this means that someone saw the body after death at the site of the murder and before anyone else went to fetch it home."

"Someone else or the murderer."

"We need to find the person who found the body and reported it."

"I've asked everyone I know, said Mabel. "No one seems to remember who it was."

"Surely there will be a record at the coroner's office?"

Mabel nodded. "I think old records are kept at the castle somewhere."

"Not every case is recorded though," said Gabriel with a tinge of sadness. "Peasant children are not deemed important enough for records to be kept about their demise even if their deaths are sudden and unexplained."

Mabel clicked her tongue in annoyance.

"I was all ready to fly up to the castle and get into the clerks' room."

Gabriel looked back at her over his shoulder, "I tell you what though. I bet the county constable has a record. He's a stickler for record keeping, I've heard."

"Sir Aumary Belvoir?"

"The very same."

"I wonder where he keeps his past investigations?"

"He has an office in the castle."

"And he lives in Durley not too far away," added Mabel. "The record will be at one place or the other."

They turned northwest at the first opportunity and soon came upon the outskirts of the village of Durley.

It was slightly bigger than Bedwyn and houses were clustered around a green and strung out on two major roads. The manor was behind a sturdy wall at the western end.

Mabel asked Gabriel to wait for her in the trees and she rapidly became a tiny sparrow and flew from the cover of bush to bush and into the manor courtyard. Where would the Lord Belvoir keep his records?"

Perhaps in a chest in the church?

Ah no. The church was closed and had been for some years owing to the Interdict. This death happened in the summer of the previous year and so records were likely to be held in an office somewhere else.

Mabel flew into an elder bush growing up the manor wall and settled in amongst other sparrows. There were no leaves on the tree now, so she pushed her way nearer to the wall and watched and waited.

After a short while a man came out onto the top step of the manor house. He was tall with curly black hair and wore a good quality blue cotte with an embroidered band around the neck and sleeves.

"Here we are my little friends," said Sir Aumary Belvoir, as he scattered some crumbs from his dinner all along the base of the wall. The resident sparrows seemed to recognise this as a daily occurrence and almost to a bird, flew down to graze on the offering. One sparrow did not fly down.

Instead, Mabel followed the constable into the screens passage as he returned to the building and quickly flew into the first room, landing out of sight on the cross piece of the base of a daybed which lay against the wall.

How long would she have to wait for him to vacate the office?

Damn. He had a pile of parchments in front of him and was working methodically through them, reading, (reading silently, she noticed—how clever was that?) and sealing them. This looked like a long drawn out job.

He had left the door open and Mabel could see the comings and goings of the great hall. Marching towards the office was a small child of about seven.

"Papa?"

"Yes Simon?"

"Can you tie that knot for me again? I've forgotten how to do it."

"The falconer's knot?"

"Yes. The one you showed me yesterday."

"Where's your rope?"

"In the hall."

Sir Aumary Belvoir stood up. "Come, let's go for a drink and then I'll show you again and maybe another knot too."

Mabel heard the door close and the key go into the lock.

Now! Where would the record be?

She flew up onto the table and cast her beady little sparrow eyes over the room. She was standing on a piece of parchment. She lifted her left leg and looked down at the writing. It was in a tidy clerkly hand.

'Deposition by Mistress Mabel Wetherspring of Bedwyn.'

'Well, well', thought Mabel, 'It's the account I gave the constable about finding the body of little Archard.' He must have taken the notes he'd made and had them written up.

The little sparrow jumped from line to line as it read the words, her own words, written down on the parchment.

Then there was an extra line or two.

'It will be recalled that over a year ago another little boy was found dead in similar circumstances. I feel the two deaths may be linked.'

Ah yes, the constable had made the same connection that she and Gabriel had made.

Mabel read on, hopping from foot to foot in excitement.

'There seem to be similarities with the two deaths, not least that a plantain leaf was found over the faces of the boys.'

"Well!" cheeped Mabel. "*You* know that because *I* told you."

'The first body was found at the bottom of a steep gradient at Crofton and death seems to have been caused by a blow to the head with a rock. Dr. Johannes of Salerno is of the opinion that this blow was struck intentionally. It is unknown whether the second death was caused deliberately but Mistress Mabel Wetherspring tells me that the body was covered over with rock debris when she found it. This suggests foul play. I have no reason to disbelieve the woman. She is a reliable witness, observant and articulate.'

Mabel smiled a sparrow smile.

"The witness to the first death, however, is not so reliable and I am inclined to think that the first finder in this case knows more than he is telling. In the light of this recent death, I need to examine him again.'

The constable then went on to name the man who had discovered the first body, that of Dunstan Durwood.

And, with a shock, Mabel realised she knew the man.

*****

Mabel was so surprised at what she'd read she didn't react quickly enough to the sound of a key in the lock. A man entered the office. He had long silver-blond hair, a thin face with a sharp nose and was very smartly dressed.

She heard Sir Aumary Belvoir's voice from the hall behind him, refer to him as Henry.

"I think I left it on the window ledge, Henry," he said.

"Right, m'lord."

Mabel leapt into the air in a panic. She needed to hide.

Sadly she'd left it too long not to be seen and she flew first right and then left looking for a way out.

The man called Henry cried out. "Oh no! There's a damn sparrow got into the office. It'll make a terrible mess!"

Mabel panicked. To her utter embarrassment, she voided her sparrow bowels in fright. The man Henry had been right. She flew up to the ceiling and then down towards the window. The shutters were open and she fled at top speed, hoping to exit through the window.

Sadly she wasn't aware that Sir Aumary's office windows were glazed and that they were all closed.

Flying blindly here and there as the instinctive bird behaviour took over from her human thoughts, Mabel flew straight into a thick pane of glass.

"Ouch!"

Henry of Manton heard "CHEEP!" as the little bird fell on the floor and lay still.

*****

Gabriel was pacing back and forth. Mabel had been such a long time. What was she doing?

He paced further. Then, making up his mind, he mounted Bertran and rode directly into the village and up the main road. He stopped just before the manor gates and dismounted.

"I'd like to see the Lord Belvoir please," he said to the first person he met crossing the courtyard.

The man took his mount's reins from him.

"Certainly, sir. Who shall we say has called?" Gabriel noted that the man had a shock of bright red hair.

"Sir Gabriel Warrener from Bedwyn."

The man handed Bertran to a groom and then said, "This way sir."

Up the steps and into the screens passage, Gabriel followed the young man.

Gabriel heard, "What shall I do, sir?" the voice sounded very worried.

"Well, it's still alive, Henry. We shall just have to keep it warm and comfortable until it wakes, if it does and then let it go."

"A visitor, m'lord. Sir Gabriel Warrener," said the red headed man peering into the office.

"Thank you Cedric. Ah—Sir Gabriel. You find us at sixes and sevens."

"I'm sorry to intrude, my lord."

Gabriel looked over the shoulder of the man Henry, as the steward gave a little something into the hand of his master.

Sir Aumary reached for a small box which stood on his table, tipped out the contents and put the little something gently inside.

"One of the little sparrows which are usually to be found outside the window in my elder tree has found its way into my office and knocked itself senseless on the window glass," said Belvoir with a chuckle.

Gabriel's heart fell to his boots. "Oh—how—unfortunate."

"I'm sure it will recover. Now what can I do for you?"

Gabriel looked over the rim of the box. The little hen sparrow was hunched down with its eyes closed.

"Erm..." Gabriel had to think quickly.

"I have discovered some information, my lord, which I thought might be pertinent to the recent deaths of the two lads. The most recent in Bedwyn and a death in Crofton last year, if you are interested to hear what I have to say."

"How fascinating, Sir Gabriel. I was just thinking about these two deaths myself today."

"I have found out that it's not possible to see the river valley and the scree slope from the road at the top of the incline. The man who gave the account of finding the body of little Dunstan Durwood, cannot have been telling the truth."

"Ah..."

"The only way he might have seen the body of the child is if he had been at the bottom, in the valley itself."

"Which implies...?"

"That the man lied. And he lied, perhaps, because he had something to do with the death."

The little sparrow gave a strange cough and opened its eyes.

All three men leaned over the box to peer at it.

"Ah, it seems the creature is still with us," said Belvoir.

"And if he lied about that, might he also be involved in the death of Archard Tapscott?"

The sparrow stretched its wings.

"Shall I take it out, m'lord?" said Henry.

"I er..." Gabriel drew the box closer to him. "I have a little knowledge of birds, sir."

"Oh...?"

"Yes. I... I... erm... I have made a study...of little birds such as this... er... erm..."

"Sparrow...?"

"Yes, sparrow. Hen sparrow. Small birds like... chaffinches and... and... robins..." Gabriel was thinking frantically. "Larks and... lapwings... my lord."

"Well, well." Sir Aumary was beaming at him and folded his arms over his chest. "I heard that your expertise was with rather larger creatures, Sir Gabriel."

"Oh?" Into Gabriel's mind came Mabel as a kite, a peregrine and a sparrowhawk.

"I heard you were hunting the Beast of Bedwyn, the gryphon."

"Oh—yes—indeed. But it seems that the creature is found and

now dead and burned to a cinder, so..." Gabriel shrugged. "My task is at an end."

Sir Aumary smirked. "I am pleased to hear it."

The little sparrow chirruped in its box and tried to stand. It fell over again.

"Oh dear. I do hope that she hasn't sustained any lasting damage," said Belvoir.

Gabriel quickly butted in.

"I have some expertise with injured birds, sir. May I take her and look after her?"

"Certainly you may," said the constable. "And bring her back to her family in my elder tree when she is fit—eh?"

Gabriel picked up the box and clutched it to his chest. Mabel slid from one side of the box to the other with a startled 'Erk!'

"May I take the box?"

Lord Belvoir, a slight smile on his lips, nodded.

"Thank you for your information, Sir Gabriel. We appreciate your—observations."

Gabriel nodded a bow and hastily backed out of the room.

As he descended the steps he heard a voice say.

"Well—what an odd young man."

It was the Durley steward, Henry of Manton. "I'm sure he wasn't telling the truth about birds," he added.

"He likes birds, Henry. A man who likes birds can't be all bad."

Gabriel beat a brisk retreat before they changed their minds.

*****

The next day, Mabel had the biggest bruise upon her forehead that she had ever sustained. And the nastiest headache. Her neck too was stiff and painful. She fiddled with her nose. It was very sore. Had she broken it?

Gabriel peered at it and pronounced it whole, just bruised. He smeared some of her tumbler's cure-all over her injuries and chuckled.

"*I* now have a reputation as a bird doctor, all because you tried to fly through a closed glass window."

"I wasn't to know it was glazed. And besides, it was very hard to see. It was all green and cloudy," said a very nasal Mabel.

"Ah well—now you know."

Mabel had not really regained her wits until they'd reached Bedwyn. She refused to speak about what had happened. After supper she went straight to bed and stayed there all the rest of the evening, waking the next morning stiff and pained.

"So... what did you learn?"

"Learn?"

Gabriel drew up a stool to the fire, sat and poked the flames with a stick.

"You went to the Lord Belvoir's office to learn what you could about the man who reported finding the body of little Dunstan, didn't you?"

"Ah, yes—I did."

"Well, what did you learn?"

Mabel rubbed her sore forehead and succeeded in making her fingers sticky with the balm.

"The Lord Belvoir had come to the same conclusion we had."

"That there was something wrong about the story the man told?"

"Yes..."

"Who *was* the man?"

"Erm..."

"Aw c'mon Mabel—it's important."

"Gabriel, don't rush me. I have an almighty headache. And a sore neck."

"But we need to find him."

"I know. Don't you think I don't know that?"

"Well come on then. What's his name?"

Mabel opened her mouth. Nothing came out.

"Do you know—I—erm—I can't remember. I simply can't remember his name."

"A bang on the head does this sometimes," said Gabriel. "It helps to talk about the incident, the period of time just before the thing you've forgotten—and you might..."

"Gabriel?"

"Yes?"

Mabel lay down on her bed.

"Go boil your head!"

CHAPTER EIGHT
~ JOHN FOUR ~

They heard the hullabaloo as they were bedding down to sleep that night. Shouting and a name being called over and over. It sounded so loud in the semi darkness.

"John... John... where are you?"

Mabel padded in her bare feet to the door and pulled back the locking bar. She drew her blanket cloak over her shift and around her body, for it was a cold evening.

"What's the matter, Master Head?"

"Mistress Mabel—Mabel is that you?"

"What's the matter?"

"It's John, Little John Four."

Master Head was the village reeve. He had five sons. One, Gilbert, was the youngest son of his first wife and the only product of that marriage still living in the village. He was much older than the rest. Yes, Master Head had five sons, and four were by his second wife. Or rather he had once had them. His eldest was called John. He'd died a while ago when bullneck disease struck the village. Then Master Head had had a second son, who was found dead one morning in his cradle at the age of ten days. He had been John two. John three had fallen from a tree at the age of six and hit his head, dying after three days. John Four was the three year old son of his father's older age and now it seemed, he was missing. His mother was screeching into the darkness.

"John Four, if you don't answer me this very moment I'll..."

"Have you asked around the village?"

"Aye we have. No one has seen him since late afternoon."

"Can I help, master reeve?" said Gabriel, throwing his cotte over his head and buckling on his belt.

"That would be so helpful yer lordship," said a worried Master Head.

"I'll get dressed and come and search," said Mabel and from the corner of her mouth she said, "I'll fly about to see what I can discover." It was a good job only Gabriel had heard her words.

Flares and lanterns could be seen moving haphazardly about the village in the darkness as people searched for Little John Four.

Mabel flew above them all, penetrating the darkness with her keen bird eyes. She could see so well, even though what she was seeing was grey, silver and white. It was ten times better than a human might see at night and the darkness was not at all frightening to an owl.

She soared on bright white wings and plunged and rose over the trees. She passed Master Hogg's pigs, closed up in their pen for the night. She dipped over Mistress Peabody's hen house. She fluttered, with a tiny movement of her wing tips, over the fields now denuded of their crops and ploughed up ready for the spring sowing. Little coneys were hopping about in the ruts and furrows and they scattered as Mabel barn owl passed overhead.

No Little John Four up on the common. No Little John Four lying, (God forbid) anywhere out in the open. He hadn't fallen asleep under a tree or on one of the major lanes.

She could see people with lanterns poking with sticks into tall grasses now decaying and old nettle patches, bracken and blackberry bushes. Others were scouring the riverbank.

It was cold and set to get colder as the night progressed. Little John Four would need to find himself somewhere snug to lie, or they'd find him frozen solid in the morning.

After a long time of flying around the village, Mabel returned to the green where many folk had now collected. She found Sir Gabriel.

"Anything, Mistress Wetherspring?"

"No, nothing."

Gabriel seemed to have taken control of the search.

"It's the darkest part of the night now. We'll not be able to see much. Do we think perhaps that it's best to re-group tomorrow at dawn and start again?"

Mistress Head was sobbing into her husband's shoulder.

"We'll find him, we promise," said Matty Peabody, patting her back.

"He'll come marching home, I'm sure, right as rain, half way through the night," said Mistress Corngold.

"He's fine…" said Eadric Caerlson, who'd joined the search. "I'm sure he is."

Mistress Head turned on him. "What do you know, you turnip headed clod?"

Eadric was taken aback. He stepped away from her.

"You couldn't find Henry or little Archard! Could you?"

"Ah no but…"

"Ah—get outta my sight!"

'Now,' thought Mabel, 'That was odd.'

Eadric Caerlson's shoulders sagged as he turned and walked away.

*****

Mabel brooded all night on Mistress Head's reaction. She hadn't been rude or angry with Matty Peabody or Thomasina Corngold. Why did she so take against what Eadric had said? His sentiment had been exactly the same as those women.

The following day they all woke to a sharp frost and they had to knock the ice from their washing bowls before they could splash their faces.

The sun was just coming up as Gabriel and Mabel were walking to the green where several people were waiting, shuffling their cold feet and grasping cloaks and blankets tightly around them. All were breathing smoke, like the Beast of Bedwyn.

Master Head, wearing sheepskin mittens which covered his thumb and split for two sets of two fingers, was talking to Master Buttermere the steward, just outside the manor gates.

The reeve was waving his hands towards the river.

"And we need to look in the river and the pond."

"It's freezing, man! No one will want to go and tackle the water in this weather." Henry Buttermere was being his usual dour and selfish self.

"*We'll* do the river and pools, Master Head," said Mabel, l looking at Gabriel who nodded seriously. Only he knew exactly what she'd meant.

They peeled off from the main throng of people and walked to the pool where Henry had been found, looking back to make sure they weren't followed.

"A fish again, eh?"

"No, I think I'll be an otter. They have keener eyes and are better in cold weather. Fish aren't so active in the cold."

"Right."

Gabriel screened her from the prying eyes of the villagers and took up a stick with which to prod the banks of the pond.

"No one's looking."

Mabel slipped silently into the cold water. Thank goodness for her otter fur.

And two thousand two hundred heartbeats later, she slipped back out of the water and shook herself.

Gabriel came running up.

"Nothing," she said when she had achieved her own self again.

"Well that's good news—isn't it?"

"I'll tell you what IS good," she said with a smile.

"What?"

"I have remembered the name of the man who discovered little Dunstan."

"Who...? Who?"

"Eadric Ceorlson."

*****

Gabriel blinked. "But..."

"When I went to the Ceorlson house one night..."

"You did what?"

"I went as a little mouse to the Ceorlson house and had a sniff around." Mabel wrinkled her nose—and it hurt. "I had a *real* sniff around."

"You never told me."

"You were snoring and I couldn't sleep."

"That's not an excuse for not telling me."

"I sniffed out Eadric shoe soles."

"Ergh. Did I need to know that?"

"His shoes were stained with and smelled of the little late pink crab apples which fall from the tree growing by the Tapscott house."

"So?"

"They get trodden into the path by their goat. What was Eadric doing on their path by that tree?"

"You'll have to show me where the tree is."

In the distance, they both heard the beat of horses' hooves and turned to the main road.

"It's the constable," said Gabriel. "Going towards the manor. He'll go and speak to Buttermere first and then probably Master Head."

"Ah yes. He too has worked out that Eadric isn't telling the truth."

"He's come to interrogate him further?"

"I would think so."

"Mabel..." Gabriel took hold of the tops of her arms. "You have to get into their meeting and spy."

"Oh I do, do I?"

"You most certainly do. We need to know why Ceorlson's been lying."

She looked up at him, through her eyelashes. He was so enthused by the prospect of Eadric's interrogation. His eyes flashed. He was excited. He wanted to know. She sighed.

"Oh alright then," she said.

*****

Later that day and a little way from the Ceorlson house, Mabel saw the two constable's men walking up to the door. She lingered close by. If nothing else she'd be there to look after Godyth and her grandma if things turned at all nasty.

Godyth came to the door. There was a mumbled conversation and then she heard the girl say, "He's not here. He's out in the forest, at work."

The two men looked at each other.

"Where does he go to work?"

"He's a river man."

"What does that mean?"

Godyth shrugged. "He works on the water."

"Whereabouts lass?" said the short stocky chap.

Godyth just gestured into the forest in the direction of Crofton and shut the door.

Mabel heard the other man say, "We'll have to follow the river."

"Aye—all the way back to Crofton." He turned his eyes up to Heaven in dismay.

They turned and saw Mabel. Quickly she bent down to make it seem as if she was retying her shoelace.

"Where does that path lead to, mistress?" said the short stocky one with a brief but sunny smile.

Mabel pushed back her head cloth.

"To Crofton. The river goes all the way. It's downstream." She knew what she'd said was rather silly and unhelpful but... it was enough.

Again they exchanged a glance. It was obvious they didn't want to have to follow Eadric but how else were they going to be able to bring him before their master?

In the blink of an eye, Mabel turned withershynnes and soared up into the treetops.

Her back became a beautiful green with yellow under feathers. Her nose lengthened and became a sharp and deadly beak of silver. Her eyes rounded and turned white and her crown grew feathers of the most startling red.

The green woodpecker flew over the river with its twists and turns but at no point did she see Eadric.

On her way back, she saw the constable's men dawdling down the riverbank.

'Ah well,' she thought, 'At least I'll be able to find Gabriel before they find Eadric.' Or she hoped she would. As luck would have it she was able to land right in front of him.

Gabriel had been looking for her. "Where did you go?"

"I tried to find Ceorlson but he's nowhere to be found in the village. The constable's men have gone to Crofton to see if they can find him."

"Crofton?" Gabriel's brows rose into his hair with surprise. "Ceorlson's a tied peasant. He won't be in Crofton. Not without permission."

"I know—I sent the men on a bit of a chase. I wanted to find Eadric first because it begs the question, what was he doing there when Dunstan was found?"

"He'll be here somewhere, in the village or close by."

"I've looked west. I think we now need to look east."

They started up the river path towards Froxfield, Mabel riding pillion on Bertran. Not quite two furlongs into their journey, they spotted a boat floating on the river. A man was digging out the bank with a long handled shovel. A large man with dirty blond hair and a beard.

"What on earth is he doing?" asked Gabriel.

"There's a lot of flooding along the river hereabouts. They try to keep the pools deep so that it doesn't flood the good land. They then put the waste earth on the fields. They dig the gravel from the surrounding area too."

"Master Ceorlson!" shouted Gabriel. "A word, if you please?"

Mabel jumped down from Bertran's back.

They were totally unprepared for what happened next. Eadric Ceorlson threw away his shovel and with one gigantic leap he pitched himself from the boat onto the riverbank.

Gabriel followed on Bertran, leaving Mabel behind.

"Oh damn!" she heard him cry. "Where does he think he's going?"

It was rather an unequal contest. Gabriel and Bertran at last drove the fugitive onto the fields and away from the river and Mabel's sleek brown plumage and evil yellow eye did the rest.

She stooped at Eadric, her peregrine claws coming out to grasp hold of his clothing as he ran. He pulled both arms across his head and fell.

Gabriel soon stood over him, grinning.

"Master Ceorlson, why did you run?"

"Argh! Get it off me."

Mabel had her claws sunk into the man's brown tunic and she was none too gently pecking his hair.

"Ah Mabel—come now. Master Ceorlson submits. There's no need to try to eat him," said the knight.

*****

Making sure that Mabel was not seen transforming, it took them but a short while to secure the villein but secure him they did and with

Ceorlson attached to Bertran, his hands tied with his own belt, they clopped leisurely into Bedwyn.

"Well, well, Sir Gabriel and Mistress Wetherspring. I see you have managed to achieve what my men have been unable to do."

"Just a matter of knowing where to look, my Lord Belvoir," said Gabriel, smugly.

"Yes, well. We'll see what we can get from our man? Shall we?"

Gabriel looked a little surprised. "You want me to…?"

"Well, it would be most unfair of me to hog the suspect when you have done so much of the work in apprehending him."

Gabriel gave Mabel a wide eyed look. She knew what the look meant. He'd want her there to listen in.

The man was untied and hauled from the horse's side and taken into his own home. His mother had been farmed out to one of the neighbours so they could be undisturbed. They sat Ceorlson on a stool and stood over him.

"My friend, Sir Gabriel Warrener tells me, Ceorlson, that you cannot have seen the body of Dunstan Durwood from the top of the lane. Would you care to elaborate?" said the Lord Belvoir.

Ceorlson looked up. "Eh?"

"What the Lord Constable is saying, Eadric, is that when you made your statement some months ago about the young lad Dunstan, you may have made a mistake in saying that you saw his body from the lane at the top of the bank."

"It's a long time ago."

"We are not asking you what you remember, we are asking if you told the truth. And actually we know you didn't tell the truth because you cannot see the river from the lane," said Belvoir.

"I have personally walked that piece of lane, Eadric and I can tell you, it's not possible," added Gabriel.

His eye was caught by a small movement close to the window behind the constable. A tiny wren had just hopped over a window ledge.

'Ah—Mabel,' said Gabriel to himself. 'I'm glad you could get in to hear this.'

"I..." began Ceorlson.

Suddenly there was a screeching at the door.

A man burst into the cottage, followed by the two men Sir Aumary Belvoir had brought with him.

"Sorry m'lord, he just jumped us," said one of them, as they attempted to catch hold of the man's arms.

"You bastard!"

"What?" Ceorlson was taken by surprise.

Master Head the village reeve pushed off the two Belvoir men and went for Ceorlson's throat.

"I'll kill you. I'll bloody kill you!"

There was an undignified struggle and the small man belonging to the Lord Belvoir, punched Master Head, the Bedwyn reeve, on the cheek.

"That will do now, Tostig. I think the man will no longer be a problem," said Belvoir.

But he was wrong.

As soon as people had drawn back, the reeve went for Eadric again.

"What have you done with him, where's my boy? Where's JohnFour?"

Gabriel grabbed him around the throat and pulled him back.

"Master Head, this is not the way to do it."

Eadric's stool tipped up and pitched him onto the floor. The Bedwyn reeve went on pummeling him. Eadric Ceorlson had covered his head with his arms and was screeching. "No—I had nothing to do with it!"

"Cease this now! Stop." The Lord Belvoir waded in and gave the frantic reeve a heavy buffet to the head. It shook him and he drew back allowing the others to subdue him.

"Take him out. I'll speak to him later."

They all took a moment to recover.

"So unless you'd like us to let Master Tapscott and the young lad's father Master Head in again to beat you to a pulp," said the constable. "I think you'd better start to tell us all about these missing and dead children, Master Ceorlson."

"I don't know nothing."

"Eadric, we know that you had a hold of little Johnny Chatterwell. I saw you myself. Then you were at the place by the river where Little Dunstan was murdered. And now we find you might have taken Master Head's son John," said Gabriel. "Why—Eadric, why?"

The Lord Belvoir folded his arms across his chest and leaned against the wall. 'What must he be thinking?' thought Gabriel. He once had a five year old son who had been brutally murdered. And he now has a nine year old son. How painful this must be for him. Lord Belvoir's face, however, was totally serene.

"And then there's the body which Mistress Wetherspring found, that of Archard Tapscott."

Eadric looked up. "I didn't do any of it."

"It was so awful for Mistress Wetherspring to find that body. She'll have nightmares for years."

Eadric began to cry.

"What have you done with the boy John Head, Ceorlson?" asked the constable in a very quiet voice.

Eadric grimaced.

"Ah well. We'd better get the fathers back in to beat it out of you." Gabriel turned to the door.

"Nah!" pleaded Ceorlson.

Gabriel's hand was now reaching for the door latch.

"Please—please—sir." Ceorlson appealed to the Lord Belvoir.

"Ah no, I'm not going to stop him," said Belvoir, shaking his head.

Gabriel turned at the door, just as Eadric made a bolt for freedom, trying to push past the knight.

But Gabriel was too fast for him and with one punch to the gut,

Eadric was rolling on the ground gasping and weeping.

"Where is he?" said Gabriel through clenched teeth, grabbing the neck of his tunic.

Once he'd managed to get his breath, Ceorlson said. "He's in my shippon."

"And where's that?"

"Down by the river."

"Where?"

"At the back of my plot."

Gabriel picked up the man and sat him on the stool again.

"There." He dusted him down. "That wasn't too bad, was it?"

Eadric blubbered.

*****

They found little JohnFour unharmed in the cow barn by the river as Ceorlson had said.

Gabriel had gone with the boy's mother and the two Belvoir men, to recover the child. "It seems to me that he'd been cared for, m'lord. He was covered in blankets and had food. He wasn't bound, just locked in."

Belvoir paced the manor hall. "Well done, Sir Gabriel. One death averted."

"You think so, sir?"

Belvoir stopped, looked up at the hall rafters and said, "No."

"It doesn't hang together, does it, sir?"

Belvoir sat on a bench and sighed. "No, it doesn't. But we have to charge him with abducting the boy and keeping him."

"If he has killed all the others, why keep this one lad?" said Gabriel.

A voice broke into their conversation, "Forgive me, sirs,"

"Mistress Wetherspring," said the Lord Belvoir. "Come. Sit by the fire."

"Mabel?" said Gabriel, forgetting that he was supposed to be formal with her. The constable's eyebrow went up slowly.

"Erm—Mistress Wetherspring. Have you found anything?" said Gabriel at last.

"You ask why Eadric did not immediately kill the young lad, JohnFour?"

"He killed all the others in the same way. A rock to the head," said Gabriel.

"Maybe he was planning it...?" said Belvoir.

"Does Eadric Ceorlson seem to you like a man who plans, m'lord?"

The Lord Belvoir looked carefully at Mabel, "Go on, mistress."

"I have just spoken to Ceorlson in the lock up. He is terrified..." The wisp of a smile came onto her lips. "Particularly terrified of Sir Gabriel and the fathers of the boys. He answered my questions quite willingly."

"Ah well, you have the advantage, mistress, you know him well."

"I have known him for years, though he's only really an acquaintance."

"And would you say he is the sort of man who could kill a child in cold blood?"

"I would say that he might kill in an unguarded moment to protect his family but a child? No. He's a man of little intellect. If he was angry then a crime might be committed in the heat of the moment. A crime of his passions. But the planned murder of a child? No, m'lord. And certainly not a child he knows."

"So, how do you explain that he knew where the body of the young lad in Crofton lay?"

"Oh he told me why that was."

"He did?"

"He said that Godyth told him."

CHAPTER NINE
~ CHISBURY MANOR ~

"Gabriel's face wore an expression of complete mystification. Then the Lord Belvoir said, "You are telling us, Mistress Wetherspring, that the young girl Godyth was also present when her uncle found the body of the young boy Dunstan Durwood?"

"I am, sir. In fact, I think it was not Eadric who originally found the body. It was Godyth herself and she told him where it was to be found."

Sir Aumary Belvoir walked to the one window of the house and looked out.

"And before you ask us, sir, she did not mention this at all, when we questioned her."

Belvoir straightened his long split cotte of blue wool and cleared his throat.

"Have you questioned her about every death?" he asked, turning around, his face very stern.

Mabel looked quickly at her feet and then up at Gabriel.

"I have been unable to find her. I was going to question her on my own but she can't now be found in the village."

"Then we must set a search in motion for her," said Belvoir, his expression now turning to one of worry.

"Might we find that Godyth is yet another missing child? Another victim of this abductor?"

"Shall I begin the search in the village, m'lord?" said Gabriel.

"I think that would be a good idea, Sir Gabriel."

They quitted the house and watched as little JohnFour was hurried away home by his family.

"Please take charge. I would not have Master Head and his wife worried by this latest development. They've had enough to contend with."

Mabel looked up at this tall knight of the realm.

What a very kind man he was and how lucky they were to have him as their overlord in the forest. He was also bright enough to realise that Gabriel and she would do a better job than Master Head.

The day was marching on and hours of daylight were short at this time of year. They needed to move quickly.

"So how do we go about it?" said Gabriel as he watched the warden and his men ride off in an easterly direction.

"We ask Eadric where he thinks his niece has gone."

"Are you sure he'll tell?"

"Those two, it seems to me, are joined at the hip. He'll know and he'll tell."

Eadric Ceorlson was languishing alone in the lockup. Master Lovegrove had been removed to Marlborough castle gaol pending his trial for the murder of his wife. Eadric's face was scratched and his left eye was beginning to close where he'd been thumped. He was rubbing his shin where, Mabel supposed, he'd sustained further injury as he fell from his stool.

He was wary of Sir Gabriel and paddled away from him on the beaten earth floor when the knight entered the place.

"I haven't come to hurt you, Ceorlson."

"I have told Sir Gabriel what you told me, Eadric. That it was Godyth, your niece who first discovered the body of Dunstan by the river," said Mabel.

Eadric gave a slight nod.

"Will you tell him what you told me?"

The man ran his wrist over his nose and it came away bloodied. "She told me where to look."

"How did she know where the boy lay?"

"I di'n't ask her."

"You didn't ask her how she knew where a little boy who had been killed could be found? Did that not make you curious, Eadric?" said Gabriel.

"Nah, she knows all the children around these parts. What they're doin'."

There was something about the way he said this that made Mabel prickle with fear.

"Eadric. Why would Godyth be at Crofton?"

He shrugged. "She goes everywhere. No one can stop her."

"Like when she used to go to see her mother in Chisbury?"

"No one can stop her. Not even Master Lovegrove."

"When she becomes an adult next March, she will be confined to the village and environs. Her master will make sure she obeys," said Gabriel.

Ceorlson threw him a look and Gabriel was unsure what it meant. But Mabel knew it meant 'good luck with that!'

"If we wanted to find her now, where might she be if she's not in the village?"

"Playing with the other bairns I s'pose."

Mabel's stomach turned over. "Where?"

Ceorlson shrugged again. "I dunno."

"Eadric, can you tell me how your shoes came to be full of the mush of the late crab apples which fall from the tree outside the Tapscott house?" asked Mabel.

The man laughed suddenly and quickly. Mabel and Gabriel were surprised he was so jolly about it. "You can't eat'em."

"No, I know that. So what were you doing there?"

"Standing."

"Why were you standing there?"

"Just standing."

"It's quite a way from where you live and even further from where you've been working."

Ceorlson began to become upset. "I can't tell you. It's… it's a secret."

"Aw c'mon, you can tell me"

"No."

"Then do you think I might be able to guess?" said Mabel.

Ceorlson shrugged but at the same time he smiled which seemed to invite Mabel to hazard a guess.

"You were waiting for little Archard Tapscott to come out of the house."

Ceorlson chuckled, shaking his head. "Nah—wrong."

"Was Archard in the house when you were standing there?"

"He musta bin."

Gabriel sighed. This was getting them nowhere and he said so. But Mabel did not agree. She definitely thought that it told them something. Outside the hut, Gabriel and Mabel drew together and whispered.

"Shall I quarter the area and see if I can find her?" said Mabel.

"I don't know…"

Gabriel paced away from her. "You know the children, Mabel. Who will tell you where they play?"

"Johnny Chatterwell is the most friendly child," Mabel grinned. "When he plays he does so with everyone."

"And he's a special friend of yours, I seem to remember."

Mabel poked out her tongue.

*****

"Hoodman's blind."

"What?"

'Hoodman's blind. You know—the game..."

Mabel sat down on a tussock of grass.

"Johnny, you mean you were playing hoodman's blind?"

"That's right."

"Where were you playing it?"

Sir Gabriel hovered above them with his arms crossed like a nervous fly.

"We played in a clearing in the forest up by your house and we played by the river. But we shouldn'a bin there."

"How many of you?"

"Well there was me and Isabella and Tildy, of course."

"Your sister?"

"Yeah. She was a bit silly as she kept taking off the hood and we told her she couldn't play if she kept doing that."

"Which Isabella was it?"

"Issy Corngold."

"Any boys besides you?" asked Gabriel.

"JohnFour."

"Little JohnFour who went missing today?" Gabriel had stopped pacing.

"Who else?"

"Sometimes Alys Hardhand."

"Boys, Johnny, we are interested in the little boys." Mabel put her arm around the lad.

"Peter Swineherd. He played with us. But he doesn't like Goddy so he stopped playing."

"Why did he do that?"

"He said she was too bossy. But I got bossy sisters so it didn't matter to me. I'm used to it."

Gabriel's mouth crinkled in amusement.

"Johnny, when you got lost Eadric found you—he did find you didn't he?"

Johnny looked up at Mabel. "He's a bit light in the 'ead. Me da says he's got ale for brains."

"Well I'll admit he does drink quite a bit," said Mabel.

"Me ma says that he can't take drink and it goes into his head because there's nothing where his brain should be."

"That's as good an explanation as any."

"And he doesn't piss it all out again. It sticks there."

"Right."

Gabriel cleared his throat. "The day you got lost, who did you go into the forest with?"

"I went looking for the winged pig."

"Yes I know you did. But I don't think you were alone, were you?"

"Goddy came with me."

Mabel whispered to Gabriel. "Eadric denied that Johnny had company, didn't he?"

"To try to find the pig?"

"Yes."

"What happened then?"

"I thought I saw it and I ran away after it and when I tried to find her, I couldn't see her and I kept yelling for her. But she wasn't there."

"That must have been very frightening."

Little Johnny Chatterwell stuck out his chest bravely, "Aw no. I wasn't frightened."

"Then what happened?"

"It was night."

"Now that must have been scary."

"Nah…"

"What then?"

"I saw Master Eadric."

"Did he say why he was in the forest? So far away from where he normally works?" asked Mabel, "And from Bedwyn?"

"No. But he wanted to find Goddy, he said. And he found me instead."

"Why did he want to find her?" asked Gabriel, giving Mabel a wide eyed look.

"He said she was supposed to be at 'ome."

"And so what happened then?"

Johnny Chatterwell jumped up. "We went looking for the flying pig. Me and 'im." He pointed with a firm finger at the sky. "Master Ceorlson said that *he* believed that there was a pig and he wanted to find it—like me."

"And so the two of you walked back to Bedwyn? Did you see the pig?"

"No." Johnny sniffed. Mabel thought that this action signalled his disappointment. "We didn't."

"Where was Godyth during all this?"

"I dunno. She musta got back on her own."

Mabel stood up and took the young lad's hand. "Did she ever say that she saw the pig? Did she tell you?"

"No." Here Johnny Chatterwell's eyes twinkled, "But she *did* see the fire breathing gryphon and she said next time we went out, we could go and look for that."

"Now that would be exciting."

"Yeah."

Gabriel hunkered down in front of him. "Godyth told you she saw the Beast of Bedwyn?"

"Yeah. At Crofton."

Gabriel gave Mabel a significant look.

"She told me she'd seen it and that she thought the beast had been responsible for the death of her brother, Henry," said Mabel.

"Oh...?"

"Best you don't go out even if you are with someone, Johnny. That beast might be dangerous."

The lad's eyes grew as round as a ladle. The danger in the situation was exactly why he *would* go searching.

"You don't think it's dead then, mistress? Like what they say."

"Not if Godyth has seen it recently."

Johnny swallowed. "Can I go home now?"

"One more question. Where do you think Godyth is now? She's not at home."

"If the beast hasn't got her then I suppose she'll be out looking or something."

"Where?"

"Chisbury Copse, or Stock Farm, I suppose. That's where she said she saw it. Or Crofton by the cliff."

*****

Mabel desperately wanted to get out of the house and the village. She felt trapped there. She needed to turn three times withershynnes and become some wild animal running free, flying unfettered, feeling the wind in her fur or feathers. Leaving the real world behind, pulling off the shackles of everyday living.

She needed time to think.

Leaving Gabriel to a supper at the manor, she took off towards Chisbury Copse and wheeled around in the sky until it was almost dark. When Mabel kite could no longer see in the crepuscular light, she became a night owl and glided silently on white wings, peering into every crevice, examining every tree bole and searching every hedgerow.

Something bothered her. Why was Godyth talking about the Beast of Bedwyn? Of all the people in the world, Mabel knew with certainty that the gryphon had taken to the skies just once and it would never return. She *was* the gryphon.

Why did Godyth say she had seen it when it was impossible? Was it just as Gabriel had said, the product of a childish imagination? Or was it something else? And where was she now?

Mabel veered over the incline at the manor house at Chisbury where the body of Gelle Lovegrove had lain. Could she see a light there? Might that be a small fire?

She swooped down and landed on the ruined wall.

Blinking languidly, her white eyelids slowly covering her bright black eyes and then snapping open again, Mabel looked down on the ruin of the great hall, turning her head smoothly side to side.

Godyth had built herself a small fire and she was sitting by it, clutching her knees.

Every so often she would poke the flames and add a few twigs, a pile of which she'd made beside her.

The girl seemed perfectly happy out in the dark alone. Mabel remembered times when *she* had been out on her own in the dark. It had never bothered her either. She didn't worry about noxious night airs or demons which stalked the landscape looking for unwary souls. She was more interested in the hungry badger as he dug for worms and slugs, the calls of the night birds, like the owls and the nightjar and the shape of the sure footed fox against the moon as he hunted for carrion with his sensitive nose or pounced on unsuspecting voles in the long grass. These were her companions of the night and nothing of which to be afraid.

Mabel lifted off and took a turn around the ruin, landing a little way away. Three turns to deosil and she became Mabel Wetherspring again. So as not to startle the girl, she called out.

"Godyth, Godyth, it's Mabel Wetherspring. Can I come into your place?"

The girl jumped up and stood as stiff as an iron bar, her hands to her sides. "Mistress Mabel—what are you doing here?"

"I followed you Godyth. Everyone in the village is very worried about you. They didn't know where you'd gone."

"*You* knew."

"I guessed that maybe you'd come back to the place where your mother lived."

The girl pushed her curly locks behind her ears. "This was where she was found."

"That's right. Sir Gabriel and I found her. But you'd been here too hadn't you? You came to see her and she told you to go away."

"I went home."

"But you came back and that was when you found her dead, wasn't it? Just before we found her. I saw you running away."

Mabel came into the light of the fire. "Why did you run?"

"I was frightened."

Mabel pulled her kirtle around her. It was cold out in the countryside on that January night.

She sat down and put her hands out to the flames.

"Why were you frightened?"

Godyth looked away, uncertainty written on her face.

"You are like me, Godyth, you aren't worried by the dark, by the creatures who inhabit the night. What frightened you?"

The girl bit her lip and slowly seated herself again.

Mabel looked up at the ruin of the manor walls. The creeping ivy growing there was moving gently in the breeze and it looked like a slithering creature of the night moving slowly forward as it made patterns and shadows on the stones.

"It seems to me that you aren't easily frightened, by the night or by anything in the day. You went out with Johnny Chatterwell to search for the flying beast. That's not the action of someone who is easily frightened."

"I *so* wanted to see it."

"So did Johnny."

"We went together but he ran off."

"He told me that he thought he'd seen it and he ran away from you. And then he got lost. Is that the truth?"

The girl nodded.

"Who else wanted to see the beast?"

"No one."

"Did Henry, your brother, want to see it?"

"No."

"What about Archard?"

"He was just a baby."

"Well then, did John, little JohnFour? Was he interested in the beast?"

"He is a baby too."

"Do you know why they wandered so far from home, Godyth?"

She shook her head vehemently.

Well, it was certain, Mabel thought, she could not trick Godyth into telling her the truth.

"You know that your Uncle Eadric is in the lockup and he is very likely to be charged with stealing away little John Head. If those who are going to try him think that he also killed the other children, then he will hang for them too."

The dark brown eyes were black pools in Godyth's face. "My uncle tells lies. He's a drunkard and he tells lies."

"But I don't think he's a murderer, is he, Godyth?"

Mabel made herself comfortable on a large stone.

"Why did you say that you'd seen the Beast of Bedwyn, Godyth? You know that it wasn't true. You haven't seen it."

The child's face disappeared into the darkness as her black hair swung forward and made a curtain into which Mabel could not see. There was no answer.

"What happened when you came to see your mother? I know I have asked you this before but this time will you think about your answer and answer me truthfully? Did you see Master Lovegrove kill your mother?"

"No."

"But you saw who did?"

The girl nodded, her dark waves bouncing around her face.

Mabel pulled a few more twigs from the pile and fed the fire. It crackled and spat.

"Was it someone you know?"

She nodded again.

"Can you tell me who?"

The girl shook her head. "I can't tell you. If I tell you, he will kill me."

"How do you know this?"

"Because he said he would."

"We can protect you, Godyth."

"No."

"Why is Master Lovegrove saying that he killed your mother when it's not true and *you* know who did?"

"He is looking out for me. You'll have to ask *him*."

They sat in silence for a while listening to the sounds of the night. A dog fox screamed fairly close by; it was the mating season. A pheasant disturbed by the fox's footfall went clucking up into the bracken.

"Godyth—please tell me, who killed your mother?"

The girl sighed.

"It was my father," she said.

CHAPTER TEN
~ THE GAOL ~

She is incredibly confused, thought Mabel. She doesn't seem to be able to hang on to reality. One moment she's telling me that her father didn't kill her mother and in the next she's saying that he *did*.

"Your father cannot hurt you, Godyth. He is in the gaol at the castle in Marlborough."

The girl shook her head and although Mabel thought she had added a smile, she couldn't see it.

"No, he isn't."

"Would you like to go and see him? Sir Gabriel could take you."

"No, thank you."

"How did you know where little Dunstan Durnsford was lying dead in Crofton? Were you there when he was killed?"

"Did my uncle tell you that? I've told you that he tells lies. Especially when he's drunk."

Mabel was beginning to get chilled. Chilled in the body and the soul.

"I think we had better begin to walk home now. You know the way through the woods, you show me."

Sighing deeply, the girl doused the fire and stood.

"If you don't know the way, how did you get here?" she said.

"I know a different way. Not the way you'd come."

It took them almost an hour to walk to the village and Godyth was welcomed back with hugs, tears and admonishments by her frantic grandmother.

"Thank you Mistress Wetherspring. Thank you for returning my precious girl to me. She is all I have now."

Mabel walked slowly into her cottage and lit a lamp. Gabriel was flat out on a bench in the darkness, fast asleep.

She looked down at him, his mouth open, his hair falling over the top edge of the bench in waves, his hands locked over his belly, gently snoring like a puppy.

"I think it's time you went to lie down, don't you?" she said. "Properly. On a bed."

Gabriel woke up with a snort and Mabel thought he sounded like one of Master Hogman's porkers.

"Oh—it's you."

"If you continue to sleep on a hard bench with your feet over the edge you'll have cramp and backache tomorrow."

"Oh? So you speak from experience do you?"

Mabel poked the fire into a glimmer.

"I'll have you know as a knight, I am trained to sleep on a knife edge."

"Well sleep on this thin thread of information, Sir Gabriel," said Mabel. "I found Godyth at Chisbury manor..."

"You've been out there? All alone?"

Mabel slaked her thirst on a pot of ale. "No one knew I was there and I found Godyth on her own."

"So, no one *had* abducted her?"

"No. She walked there but I got her talking and she said something—interesting."

Gabriel ruffled up his hair and Mabel chuckled at him.

"You look like a Wiltshire horned sheep."

"What?"

"Your hair. You have two horns of curly locks," she giggled.

"Sticking out. You do look funny."

"You don't look so well kept either," countered Gabriel, smoothing down his unruly locks.

"Well, I have just walked a mile through the woods keeping my eye on a very strange young lady." Mabel took up her comb and began to run it through her waves. Then she rapidly plaited it.

"She doesn't seem to care that her father…"

"Master Lovegrove?"

"Yes, that he will very likely hang for the murder of her mother. Or that her uncle will be charged and convicted of the abduction and murder of the local children. This is a girl who until a few days ago was close to her father and even closer in a way, to her uncle Eadric."

"So what has happened?" Gabriel slid up to her on the bench.

"Something, certainly. And she seems frightened. And she knows jolly well that I know that she is lying about seeing the Beast of Bedwyn. But she persists in the lie."

Gabriel gently put his arm over her shoulder. She felt the warmth of his body rippling through her own.

"What else did she say?"

Mabel went through the conversation she'd had with Godyth, whilst Gabriel listened intently, absentmindedly and sweetly stroking her neck .

It distracted her and she found it hard to tell a coherent tale. She wanted him to stop. But she desperately wanted him to carry on.

"We need to speak to Master Lovegrove again. I have a few—new questions for him."

"Such as?"

"Well for a start, who is this person that Godyth is afraid of?"

"You think he'll know and if he does, he'll tell?"

"It's worth a try."

"I can get into the castle tomorrow," said Gabriel.

"Ah no—no—I am coming too."

"I doubt they'll let *you* in."

"I won't be coming as Mabel Wetherspring, Gabriel," she said, looking at him in disbelief. 'Don't you know me by now?' she thought.

"Ah—a magpie or a jackdaw, eh?"

"Or maybe a sparrow?"

"Ah no. Not a sparrow. Please. I'll not have you flying into any more panes of glass."

"I'll not do *that* again."

"You are the most accident prone girl I know," he chuckled.

"Know many girls who can go flying into window glass, do you?"

She stood and went over to her bed, throwing her plait over her shoulder in a gesture of pique.

"Aw c'mon Mabel."

"You won't even know I'm there."

Gabriel folded his arms across his chest.

"A magpie, a jackdaw, a pigeon, a peregrine, a cat—even a horse. Try something else, will you?"

"You'll just have to wait and see."

"I bet I can work out what you are…"

"You won't!"

"I will!"

"You won't."

"Try me."

"Alright! You're on!"

*****

The woodpecker sped with its characteristic flight through the trees of Savernake; short flapping swipes of her wings and long swooping glides until she reached the edge of the forest trees.

She watched a large horse gently moving along the London road; a buff beast with a noble head and a mane like spun gold. The man riding her looked up to the sky and she saw him shrug his shoulders.

Mabel flew through the lower branches. Gabriel wouldn't be

looking for her there. He'd look up to the open sky as he had just done expecting a kite, a sparrowhawk or a peregrine.

Mabel chuckled and the sound came out as 'klu klu klu klukluklu!'

She landed on the grassy mound of the Marlborough castle keep, scattering a scourge of starlings already poking their beaks into the earth. To encourage the illusion that she was in fact a green woodpecker, she too poked her beak into the grass.

"Ugh! Pah!" She spat out soil and clacked her beak together, her long tongue flicking in and out. "Ugh. Why did I do that?"

Something ran up her beak. She tried to work out what it was. It wasn't until it was quite close to her nose that she realised it was an ant.

Cross eyed, she spotted it marching down the length of the blade of her beak and shook her head.

'Now concentrate, Mabel!'

But the ant would not be deterred. It ran onto the underside of her beak. Mabel knocked it on the ground. 'Get off!'

But the little creature was tenacious.

'Don't make me eat you. *Please* don't make me eat you!'

The ant continued to run around her beak. Mabel followed it with crossed eyes.

'Right. I warned you.'

Mabel's long tongue came flicking out and in an instant had grabbed the ant. Could she swallow it? She kept her beak closed for a while. 'Now what?'

"Ugh no! Creepy crawly things! No! Not squirmy things—no." She couldn't. She couldn't swallow it! It was running around her mouth and tickling.

She spat it out and in the next moment lifted off from the grass.

She needed to get into the castle keep and she wanted to do that before Sir Gabriel got there.

She knew that Master Lovegrove was being held in the gaol and that the gaol was deep in the keep, the massive white painted tower which dominated the town. She hopped towards the base of the building.

There she saw some metal grills set into the wall quite low down.

This must be where the cells were.

She pressed her head to the grid and peered in with a white eye. It was very dark. How could she see if Master Lovegrove was in there?

She tried to squeeze through the grill. Ah no, the squared bars of the grid were just a little too close together.

Right: only one thing for it. Mabel chuckled to herself. Gabriel would never guess this one! She'd win the bet without a doubt.

*****

Sir Gabriel handed Bertran's reins to a groom.

"I'll call for him in a moment—I won't be long. Where can I find the gaol master?"

He was easily found and Gabriel was pleased to see that the man was friendly, clean and personable.

"Ah yes. Sir Gabriel Warrener. The Lord Belvoir has spoken of you."

"Favourably, I hope?"

"Oh yes indeed." There was a slight smile on the older man's face, "He was concerned that you might be injured when tackling the Beast of Bedwyn, I gather."

"Ah—Master Gayle, I have not yet managed to find the creature. Indeed I think it a figment of the imagination of a whole village."

Master Gayle jiggled his keys and removed his coif to scratch his white hair. "Really? Well, well. He also tells me you are an expert in birds."

Gabriel cleared his throat. "Might I see the prisoner, Phillip Lovegrove?"

"Certainly you can."

The key grated in the lock and Gabriel ducked under the lintel into an almost complete darkness.

Master Gayle struck some tinder and a small circle of light flickered around him and sent his shadow scooting up the wall.

"Just let me light some candles."

Master Lovegrove shielded his eyes from the light flashing in front of him. He'd been here in this semi darkness for three and a half days and he could not bear the sudden brightness.

"Someone to see you, Master Lovegrove. Shall I leave you, Sir Gabriel?"

"Thank you. We have private business to discuss, Master Gayle. I will call you when I need to leave."

The door rattled shut.

"Lovegrove, it's Sir Gabriel Warrener. I have come to ask you some more questions."

Lovegrove stood shakily. "Questions, sir? I—I have answered questions."

"Yes, but now we have new evidence and we need to speak to you about it."

The man seemed wary.

Gabriel looked around. The roof was barrel vaulted and painted though it needed a further coat of whitewash, for it was growing mildewed and green. Around the perimeter of the small room was a stone bench which served as both seat and bed. The floor was beaten earth. He could smell the bucket which had been provided as a privy for Master Lovegrove. He moved away from it.

Passing through a dark patch, he hissed through his teeth, "Mabel, Mabel are you here?"

He heard no feminine reply but that of Master Lovegrove's, "I beg your pardon, sir?"

"Nothing—no—er—nothing."

Now he had adjusted to the gloom, Gabriel fixed the prisoner in a small patch of light coming from the outside through the grill.

"Are they treating you well?"

Master Lovegrove snorted. "Oh. It's a palace, sir. Three meals a day, bread with all of them and as much water as I can drink. And the accommodation is most..."

"I didn't need an answer, Lovegrove."

"No, sir."

"But I do need an answer to this. Why did you swear to the killing of your wife Gelle, when you did no such thing?"

Phillip Lovegrove flinched. "Because..."

"Ah no. I will not accept it. The truth please."

The prisoner fell silent.

"Lovegrove, you will not know that your brother-in-law, Ceorlson, has been taken up for the murder of your son Henry and for the abduction and murder of some further children of the village."

Lovegrove's face was puzzled and horrified by turns. "No, I didn't know. And it cannot be true—none of it."

"He was found hiding one young lad away. The reeve's son, JohnFour. He was caught red handed."

"No! Eadric may be a bit simple but he'd never harm a child. I cannot believe it."

"Mistress Wetherspring, are you here?" said Gabriel again a little louder. 'I thought we'd do the questioning together?"

Mabel stepped out into the light. "Yes, I'm here. I followed you in."

"Ah yes—right."

Lovegrove had jumped out of his skin. "Mistress Wetherspring. Where did you...?"

"Hello Phillip. I came to see that there was fair play. And to ask a few questions of my own."

Gabriel gave Mabel an exasperated stare.

"Master Lovegrove, we have been speaking to Godyth," she said.

"Oh God, no." The man immediately lowered his head and they couldn't see his expression.

"Who is it she is afraid of, Phillip?" said Mabel gently. "Because I am certain she is afraid of someone—and it's not you or her uncle."

"No—no one."

"She doesn't seem to care that you will hang or that her uncle will be charged with the murder of the children."

"You must not speak to Godyth."

"Why not?" said both Gabriel and Mabel together.

"She is—she does not tell the truth."

"She seems very—confused about the night that her mother was killed. First she tells me that you did not kill her and then she says—yes, you did."

"You cannot trust her."

"You are telling us that we cannot—*you* cannot—trust your own daughter?" said Gabriel.

"She's just a child."

"She will be twelve in two months. Then she will be considered an adult, with all the responsibility that the age of twelve carries."

"No."

"An adult, capable of bearing all that the law may bring down on her."

"No!"

"Who killed your wife, Phillip? I think you know."

"No—I did it—*I* did."

"Who killed your son Henry?"

"I…"

"It wasn't you. You were in your house when it happened. You have an alibi and I cannot believe we have two murderers in the village. That's too much of a coincidence," said Mabel, coming closer. "Isn't it?"

"Anything you can tell us would be helpful," said Gabriel.

But Master Lovegrove was silent on the subject and began weeping.

Mabel went down on her knees before the man.

"Come, Phillip. You have known me for a long time. You are a good man. I know you are. Life has been most unkind to you but with the strength of God and your family you have come through it. Don't throw away your life now."

Gabriel gave her another exasperated look.

"It's no good. We might as well go," he said.

Mabel rose and looked down on Phillip Lovegrove. "Phillip, answer me one question *truthfully*."

The man wiped his snotty nose. "If I can."

"You are not Godyth's father, I think. Tell me. Are you Godyth's real father?"

The man's face was stricken. His eyes grew large and terrified. Then his whole body slumped.

"No—no." He shook his head.

"Who is her father?"

"I—I can't say."

Gabriel's mouth was open. How did Mabel know that? How had she guessed the truth?

"Well, if you will not tell us, we shall have to go and leave you to your fate."

"She was pregnant when I met her."

"You married her, knowing this?" said an incredulous Sir Gabriel. "Aye—I did."

"You didn't care that Gelle was having another man's child?"

"No, I didn't. I loved her."

"Who was the father of the child?" asked Gabriel.

Lovegrove merely dropped his chin to his chest.

"Phillip. We are trying to help you. And we can't do that if we don't know the whole story."

"It's not what you think!" burst out Lovegrove.

"What is it you think we think?" said Gabriel.

"That I was a jealous man and..."

"Phillip. You have admitted to killing your wife in a rage. But as far as I understand it, you are not the sort of man who has a short temper," said Mabel. "Why do you suddenly break and kill your wife, after six years? Why have there been no rumours in the village about your temper? Your children have been safe with you for six years. Why now?"

Lovegrove rose and looked out of the tiny gridded window.

"After Godyth was born, Gelle just had no interest in the child. She left her to lie in her own filth, she'd forget to feed her. It was as if Godyth was not her own child."

"So this is where Gelle's mother came in. She had to look after her?"

"Gelle wasn't like this with the others?" asked Gabriel.

"She was not a particularly good mother, no, not ever," said Lovegrove. "Not with any of them but although she was distant and wasn't very loving to them, she played her part."

"It was only Godyth in whom she really wasn't interested?" asked Mabel.

Lovegrove sniffed and nodded his head.

"Then when little Nalle came, my wife disappeared and I couldn't find her."

"I hear that after their children are born, some women become ill and withdrawn," said Mabel. "This malaise passes after a while, I'm told."

This was all news to Gabriel for he'd had no experience of such things. He looked from one face to the other with an uncomfortable feeling in his chest.

"It didn't pass. She never returned," Lovegrove wiped his eyes. "And when Godyth was a tiny baby, she not only neglected her but she did try to kill her on several occasions. I managed to stop her—or her mother did."

"What did she do?" whispered Mabel.

"She tried to strangle her."

There was a terrible silence as Mabel and Gabriel took in this horrible news.

Eventually Lovegrove sighed. "And then she was gone. Gelle was gone for good."

Mabel sat down on the stone bench and closed her eyes.

"But the older Godyth got, the more she wanted to see her mother?" she asked.

"I wasn't able to stop her. I tried. She'd find out where she was and she'd visit even if Gelle told her she wasn't wanted."

Gabriel sat by Mabel and leaned forward, his arms on his knees. "Who told Godyth where her mother was?"

Lovegrove bit his lip.

"It wasn't difficult to find out. It was all over the village, all over the forest that Gelle Lovegrove was a prostitute living in Ramsbury." The man covered his face with his hands. "And then recently that she'd gone out to Chisbury."

"That's where I found Godyth last night, Phillip. She'd gone back to where her mother had lived."

"Aye, she's drawn to the place. There and Crofton."

Suddenly he'd taken in a huge breath and squared his shoulders.

"When I went to see her to bring Godyth back, there was another man there."

"A client of Gelle's?" asked Gabriel.

Lovegrove snorted, "Nah!"

"Who?"

"Just a man with pale hair and a beard. Just a man."

"And you don't know him?" asked Mabel.

There was something about the way in which Phillip Lovegrove slumped on the hard stone bench. Mabel *knew* she had to push him.

"*Do* you know him?"

Tears trickled down Lovegrove's cheeks.

"Gelle was lying on the earth and the man had a stone in his hand."

Gabriel bounced up. "*He* killed her?" His voice was full of incredulity. "Why didn't you tell us this before?"

"I—wanted to."

"Why put yourself under suspicion? We could have been looking for this man. All this time we could have been searching..."

"Who is this man, Phillip?" said Mabel.

The agony visible on the man's face made a bitter taste come into Mabel's mouth. He struggled for many moments with his lips, trying to make words and then he said, "I do know him. Of course I know him."

"Who is he?"

Lovegrove's eyes came up to meet Mabel's and there was horror in them.

"He's Gelle's father," he said.

*****

The man who paced around the derelict cottage at Stock Farm was furious.

Lovegrove had been removed from his house in Bedwyn and there was no way he could get into the castle gaol to deal with him. It would have been easier at the village. Why did he not act sooner? He just had to hope that Phillip Lovegrove would be found guilty and hanged. Damn that Wetherspring woman. If she hadn't poked her nose in, he might have been able to put an arrow into Lovegrove. He'd just been a little too slow. That's all.

*****

No sooner had Lovegrove ceased speaking than there was a sudden rush of air into the base of the keep.

"Everything alright, sir?" said a voice.

Mabel quickly stepped back into the shadows so she wouldn't be seen.

A pot bellied, bearded and rubicund man came into view through the cell door. He lifted a lamp. "I thought I 'eard crying…"

"It's alright. Everything is under control," said Gabriel. "Thank you."

The man came forward. "Not giving you trouble is 'e, m'lord?"

"No. Not at all. I—er—I don't need any help, thank you."

The man turned to look into the jet black corners of the room. "I thought I 'eard a woman's voice..."

Mabel turned withershynnes three times and in her head she said, 'I wish to be an ant.'

Her waist shrank to a mere thread and her whole body fined down to less than a half an inch. Long antennae grew from her head and she scuttled further into the darkness. The man followed, peering into the corners of the cell.

"No, my good man, it's just us two here," said Gabriel, flicking an admonishing look at Lovegrove which said 'keep quiet and say nothing'.

Gabriel's eyes took in the interloper. Ah, he recognised him. He was one of the gate guards. The one called Bunce, he thought.

"Bunce, isn't it?"

"Aye sir, it is."

"Well, thank you. We can manage now. You'd best be back to your duties. I'm almost finished."

Bunce swivelled on his rather tatty boots and made for the door.

Gabriel had seen Mabel's diminishing form creep into the darkness. He'd sworn she'd become an ant. But—no—surely not.

The soldier made his way with a heavy tread back to the door.

At that same moment, Mabel ant made a dash for the light.

Gabriel watched helplessly as Bunce's large foot came down on the very spot where she had scurried. The. Very. Spot.

"MABEL!" he cried. "Oh no—MABEL!"

CHAPTER ELEVEN
~ THE ANT ~

Gabriel desperately wanted to cry out loud. "Get your foot off Mabel!" But he knew he couldn't. And anyway, with such a very heavy tread, Mabel must be nothing but a mushy mess on the bottom of the man's shoe. What was the use?

"I beg your pardon, sir?" said Bunce.

Gabriel bent double to look at the flagstone where an instant before Mabel ant had run. He had to close his eyes. Oh he *couldn't* look.

"You alright, sir?" said Bunce, peering down at him.

"Ah—yes. I—er—thought I saw—something on the floor here."

Bunce stepped back.

'Oh no! Not further pressure!' thought the knight.

"Nope—nothing there. Nope," said Bunce, swivelling on his sole to lock the door to the cell.

Opening his eye—just the one—Gabriel could see no horrible mess on the flagstone.

Maybe she'd managed at the last moment to avoid him. No, he'd seen what he'd seen. Bunce's foot had gone splat onto Mabel ant, *right onto her.*

His heart had jumped into his mouth, the back of his throat constricted and he knew this meant tears were not far away. He felt nauseous. His heart was thumping. He was hot.

"Ah Bunce, where are you headed now then?" he managed to croak.

"Now, sir? I'm going to 'ave a pint with my mate in the storeroom where 'e works. I'm off duty now, you see." He locked the door after Gabriel.

"Might I join you, do you think?"

Bunce looked surprised. "Ah sir, I doubt our ale will be what you're used to."

"On the contrary, my dear fellow, it will be—most welcome." Yes, thought Gabriel, if Mabel *is* dead then I shall be drinking myself to death tonight, poor ale or no poor ale.

Bunce stomped up the steps of the keep and into the lowest storeroom.

Oh—every thud was torment.

'I have to get her off his sole, even if she's squashed to a pulp—I have to,' said Gabriel Warrener to himself, shaking inside.

*****

Mabel's vision shrank to a few inches in front of her nose. She waved her antennae about to see if she could work out where to go.

Then, everything went dark.

She heard voices. Or she thought she heard them.

"Ooo orai ir?"

"Ah...e. I...er...or I aw...ome ing on a or ere."

Mabel shook her head. There was something wrong with her ears as well as her eyes. She wasn't hearing what people were saying.

"oe...o ing air...oe."

She wriggled side to side but found that she was wedged tight into—something.

Then after a little more of the noises she couldn't understand, though she did think that one of the noises was Gabriel, she found herself rising up from the ground and falling again rapidly.

144

'Argh!' She felt sick.

She put out all six of her legs and hung on to whatever it was that had her contained.

Up she came again and then down.

"igh I oin ou, oo ou in?"

Good Lord, what language was that? It was all vowels.

She tentatively took one of her six legs from its purchase on the wall of the thing which held her and groomed her ears—or where she thought her ears should be.

..."I ill ee ...ost el o."

Then Mabel realised that she *had* no ears. What she was hearing were vibrations in the air and from the ground. That was why she couldn't understand the words.

Once more she flew through the air and, hanging on tightly to— whatever it was—she was jiggled and jostled about until the thing stopped and she 'heard'.

"eul ay eer. Ial e us um ink."

'Ink?' thought Mabel, are we in the scriptorium?'

Once again she was rattled from side to side and had to hang onto the rough surface of the thing which held her.

Her antennae picked up an unpleasant smell.

'Phor! That smells like one of Master Platt's overripe cheeses.' He was the head cook at the Bedwyn estate.

Now it was dark again and she could 'hear' more conversation, all in vowels.

Then it came to her. "You wait here. I'll get us some drink," was what the voice had said.

It was now saying, "There you go m'lord, best castle ale that is."

So Gabriel *was* there. Oh how happy she was about that.

She hung on tight and wriggled her feet into more comfortable positions. All six of them.

Then daylight flooded in.

If she'd been a person, she would have blinked. Her eyes, which gave her a picture of the world which was a bit odd and fragmented, were suddenly blinded by a strong light.

*****

Bunce had put his feet up on the table. Then he decided that it perhaps wasn't a good idea with a knight looking at him.

He was about to pull them down again when Gabriel said,

"Ah no—you put your feet up, Bunce. It must be hard work all day, standing by the gate."

"That it is, sir. Mortal 'ard on the sole."

Gabriel fixed his eyes on Bunce's right boot sole as he crossed his ankles and sat back on the bench.

"My mate'll be 'ere in a mo."

"Good."

Gabriel scoured the sole of the man's boot.

His face got closer and closer to it.

Phew! The man had sweaty feet. It smelled like the rancid cheese Master Tipfinger put into some of his special dishes. Master Tipfinger was the head cook at the estate at Rutishall.

"Why don't you take your shoes off, Bunce?" said Gabriel. "Give your feet a rest."

"Oh aye, I'd like to do that but, well—beggin' your pardon, sir an' all that…"

"Ah no. I don't mind at all. I wouldn't tell you to do it if I didn't mean it."

Bunce thought long and hard.

Gabriel agonised over Mabel in those few moments.

'If he won't take them off, I shall order him, or I shall rip his shoe off his foot myself.'

"Well, this is uncommon kind of you, sir," said Bunce with a grin, bending down to undo the lacings.

"But I warn you…"

Another voice broke into the conversation.

"His feet are awful smelly. Best he keeps his shoes on, m'lord," it said.

"Ah. Sir Gabriel Warrener, this is my good friend, Roger Pennyfeather. 'E is employed 'ere, in the stores."

The man bowed.

Bunce put his feet up again.

Gabriel was sweating with anticipation and fear.

"Bunce, I'd like to have a look at your right shoe. Can you take it off please?"

"What sir? Why?"

"Just do as I ask."

Bunce screwed up his mouth and nose and put down his ale cup very slowly.

"Well alright. But don't say I didn't warn you."

He squeezed the leather together just above the sole and pulled.

Gabriel grabbed the shoe.

All along the sole at the level where the toes met the main part of the ball of the foot, was a long crack.

"This must let in water, Bunce," said Gabriel trying to be calm. "They're cracked—here." He pointed.

"Aye they do. I can't lie about that. But there's years left in 'em yet. Years!"

Gabriel brought the noxious footwear up to his eyes.

"Mabel, Mabel... are you there?" he whispered.

The two men looked at him in total confusion.

"Er—sir?"

Gently Gabriel flexed the shoe's sole.

"Tell you what Bunce. A man can only wear one set of shoes at once. How about you take mine? I'm feeling generous today."

"Aw, no sir, I couldn't possibly..."

"I insist." Gabriel was unlacing his own brown shoes. He pulled them off. "I have more shoes than I can possibly wear." This was an absolute lie.

"Here—with my—erm... Here, a gift. I am sure they'll fit you."

"Well, that's uncommon good of you, m'lord."

"I'll take yours with me."

"If you must, sir."

Gabriel bundled the shoes under his arm. "Right. I'll be off then. Thank you for the ale."

Which he hadn't touched, of course.

*****

Mabel was thoroughly dizzy with the toing and froing. First she was on her head, and then on her tail. Again she felt herself moved but this time it was more a joggling than a large scale movement up and down.

Her antennae smelt horses. Her eyes saw clouds or at least she thought they were clouds.

Then she was amongst grass. She could 'smell' it and everything was still. She could hear Gabriel's voice but she couldn't work out what he was saying.

She tried to pull herself from the things which kept her trapped. Suddenly a bright blue eye came very close to her.

"Mabel?"

"Gabriel!"

Sir Gabriel flexed Bunce's shoe sole and blew on it.

Mabel flew through the air landing on her back on the soft grass, wiggling her legs in the air..

She righted herself and checked all her appendages. She cleaned her antennae, she snapped her jaw a few times to make sure it still worked.

In a trice she had turned deosil and had said, "I wish to be Mabel Wetherspring again."

Mabel managed the transformation but it took a while. From

such a small animal to a much bigger one usually took some time and a great deal of effort. Eventually her two human feet hit the grass and she fell backwards, dizzy and rather exhausted.

The first thing she heard with proper ears was,

"Mabel Wetherspring! If you ever do anything like that again—I'll kill you!"

*****

Mabel stared up at the sky.

Her leg hurt. Her arm hurt. Oh, she ached all over. Probably with the effort of keeping herself braced safely in the crack in the shoe, which she now realised was where she'd been.

"Whatever possessed you to become an ant?"

Mabel pouted, "I didn't think you'd guess that one."

"Well, no I surely wouldn't because it's inordinately stupid!"

"Are you calling me stupid?"

"Well—yes, I suppose I am."

Mabel seethed.

"I couldn't get into the gaol so I crawled through the grill as an ant. I was sure no one would see me as small as an ant."

"No they didn't. Of course. But you were a half an inch from being squashed like a—like a bead of bread! I was so worried."

"Well, I'm alright, aren't I?"

"Mabel, do you not realise how frightened I was that you'd been killed?"

"You know I can look after myself." As she said this, she felt a bit foolish. It was obvious in this instance, she hadn't been able to.

"You must stop being so foolhardy with your transformations."

"You're not the Lord Stokke, you can't tell me what to do. He is my lord, not you."

"I am your friend, yes, but I am a knight and I outrank you. So, yes, I *can* tell you what to do. He is my lord too and my authority comes from him."

Mabel turned her back and started to walk home.

Two furlongs, two yards, two feet and two inches away from Gabriel, she turned withershynnes and became a pigeon. She flew in high dudgeon, all the way home.

*****

Gabriel plodded home to Bedwyn on Bertran. He now regretted his last words to Mabel; it was just that he had been so upset, so worried about her. She didn't seem to understand this. Why couldn't she understand?

He'd speak to her, be a little more conciliatory when he got home.

But when he tried the door to the cottage, it was locked.

"Looks like I am sleeping in the hall tonight," he said out loud.

He waited. He waited a long time. Then he heard the locking bar go up from the inside and he lifted the latch and pushed the door.

Mabel was standing a few feet into the cottage in the semi-gloom, her arms crossed over her bosom.

Gabriel took a deep breath.

"I'm sorry," he said.

She turned her back and walked purposefully to the fire and poked it with an intent to kill it, he thought.

'Ah well. At least she isn't killing me.'

Trying to keep things on an even keel, Gabriel took off his sword belt and his supertunic and said nothing more.

"There's pottage in the pot," said Mabel sharply.

He was going to say that tonight he'd eat in the hall but that wasn't going to go down well, he thought. So he didn't.

"Right," he said in the blankest voice he could manage.

Mabel turned back to him.

She looked at him from head to toe.

"Gabriel, what happened to your shoes?"

"Ah—that's a bit of a long story."

Mabel smiled.

"We have all evening," she said.

*****

One of the things they discussed without getting irritated with each other, was what Master Lovegrove had said.

"We heard him correctly, didn't we? He said that he wasn't actually Godyth's father."

"That's right."

"And that the person who was there at the killing of Gelle, his wife, was Gelle's father?"

"Why would he kill his own daughter?"

"We need to find out who her father is, Gabriel. That's our next task."

He sipped hot pottage from his spoon. "How do we do that?"

"Ask around Bedwyn."

"He might not be a Bedwyn man. Surely if he was, you'd know and I'm guessing you didn't know who he was."

Mabel chewed the side of her mouth. "No, I don't know Gelle's father. She came here to marry Lovegrove from one of the other villages in the forest. The Lord Stokke gave permission for her to come but I don't know where from. I was only young at the time."

"Not the sort of thing a youngster is interested in."

"No, and I never got to know her well. She was a lot older than me."

"She doesn't sound like the sort of person you'd really *want* to get to know."

"Like I say, she was always a bit odd." Mabel screwed up her nose. "I wonder why she was so—odd?"

"Was there anyone in the village besides Lovegrove who knew her well?"

"Joan Hartshorn was her neighbour for some time. I wonder if she can enlighten us? The Hartshorn cott is close to Lovegrove's"

"Then tomorrow, we shall go and talk to her."

Gabriel unrolled his palliasse and lay it on the floor as far away from Mabel's bed as was possible. She noticed the distance but said nothing about it.

"Goodnight Sir Gabriel."

"Goodnight Mistress Wetherspring."

*****

Sir Gabriel was on his back breathing deeply with a slight stutter when Mabel carefully inched out of her bed. It was cold and she shivered, quickly pulling on her shoes and tying up her hair and with one more glance at Gabriel, she turned withershynnes.

The little mouse scurried across the floor and flattened itself to creep under the door.

She hadn't wanted to risk opening it in case Gabriel had heard her. She ran on little pink feet to the water butt and crouched in the shadows for a while.

Her little mouse heart was beating faster than a man could ever imagine. Twelve beats to every one of a human's. She closed her eyes and imagined how her own, Mabel heartbeat felt. Much, much slower even in anxiety.

She looked up. Thank goodness Master Nightowl was nowhere to be seen. She stepped away from the wooden base and turned withershynnes again.

'I'd like to be a long eared owl.'

Mabel had seen these amazing birds on the commons in the forest. The tufts on their heads made her laugh. They weren't ears at all but were simply a feathery device to make them look taller and bigger.

She preened her mottled rust-brown feathers, flexed her distinct white eyebrows and opened wide her striking rust coloured eyes.

Although it wasn't summer and there was no need to call, she opened her beak and "wheeyoo, wheeyoo!" came out in a low moan.

Mabel knew that when hunting, the owl swept through open country, flying to and fro in a zig-zag pattern while scanning the ground for food. But she did not feel the need to do this now, although she'd spotted a tiny lone shrew scooting along the bottom of the hedge which surrounded her garth, she would leave him to his own hunting.

Off she flew and gently drifted over the thatch of Master Hartshorn's house. She twisted her wings and flew over the village to the house belonging to Mistress Ceorlson.

She touched down on the thatch, folded her wings and listened. No one had noticed or heard her. The village was almost silent. She stretched her neck and settled herself to eavesdrop.

A mumbling came from the inside of the cottage and Mabel recognised the voice of Mistress Ceorlson.

"Godyth, you must understand, you have to put it all behind you now."

"What do I have to put behind me?"

"What has happened to you. It's the way of the world. Us women..."

"I'm not a woman yet."

"No, but soon you will be. I will help you as much as I can, when you are twelve."

Mabel realised that the two inhabitants of the cottage were lying in their beds talking quietly to each other.

"Us women—we have to put up with so much in life."

"Why do we have to?" said the younger voice.

"Because God has ordained it. He wants us to do as he wishes."

There was a rustling and Mabel had a vision of Godyth sitting up in bed.

"And how do we know what he wishes?"

"The priests tell us. They know what God wants because they can read the Bible and have a direct connection with God and his saints.

You know this Godyth."

"I know. Yes."

"God's creation, Eve, was a wicked person, Godyth and she had to be punished for what she did."

"I know—that's why we women are punished by God. We are the daughters of Eve."

"I'm glad you have learned something."

"Of course I have," said Godyth flippantly.

"Good."

"And men? Do they have to do what God wants them to do?"

"Of course they do."

"But they can do so much more than we can."

"That is just the way of the world, Goddy."

"Boys are horrible. They grow into horrible men."

"Go to sleep, Goddy," said her grandma.

"I don't want to go to sleep."

Her grandma sighed. "I must admit, I cannot sleep either. I fear for your father and for your uncle. They are both in great danger of losing their lives."

Godyth was silent and Mabel could detect a strange atmosphere suddenly coming over the cottage like a miasma.

"He won't come again," said Godyth almost to herself. Mabel thought she'd misheard but no she hadn't, for the child repeated what she'd said.

"He won't come again."

"What's that Goddy?" asked her grandma.

"Nothing." There was more rustling as the child settled into her straw mattress.

Mabel frowned, as much as a long eared owl can frown. 'What did Godyth mean that he would not come again?'

After listening for further speech, Mabel lifted off from the thatch and swooped over the cherry orchard.

Who was *he*? Master Lovegrove, perhaps? Mabel did not think

Godyth was talking about him. Her uncle maybe? Was she just voicing the fear that neither men would come home, for they were both to be tried for murder? She rose over the oak tree in her garth. No, Mabel would not go home just yet.

As she flew once more over the river, a ribbon of purple in the complete darkness of the night, Mabel caught sight of a shadow, a darker shape in the inkinesss of the already black and almost moonless village. Just a few stars pierced the heavens and gave light beside the nail paring of a moon.

She rose up over the reeve's large cottage and dipped down over the smaller Hardhand property.

The shadow scuttled along the path, taking advantage of the deeper shadow by the hedge. Then, bent double, she saw the person stop and look around. She couldn't recognise the man but a man it was. His face was all hard planes, grey and black but she noticed that his long hair was light coloured.

She resolved to follow him and keep him in sight, for it was obvious he was up to no good.

She flew to the nearest tree: a large sycamore unusual in the village. She looked down on part of the village green. The man was scrambling at a pace over the open ground, again bent double. He then waited. He stopped before the house of Mistress Ceorlson. He hesitated. He ran his hand through the silvery hair.

Her owl eyes were, of course, ten times superior to her human eyes but it was still hard to see what he was doing. He was whispering to himself very quietly. Even with owl ears, she couldn't work out what he was saying.

In total silence she dropped from the sycamore tree and landed once more on the roof of the Ceorlson house.

Now she could see him well. A thin face, hatchet like, with a pointed nose and deep set eyes. Not a good looking man but one particular thing struck her. He had a very long neck. Where had she seen this phenomenon before? She knew she had.

The man was trying the door, gently. It was locked and barred.

Mabel rose up from the roof and cried out in warning. "Wheeyoo, wheeyoo!"

The man looked up and saw the owl. He cursed.

Mabel flew down in a low swoop and made for the man.

"Wheeyoo, wheeyoo!"

He looked up, following her path and turned, fleeing across the village green.

Of course an owl's cry was not going to make people wake out of their sleep and get up and see what was happening. They were used to such noises of the night; the dog fox's scream, the owl's hooting, the lowing of the cattle in the barns, the bark of a dog...

They would simply mutter, turn over and go back to sleep.

But Mabel *was* awake and she *could* follow this man.

He went back the way he'd come and she tracked him by flying over the Peabody house, over Master Chatterwell's and between the cottages of John Swineherd and the Brockmans.

The man gained the road out of the village and ran, looking back behind him every so often. He didn't notice the pigeon sized owl flying after him about twenty feet from the ground.

The man left the main road and passed through Shawgrove copse. He was blowing now and had to stop to catch his breath.

Then he slowed and walked.

Mabel circled overhead.

The man ducked through a hedge and was momentarily lost to her sight.

He was in the vicinity of the buildings at Stock Farm.

She picked him up again as he strolled nonchalantly into the farm and disappeared amongst the many buildings of the farmyard.

Who was this man and why had he tried to get into the Ceorlson house?

Here was a completely new character in this tangled web of clues and Mabel was totally perplexed.

She flew directly back to her cottage, crept into her house and fell into bed.

She noticed that Gabriel had not moved an inch.

CHAPTER TWELVE
~ THE NEIGHBOUR'S TALE ~

It seemed that the dawn came as soon as Mabel closed her eyes. She had slept poorly and her eyes felt raw and sore. Before she dressed she went to her shelf of remedies and took up a little bottle. This was a tincture of eyebright which would help ease her eyes. She leaned over Gabriel to reach her shelf.

'My! The muscles of his upper arm and shoulders are...'

Gabriel was still asleep, his torso naked, one arm flung out of the covers as Mabel poked the fire into life and fed it with twigs. It was cold today and she shivered, wrapping her cloak around her shift.

She licked dry lips.

Gabriel groaned and stretched his arms above his head. He yawned and as he exhaled, his breath made a plume of white vapour. The hairs on his arms glistened gold.

"Come and sit by the fire. It's cold today," said Mabel quickly. "Too cold to go about the house without a blanket."

Gabriel snatched up his cloak which he had laid over him on the top of his blankets.

"I'll dress. It'll be warmer." Then he went outside to the privy.

When he returned, rubbing his hands together and blowing on his fingers, Mabel was stirring a pot of warmed ale.

"I have something to confess."

Gabriel threw on his gambeson.

"Oh, don't tell me..." His arms flailed about and Mabel jumped up and pulled it down, "Confessions usually mean..."

"No listen. It's important."

"It always is—with you."

"Ah well, if you don't want to know."

"I don't know if I don't want to know. There's a lot I don't want to know, because when I do know it, it makes me nervous."

"I went out last night. To listen in at the Ceorlson house."

"Oh?" he said, wrapping his hand around a mug of ale. He blew on it. "I didn't hear you."

"No. You were fast asleep and snoring."

"I do not snore."

Mabel pulled a disbelieving face.

"I heard Godyth and Mistress Ceorlson talking. Godyth said something odd."

"The child is completely odd. Why should she not add to her oddness?"

"She said..." Mabel went on, "He will not come again."

"He will not come again? *Who* will not come again."

"The way she said it, it seemed to me that she was *not* talking about her father—or rather the man who raised her—or her uncle."

"Who then?"

"I don't know but as I was sitting there listening, I saw a man creeping up to the house. He tried the door."

Gabriel sat up straighter.

Mabel went on to explain what had happened.

"What did he look like?"

"He was silver haired and pointy faced, like a rat and he had a very long neck."

"What do you think he was doing there? Do you know him?"

"No. I've no idea what he wanted but whatever it was, it was suspicious. No one tries to get into a house in that way after dark. But

I am going to go to Stock Farm to look around and see if I can spot him again. That's where he disappeared to."

"Be careful Mabel."

"You mean you aren't going to tell me that you want to come too?"

Gabriel shrugged. "No, I think you'll be able to do the job perfectly well on your own as a pigeon or a magpie or whatever you want to be. You can look after yourself, remember?"

Mabel counted to ten. Now, why didn't she believe him?

"Besides, *I* have a job to do, don't I?"

"Oh?"

"I'm off to quiz Mistress Hartshorn about Gelle Lovegrove—unless you'd like to do that. It would be a safer option, I think, than tackling an unknown man at an unknown place. I could, of course, go to Stock Farm instead of you."

"I am perfectly happy, thank you, watching an unknown man and trying to work out his involvement in this series of murders. If there is one."

"Right. So, what animal are you thinking of being for this—task?" asked Gabriel with a touch of mockery.

"I haven't yet decided," said Mabel. "But when I followed the man to Stock Farm last night, I noticed that they were rather overrun with mice and rats."

"Ah yes. You'd notice something like that if you were an owl, wouldn't you?"

"I thought they could do with a bit of help from a cat at Stock Farm. What do you think?"

Gabriel tutted.

"Good luck. I'll see you back here for dinner. Unless of course, you've had mice for dinner."

*****

Gabriel desperately wanted to follow Mabel to Stock Farm but his pride wouldn't let him. Besides, as he'd said to her and they had agreed, he wanted to go and ask a few questions of Joan Hartshorn.

He neared the cottage and heard an argument in progress— Young Thierry and Master Wilfred. Both men were foresters, owing service to the Lord Stokke. It seems they were arguing about where they were going to be working that day.

"Wilton Brail—he said Wilton Brail copse."

"He did not you deaf ol' bastard, he said Brail Field copse." This was the younger man.

"Nah! The reeve said that if we had the time, we could go up to Haw Wood by Stock Farm afterwards. Now, as you well know, if we work at Brail Copse, we'd find it a bit of a push to leg it to Haw Wood, even if we did have time."

"Yeah! And what does ol' lazy braies know about distances and time? Stuck here the whole day."

"It's not him, you pillycock. He has instructions from the lord."

"Alright. What does the daft lord know about getting from Wilton Brail or any Brail copse for that matter. He never walks anywhere. It was the nearest place, obviously."

"You watch yer mouth when you talk about Lord Stokke!"

Thierry Hartshorn seemed to have the upper hand. "Pah! You go your way, I'll go mine."

His father blew a raspberry between his lips.

"We need to stick together."

"I'm not going all the way out to Wilton Brail, to walk all the way back to Haw Wood!"

"Alright you go…"

"It'll be dark before we can get it all done. And I'm not going anywhere near Stock Farm in the dark!" said Thierry.

"What's wrong with Stock Farm eh?"

Thierry lowered his voice. "You know as well as I do."

"Aw—don't be so foolish!"

"Foolish? The man's mad, you know that."

Gabriel neared the cottage and put his ear to the door.

"That's why we need to stick together."

"He doesn't care who's where. The whole of God's angels might turn up and he'd not care. If he's drunk and he is most of the time, then being together ain't going to help us," said Thierry

"He's only an ol' drunk."

"He's a bloody demon."

"Aw c'mon Ti. You know we have to do what the reeve tells us. It's the rules."

"Yeah, well I ain't going nowhere near Stock Farm."

"We'll be fined."

"Then I'll pay the fine. I won't end up dead like poor Leofwin..."

"It was never proven."

"Yeah, well—there was plenty of proof. He just got away with it."

Gabriel's head was suddenly filled with voices—all of them clamouring—all of them questioning.

'Who? Who's the demon at Stock Farm? Who was Leofwin and why did he die?'

"I am not going anywhere near Stock Farm. We'll go to Brail Field Copse and mind our own business." They were suddenly silent.

'No, no, don't! Keep going—I want to know who the demon is!' said Gabriel to himself. 'Mabel has gone to Stock Farm.'

A woman's voice rode over the two male Hartshorns.

"If you two don't quit yellin' I'll take my broom to the both of you, now git!"

"But ma."

"Go! You'll be late getting there now and you'll have to run all the way."

There was a swishing sound and a sort of rustley slap.

"Argh!" Thierry had received the promised swipe with the twig besom.

Gabriel, leaning on the door, his brow sweating and his ear pressed close, suddenly fell inwards.

He just about managed to right himself.

"Ah—yes," he said lamely.

The two men looked at each other.

"Sir Gabriel, m'lord?" They both touched their forelocks. The younger man snatched off his coif.

"Can we help you?"

"Er—no, it's er—Mistress Hartshorn I have come to see..."

"Right."

"I er... um... was leaning against the door because... I erm... have a stone in my shoe."

"Right."

The two foresters nodded and, casting a glance at the terrible state of the knight's shoes (they were Bunce's of course), jogged off past him, looking back once.

Damn! He'd wanted to ask them who lived at Stock Farm.

Mistress Joan beckoned him inside the house.

"Forgive those two m'lord. Theym'z always arguin'. Two stubborn grown men in the same house. It's not a good idea."

"Ah no." Gabriel thought about his own position. He and his father. Hmm. He could relate to that.

"I wonder if you could spare me a little of your time, mistress?"

"What would you be wanting my time for, Sir Gabriel?"

"Is there anything you can tell me which might throw some light on the death of your neighbour Gelle Lovegrove?"

The woman walked around her small cottage. Gabriel thought that she was rather nervous. And that was odd.

"Gelle? I thought it had been proven that her husband killed her?"

"Well, no. There is some doubt owing to—to—new evidence. The authorities have asked me—Mistress Mabel Wetherspring and me to look into it because there are a few—loose ends."

"Loose ends? What's a loose end?"

Ah... not all the facts add up."

"Oh. Well. I can't say much."

"Anything would be useful."

"I knew her, of course."

"Mistress Wetherspring said that she was a bit odd."

Joan Hartshorn laughed out loud. "She was. She was a few apples short of a tart, that's true, but it was only later she started to be really odd."

"What did you notice?"

"She didn't want to know anything about her childer for a start."

"Her husband told me this."

Joan leaned forward. "She even tried to, you know..." she made a movement which, to Gabriel, looked like someone trying to strangle another person.

"That too I've heard," he whispered.

"Now I am not saying there's not been times when I haven't wanted to strangle my own childer—or Master Hartshorn. But I have always stopped short of actually doing it—always!"

"Naturally."

"She talked to herself a lot. That's not right in the head."

"It isn't?"

Gabriel vowed to stop talking to himself.

"Not when she does it in two voices."

"Two? Voices?"

"Her own voice—and then another's. Answering."

"Good Lord. Is this why people thought she was possessed? Why she left the village?"

"Mighta had somethin' to do with it."

"Mistress Joan, do you think that Lovegrove is capable of killing his wife?"

"They argued a lot."

"Ah, did they?"

"Livin' s'close, you can't help but hear."

"What about?"

"Mostly about young Godyth."

"What was said about her?"

"Oh all sorts."

"Can you be specific?"

"Oh no—nothing—spefisix…"

"No, I mean… what did they say about her, exactly?"

Joan was definitely reluctant to say anything. Her mouth worked but nothing came out. She began a sentence and then chewed her nail.

"C'mon, Joan. Master Lovegrove's life is at stake here. Do you want to see him hanged for something he may not have done?"

"I can't. I'd just bring—it down on me and mine."

"What?"

"The bad luck. The curse."

"What curse?"

Gabriel's little voice said, 'Oh God, Mabel's probably walked into a curse.'

"The curse of—the Fryxells."

"The what?"

Joan whispered, "The Fryxells. It all began with Henry Fryxell, senior."

A horrible feeling was rising up under Gabriel's breastbone.

"These Fryxells… they don't happen to live at Stock Farm nowadays… do they?"

"No—why should you say that?"

The horrible feeling rapidly dropped into his boots.

"Nothing. So what has this curse got to do with Gelle Lovegrove?"

Joan Hartshorn wiped her hand over her forehead and grasped hold of the tail ends of her head cloth as if she would keep a lid on her head.

"Mistress, please—it's very important."

"Theym'z all mad."

"Mad—who are?"

"All those who are cursed."

"I am getting a little fed up with this. Who are the cursers and who are the cursees?" said Gabriel crossly.

"Eh?"

"Who is it doing the cursing and who is in receipt of the curse?"

"Oh... well, sir." Joan sat down. "You don't mind if I sit down, sir, do you?"

"You can stand on your head, if it will make you tell me this story more quickly, Joan."

"Oh no, Sir Gabriel, I don't want to do that... Why, my kirtle would end up all over me... and I'd be showing me..."

"For Heaven's sake woman!" He took one pace towards her.

"Argh... alright... Gelle Lovegrove was a Fryxell before she was married."

"And you say, they're all mad."

"Aye sir, they are."

"How does this madness—how does it show itself?"

"Well in some it's just a wandering in the wits and a not really being quite all there... you know."

"Like Gelle?"

"Aye, like her."

"And in others?"

The woman crossed herself. "In others it's a terrible temper. Like a demon takes possession of you."

"So, that would mean that you might be angry all the time and try to take it out on the people nearest to you?"

"I don't know what the demon makes you do, sir."

"But you think that the family, Gelle's family, is possessed."

"Why else are they so—angry and dour all the time?"

"Gelle described Godyth's father as a 'devil'," said Gabriel.

"Master Lovegrove?"

Gabriel thought back to the conversation he'd heard earlier that morning, through the door.

"Joan, who was Leofwin?"

The woman hissed through her teeth.

"Ah... that's a name we never..."

"Who was Leofwin?"

"He was the man who originally ran Stock Farm."

"Was he a Fryxell?"

"Aye, he was."

Gabriel took a turn around the house. "He was killed, wasn't he?"

It was obvious that Joan didn't want to answer. "There was no evidence."

"Who do you think killed him? Leofwin?"

"A stake was driven right through his heart." Joan Hartshorn shivered. "I 'spect it was a demon who did something like that."

"Who was suspected?"

"Ah no—you cannot make me utter his name. We never speak it here. In Bedwyn."

"Master Stock? Is he a Fryxell?"

Joan wrung her hands and looked all around the small cottage. "Ah sir. I hope the demon isn't listening."

"And he *does* live at Stock Farm?"

"He—stays there? I've heard."

"What do you mean, he stays there?"

"Well it isn't *his* place but since Leofwin's gone—there's no one to tell him otherwise."

"Gone. With a stake through his heart."

"He stays there, we think. There's no one else there."

"Does he come to the village?"

"No, never. If he did, we'd all drive him out."

"Can you describe this man, Mistress Hartshorn?"

"Oh no—I can't do that. There's no doubt if I did that, he'd hear me and—he's a demon, see."

"Mistress Wetherspring might be in danger. She's gone to Stock Farm. She's gone to speak to Master Stock himself—I think."

"Lord love her! Doesn't she know the place is damned?" Joan crossed herself vigorously.

"Obviously not."

"Oh—oh—oh."

"Mabel, Mistress Wetherspring is in danger?"

She nodded.

"What does he look like?"

"I only saw him once, but he has a pointed nose and a chin that sits back from his mouth like a gargoyle on a church."

"And a very long neck?"

"Aye that he has."

"Tell me, you are sure he's related to the Fryxells?"

Once again, Joan crossed her breast, more slowly this time, "Aye... he's a bastard son."

"How old is the man?"

"Oh that I can't say."

"Has he silver hair?"

"Aye—when I saw him that once—he did."

"What connection does he have to Gelle?"

"That's the sad thing, sir."

"Sad?"

"He's Gelle's father, m'lord."

CHAPTER THIRTEEN
~ THE BARREL ~

Mabel kite flew high over the trees the short distance to Stock Farm. It was strange; the place was quite close to Bedwyn but she'd never been there before her nocturnal visit the previous night. She knew very little about the place or about the people who'd inhabited it.

Sitting in a tree, contemplating a number of rather derelict buildings, she was suddenly thrown back to her childhood and her father telling her mother a tale about the Fryxell family who'd lived there.

They were shunned by the locals. Her father told a tale of a curse which made the men mad and the women simple. Lying alone in her bed, listening to her parents whispering, Mabel had been fascinated by the tale. And then, as the years passed she had forgotten it and the name Fryxell was erased from her memory. Until today.

Today she remembered that conversation and the fact that the Fryxells had all died violent or nasty deaths.

She hopped down and turned withershynnes three times. 'I wish to be a cat.'

The red tipped wings of the kite shrank to produce grey legs. The fierce dark head of the bird widened and the beak disappeared into a black nose whilst at the same time, the wicked yellow eyes softened to green with a centre becoming a black slit. Little pink lined ears grew on the top of her head and long white whiskers popped from her cheeks. Satisfied at last with her new body, Mabel ran her pink pads along those whiskers, licked and rubbed damp paws along the backs of her ears.

She slunk along into the farmyard, her head down, her eyes alert and found the large barn where she'd seen so many rats that night before, but today, they were all in hiding.

She jumped up onto a fence post and balancing perfectly, perched there and watched some sparrows hopping about in the overgrown garth of the farm.

There didn't seem to be anyone here. In fact the farm didn't seem to be in use at all. It was so dilapidated, thatches falling in, mossy and thinning, fences broken, wattle exposed, walls drooping and no crops or animals in sight.

Hmm, so where did the man of the previous night disappear to?

She padded around sniffing with her excellent cat nose. Aha! She could smell a human, a none too clean human. He'd definitely been here.

Right in the centre of the farm buildings was a neglected cottage with a door half hanging off one of its hinges.

Mabel prowled around and found a window, rather than enter through the gap in the door and be surprised to find someone hostile waiting for her. She stretched up, clung to the window frame with strong cat claws and peered into the dark interior.

No one was there. Should she go in? It did look as if someone *had* been living there.

It would be easier for her, if she had to open anything or pick up something to have human form, so Mabel turned three times deosil and stood looking in at the unglassed window as herself. If she was surprised and spotted, she could always melt into the shadows and turn into a cat again.

Taking her lip in her teeth nervously she inched forward.

"Mistress Mabel!" said a voice she knew. "I didn't think *you'd* be here!"

She turned with a surprised intake of breath.

"Johnny! Whatever are *you* doing here?"

*****

Gabriel ran as fast as he could towards his horse and saddled it. He had to get to Stock Farm. He thought he had worked it all out. His head was buzzing. Gelle's father, Master John Stock, otherwise Fryxell, had killed his own daughter. And if Gabriel was right, the madness in the family had not stopped with him.

As he rode along the main road and through the forest, Gabriel turned over in his mind all those facts which he knew about the latest murders in Bedwyn. It *had* to be.

He *had* to be right. Nothing made any sense otherwise. It had been said that Gelle had sent Master Stock packing. Mabel had told him about the fact that Gelle Lovegrove had utterly disliked Master Stock.

And yes, Mabel *was* in danger. Oh, how he hoped she'd not gone poking around as herself! 'Stay a cat or a bird Mabel. You'll be safer then.'

The image of the man with a stake through his heart stayed with him as he pounded down the dark green lanes. And gradually, the nearer he got to Stock Farm, the image changed.

It became that of a woman in a blue kirtle, with light brown hair and a snub nose.

With a sob, Gabriel urged Bertran into a faster gallop.

*****

"You haven't answered me," said Mabel. "What are you doing so far from home?"

"I—I—I—" stammered Johnny.

"Johnny?" she urged.

"I came to find the pig with wings."

"What did I say to you, young Master Chatterwell?" said Mabel, catching hold of his arms.

"You said the gryphon was dangerous but you didn't say anything about the flying pig. And Goddy said this was the last place it had been seen."

"I said you had to stop searching."

"Stop searching for the burning beast. That's what you said. The pig with wings i'n't dangerous. Is it?"

Mabel suddenly had a terrible feeling.

"Did you follow me?" She fervently hoped he hadn't.

"I saw you just now."

"You didn't follow me from Bedwyn?"

"No. How could I? I never seen you till just now. I saw the cat go up to the window and then I saw you."

"Right. Well—I have had a look around and I can't see the pig."

Johnny beamed an impish grin from ear to ear.

"I knew you'd come looking for it when I saw you staring in the window," he said.

Mabel took hold of Johnny Chatterwell's arm and spun him round, none too gently.

"And so we'll just take a very quick look in here—and then you and I are going home."

"I suppose a pig with wings has to sleep sometime," said Johnny. "And this old place might be the sort of house a pig would like."

Mabel muttered under her breath, 'A human pig maybe.'

"Right, in we go."

She took hold of the edge of the door and pulled it, lifting it from the floor where it had dropped. She set it back upon its broken hinge.

Johnny peered around the jamb, just his forehead and eyes visible.

He whispered, "It's mortal dark in there Mistress Mabel"

Mabel pulled the door further with a screech of wood. There was no telltale movement in the cott. Not even the skittering of a mouse.

"No pig," said Johnny, "No bloomin' pig." He sounded so disappointed.

"Well someone has been here. There's food and..." Mabel picked up a wooden mug, "And someone has poured some ale recently."

"Pigs eat anything," said Johnny. "But I don't think they drink ale, do they?"

"Especially not from a mug."

"Is it the person who owns the flying pig, do you think?"

"I suppose it might be," said Mabel, picking up a stick and turning over the ashes of a fire. "These ashes are quite warm."

Johnny had a moth-eaten blanket in his hand.

"Ah look! The pig has a blanket!" he chuckled.

A croaky voice suddenly hissed at them.

"Who's calling me a pig?"

Both Mabel and Johnny spun round to the door through which they'd entered scant heartbeats before.

Johnny dashed behind Mabel.

"Well, you must admit, Master Fryxell, the place does look rather like a pigsty," said Mabel cheekily. "It is Master Fryxell sometimes known as Stock, isn't it?"

The man came further into the cottage.

"We are sorry—if we..."

"You're not sorry at all," he said, not allowing her to finish.

The man was dishevelled and dirty. His face was thin and his receding chin stubbly and set on—what seemed to Mabel to be—an unnaturally long neck. His shoulder length silver hair was also receding.

Suddenly Johnny developed a surge of bravery. He stood up straight.

"We've been looking for the flying pig. Have you seen it?"

"Flying pig? No—no flying pigs. But I have discovered two nosy beasts rummaging through my house."

"We needed to ask you some questions, sir," said Mabel, inching towards the door, her hand on Johnny's arm.

"There's nothing you can ask to which I will give you an answer, you nosy cow!"

Johnny was outraged at the insult.

"Don't you call Mistress Mabel Wetherspring a cow! She's a really nice and very clever lady!"

The man made a grab for Johnny and lifted him off his feet by the neck of his tunic.

"And you are a rude and cheeky little hoglet."

Johnny was going pink in the face and wriggling. "Gargaale... grrargh."

"Put him down. He's done nothing to you," yelled Mabel.

"Doesn't need to. I don't like children. I don't care what I do."

"Is this why you have been going around Bedwyn village," said Mabel, "Killing them?"

Johnny gave a little strangled scream.

The man, whom Mabel had guessed correctly, was John Fryxell, laughed.

"Me? Nah! Though I'm not saying I'd not like to."

"What were you doing at the Ceorlson house last night?"

The man dropped Johnny to the floor in surprise and Mabel instantly stooped to scoop him up, pulling him close to her.

The boy was breathing hard and trying not to cry.

"I watched as you tried to get into the Ceorlson house yesterday. What were you doing there?"

"None of your damn business."

"Well, you weren't making a social call. It was far too late for that and you found the door and shutters bolted. It annoyed you, didn't it."

The man chuckled nastily. "And so you had to come and see where I lived, to have it out with me? Eh?"

"I wanted to ask you if you had seen your granddaughter lately? And what you wanted with her last night?"

174

"Godyth? Why?"

Mabel took hold of little Johnny and rubbed his neck where the man John Fryxell or Stock or whatever his name was, had half strangled him.

"She was in the house last night. Was it her you wanted to see or was it your wife?"

"Wife?" The man laughed out loud. "Wife?" He bent to the floor and picked up a coil of rope. Mabel noticed he now had a knife in his hand.

"She's not my wife."

"Mistress Ceorlson, is the mother of Eadric and Gelle—is she not? And you are Gelle's father so she must be your wife."

"Who says we were married?"

Stock promptly leapt forward and grabbed hold of Little Johnny again. Although taken unawares, Johnny kicked out but a buffet to his head turned him into a limp bundle in the man's arms.

"Come any closer and I'll slit his throat."

Mabel backed to the wall. "Leave him be. He's an innocent in all this. Let him go." Mabel's eyes searched Johnny's body in the darkness of the cottage. He was still alive and breathing, just dazed.

"I have no intention of letting either of you go."

"Why did you kill Gelle? What had she done to you?"

"Who says I killed Gelle?"

"I think your granddaughter knows the truth."

"Truth?" yelled the man. "She wouldn't know the truth if it jumped down her throat!"

Stock then wrapped the rope around a barrel which lay inside the cott, sat a moaning Johnny down, stretched his arms around it and secured them. Poor lad, he looked as if he was embracing it. Then he did the same with his feet. All the time the knife was close to the boy's neck.

"Now it's your turn."

Stock moved forward but Mabel ran to the other end of the

cottage and into the dark shadows. Sadly she had no time to turn withershynnes before the man caught hold of her, wrapping strong arms around her. Mabel kicked out with blows to his shins but he bore them as if she had merely blown on them.

He turned Mabel round to face him and took a long look at her, screwing up her mouth with rough fingers. His breath was rank.

"You're not bad. I might have had you later. But there's no time."

He then proceeded to rope her to the other side of the barrel.

"Like you had Mistress Ceorlson?"

"Ah ...that was a long time ago."

"So you admit you are Gelle's father."

"But not Eadric. I won't admit to that fool. He's a Ceorlson through and through. Idiots, the lot of them."

"They may be idiots but they're not murderers."

"You sure about that?" said the man, pursing his lips. "What's your name...? Mabel?"

He was not answered.

"You sure that the Ceorlsons are not murderers?"

"I have a feeling the Ceorlson bloodline is not tainted but Fryxell blood is," said Mabel, braving it out. "Undoubtedly."

"Shut up!" said Fryxell as he gave Mabel a blow to her head. It stung but she kept her wits.

He crossed to the table and drained the ale pot.

"I shall leave you now. And by the way, there are no people nearby. No one to hear you calling out. And no one ever visits. This is the end of you both." He smiled sweetly. "It was nice meeting you."

He opened the door wide.

"And yes. I did kill my daughter. She was going to blab and I couldn't have that. She too was a nosy bitch. And you know what happens to nosy bitches? Well, if you don't, you are gonna find out now."

He pulled the door closed and Mabel heard a screech of wood as he secured a bar across it.

That didn't bother her. She could get under the door easily if only she could get free of this rope.

She heard poor little Johnny moaning.

"It's alright Johnny. You just rest. I'll get us out of here."

But it was hard to see how she was going to turn withershynnes to become any animal, anything, roped to a barrel.

She strained against the rope holding her around it. It was very tight and the coarseness of it chafed her wrists and ankles.

She pulled and pulled then had to rest.

"Oh fiddle faddle," she said. "There must be a way!"

*****

Throwing his leg over Bertran's ears, Gabriel bounded down from him to the edge of the farm buildings. This had been quite a holding once—quite a large group of properties. It would take him some time to investigate them all.

Perhaps he should call out? He quickly decided against it. If Fryxell was here, he would know that Gabriel was looking for Mabel and if he was close by, might do her harm.

He looked out across a small green where there was a well. Was that a human shadow crossing its slatted planks of wood?

He bent double and stealthily ran to a canopied door of a barn where grains had no doubt once been stored. Flattening himself against the building he peered around the corner at the well.

No one. There was no one there.

Suddenly there was a noisy flurry. A clamour of rooks. They flew up cackling, disturbed by some movement behind a cottage where the thatch had fallen in.

No one could hide in *there*. There was no room. There was too much debris.

Was one of those rooks Mabel?

Gabriel looked up and hissed quietly, "Mabel! If that's you, can you make yourself known."

The birds merely looked on and Gabriel decided they were just rooks.

He drew his knife and padded gently into the centre of the small green. No one followed. He could see no one.

Out of sheer habit, he looked up to the sky. Was Mabel a kite? He could see one high up in the cloudless firmament. It would be like her to reconnoitre the place from above.

He waited for the cry 'Wheeooooeeoooeooooeop,' but it didn't come.

He almost wanted to holler and imitate the bird himself but it wasn't wise to betray his presence.

There was nothing for it. He had to search every building.

Little did he know that he was watched. Carefully and quietly watched by youthful eyes which saw everything with utter clarity.

*****

Mabel held her breath, gritted her teeth and tried to break the rope holding her. She almost succeeded in breaking her wrists.

She peered around the barrel.

"You alright, Johnny?"

"Yes," said a snuffly voice. "My legs ache."

"Ah well, wriggle them about a bit. Try and get the feeling back into them."

She felt Johnny moving about at the back of the barrel. It was one of those really huge ones which were known as tuns. The barrel moved a little.

"Johnny, now listen very carefully," said Mabel. "We are going to tip this barrel over."

Johnny sniffed. "How can we do that, mistress?"

"We are going to rock it. We have to be careful or it will tip where we don't want it to tip and it could hurt us. The barrel is almost empty and won't be as heavy as you think."

He sounded unsure but he gave her a sniffly nasal, "All... right."

"Now upon my count. We need it to go towards the door. The top of it has to be facing the door. Do you think you can do that?"

"Yees"

"One, two, three..."

They rocked sideways several times and upon the fifth movement the barrel began to tip on the side of its bottom rim.

"Again! Harder."

She was right, it was not as heavy as one might have thought.

Slowly, it tipped over and the splintered top went rolling over the floor. They were now attached to it with one of their feet in the air each. But Mabel's hand, being on the end of a longer arm, was trapped underneath.

"Argh!"

"Whassamatter Mabel?" cried Johnny. "You alright?"

"Quickly Johnny, you are closer to the bottom of the barrel. Wriggle downwards."

Mabel felt the lad sliding the rope down to the bottom of the barrel.

"It's hard but... it is... going."

"Good. When you get it to the bottom the rope will come off and you'll be able to stand and get your arms free too."

"How can I...?"

"A barrel is fatter in the middle than at the top or base, Johnny."

"Haha—like a piggy!"

"Yes, just like a piggy. If you tie something around the fattest part you can slide it down to the narrowest and—there you are." Her hand was hurting badly and she whimpered in pain.

Johnny wriggled down the barrel and came crawling around to her side.

"Aw—this is a big barrel. It's the biggest I have ever seen."

179

"Now we need to roll it over. Help me."

Johnny pushed and strained.

"Ah no, Johnny. Do you know that the strongest parts of our body are our thigh muscles? Sit down and use your legs."

Johnny put his sloppy shoes to the barrel and pushed.

"Heehee!" he yelled. Mabel was helping him by pushing forward hard.

Her hand came free.

"Now can you untie me Johnny?" Together they untied the rest of the ropes.

She sat for a while cradling her hand. That would hurt even more, for sure, tomorrow.

"Now for us to get out."

"The man has barred the door," he said in a wavery and very childish tone. She needed to keep his spirits up.

"Johnny, shall we play a game?"

His apple cheeks, made redder by his exertions and by excitement, glowed in the poor light, although she did see the signs of a tear-track or two on his grubby cheek.

"What sort of game?"

"Hide and seek."

There was suddenly a twinkle in his eye.

"I will hide and you will try to find me." She took hold of his shoulders and turned him round. "Now close your eyes and put your hands over them and count to ten."

"I can count to twenty, mistress!" he said proudly.

"Well you *are* a clever lad. Twenty it is then."

She listened as he began his counting.

"Three, four, er... five..."

She turned withershynnes. "I wish to be a mouse."

"Seven, eight."

Her whole body fell to the dusty floor and shrank to less than a tenth of her human size. Even before she was completely transformed, she began to scurry to the ill-fitting door.

"Twelve...erm..." said Johnny Chatterwell.

Mabel smiled a mouse smile. 'Dear Johnny.'

"Twelve... erm, threeteen, fourteen... fiveteen, sixteen."

She ducked under the broken panel of the door. Immediately she turned deosil and made a grab for the large piece of wood which constituted a locking bar and lifted it. Her hand ached enormously.

"Eighteen, nineteen... and"

"Twenty," they both shouted.

"Now come and find me," said Mabel, pulling the door open.

"Cor! That was very clever," said Johnny. "I thought I might have to go on to eleventy five."

"You didn't need to. You found me." She grabbed him and gave him a huge hug.

His face was glowing, his eyes glittering.

"Aw Mistress Wetherspring," he said, "That was *such* an adventure."

"Yes, indeed it was." She tried not to grimace as he caught hold of her bruised hand.

She laid her good arm over Johnny's shoulder.

"Mistress Mabel?"

"Yes?"

"Did that man really kill Goddy's ma? We did hear him say that didn't we?"

"Yes I think he did, Johnny."

"Cor—you wait till I tell the others. They won't believe we was captured by a murderer!"

*****

Gabriel spotted the man ambling nonchalantly to a pony which was tied to a tree at the edge of a nearby copse.

He instantly recognised him from Mabel's description.

'Fryxell. Or is it Master Stock?' he said to himself. 'Gelle's father.'

He watched as the man untied the reins and walked off through the derelict buildings leading the pony.

Gabriel was conflicted. Should he try to find Mabel or should he follow Fryxell?

No, Mabel might be in trouble. He'd find her first and then no doubt if she was alright, *she* could follow him.

Just as he was about to nip behind a building which looked like a cow byre in order to stay hidden from Fryxell, he heard a voice. A light high pitched voice.

"Grandfather!"

Gabriel ducked down. Where was the voice coming from?

As he peered through a knot hole in a plank of wood, Gabriel could see Fryxell's body stiffen.

"What do *you* want?"

"It is true, what she said, isn't it?"

The voice was slightly echoey as if it came from a huge space.

"What *who* said?" Fryxell was frantically looking around to see if he could identify exactly where the voice was coming from.

"Mabel."

"Nah, girlie. She's a liar."

"I saw you."

"Then why are you asking me if you already know the truth?"

"I want you to say it?"

"Say what?" shouted the man making for the well which stood in front of a decrepit cottage.

"Say that you killed my mother."

The man Fryxell laughed. "The acorn doesn't fall far from the tree! Your mother was trouble and so are you."

Gabriel had to shift his position to keep the man in sight.

Unfortunately as he did so, he managed to bang into an old wooden bucket which went rolling over the earth of the barn floor.

The Fryxell man braced himself.

"Who's that?" He pivoted on swift feet. The man scoured the yard with eyes constricted against the light.

Gabriel held his breath and peered once more through the tiny hole. There close by the house wall stood Godyth Lovegrove. It seemed she had been hiding in the disused well.

"Very clever girlie," said Fryxell. "Very clever!"

Godyth's face was stony.

"You killed my mother. I saw you with the rock in your hand."

"I told you. I came upon her and picked up the rock—someone else—"

"It was you. I know it was you. I heard you tell Mistress Mabel, just now."

The man licked his lips. "Did you now?"

"I heard you shouting at ma, that night."

"Ah—I was always shouting at her. And she at me. That was nothing!"

Godyth stared at the man with evil brown eyes, peering through the curtain of her dark curly hair.

There were further words but Gabriel couldn't hear properly for the raucous noise of the crows wheeling overhead. He tiptoed to the edge of the barn.

"I should have got rid of you that night. But I was a fool."

Godyth moved closer.

Gabriel couldn't see her hands. They were at her back. What was she doing?

All at once a child's voice cried out.

"Goddy—Goddy, *there* you are!"

Godyth stepped back. "Johnny, what are you doing here?"

"When I lost you, I found Mistress Mabel." It was only then that Johnny noticed Master Fryxell standing in the shadows. His eyes grew round and frightened. His usually happy, glowing face paled.

"Godyth—*he* tried to kill me and Mistress Wetherspring." He pointed.

Johnny Chatterwell stood by her and looked up at her with a sad expression. "Be careful. He'll try to kill you too."

Gabriel hesitated. 'Where was Mabel? Surely nothing had happened to her.'

Fryxell chuckled, "And why would I want to do that? Godyth is my granddaughter."

Mabel stepped out of the protection of the cottage wall.

"Not only are you her grandfather, Fryxell, you are also her father," she said. "Aren't you?"

*****

Fryxell moved like a cat (and Mabel should know.) He grabbed Johnny once more and wrapped a strong arm around his throat. Poor Johnny gurgled and went puce in the face.

Mabel watched Godyth carefully but didn't interfere. She could see the resemblance. And the long neck, a feature shared by them all, Fryxell, Gelle and Godyth.

"It's true isn't it Fryxell?" she said as she threw a look at Godyth to see how she'd reacted.

The girl stood, her hands behind her back and smiled sweetly.

"Her mother's father is also *her* father."

Anyone watching would have found it impossible to tell by her face if the girl knew or not. But Mabel knew that she did.

Fryxell backed away, taking Johnny with him.

"I'll be back to kill you—all of you. You'll never know when. I'll be there—waiting for you."

Oh if only Mabel could turn withershynnes and become a wolf, she would deal with him! But sadly, she couldn't do it in front of Godyth or Johnny.

Fryxell's manic laughter echoed around the yard and as soon as he'd disappeared, Mabel ran for the back of the cottage.

She'd show him!

CHAPTER FOURTEEN
~ THE BEAST OF BEDWYN ~

Gabriel was just about to draw his sword and leap out of his hiding place to follow and intercept when there was the sound of a flapping of huge wings.

Godyth turned her head slowly to the sky. Her face moments before, so rigid and expressionless, registered utter surprise. She was rooted to the spot as her stare followed something crossing the sky. Her mouth fell open in a perfect 'o' of amazement.

Gabriel followed her gaze.

He wasn't quite so amazed but he was perplexed.

Rising into the blue of the sky and above the trees surrounding the farm, was a huge winged beast.

He swallowed. Mabel again? Or was this *really* a gryphon? This time the Beast of Bedwyn had the head of an eagle and the sandy coloured body of a lion with huge leathery dragon wings. He *had* told Mabel the first time she'd become a gryphon, she'd had it wrong.

It circled overhead and disappeared over the trees of Savernake with a sound like the pumping of a hundred bellows.

Gabriel swallowed again and threw a quick look at Godyth. "Go home, Godyth. I will follow and try to reach Little Johnny. I'll speak to you later."

"It's the beast of Bedwyn!"

"Er—yes—I'll go after them—and—and try to—to—er—catch it."

"I saw you."

"What?"

"I saw you, creeping up and hiding. Just now."

"Did you? Erm—did you follow Mistress Wetherspring?" he asked in a worried tone. Please God she hadn't seen her transforming.

"No. I followed Johnny."

"Why?"

Godyth shrugged her shoulders. "I knew the beast would be here."

Gabriel laughed.

"No..." He leaned forward. "No, Godyth, you didn't. I know for sure that that is untrue. It's not possible."

He grasped her arm. "Go back to Bedwyn. We'll need some folk to follow Master Fryxell. Go and talk to master Reeve. Tell him what's been happening."

She reluctantly sloped off into the yard and Gabriel watched her go.

Her expression was one of pure hatred; her eyes, peering up under her eyelashes, dark and full of hostility. He hoped it was for her grandfather and not for him. She walked backwards and her eyes followed him as he turned to wind his way through the farm buildings. If he'd been able to see it, he would have watched Godyth slip into an alleyway and disappear.

Gabriel peered around a corner. He couldn't see anyone and he searched the sky for the Beast of Bedwyn. He must stop calling Mabel that... it's just it had a nice ring to it. He chuckled to himself. Now to catch up with Fryxell and Johnny and of course Mabel.

Once again he peered around the corner and with no warning something hard came down on his skull.

It was a poor blow to the side of his head at the temple, but it was enough to incapacitate him and he fell to his knees, momentarily stunned.

When he'd come to his senses, there was no one in sight.

*****

Mabel pulled the great leathery wings back and forth with strong muscles. This time she had it right. This time she really *was* a gryphon.

She scoured the ground with her amber eyes; the rim of her lethal beak shining yellow in the weak sun. She caught a glimpse of her outstretched saffron coloured talons and noted her beautiful red-brown feathers. She knew she was powerful and as an eagle, was the larger of the sexes. As a gryphon, she was unbeatable.

Once more she quartered the ground, flew over Shawgrove Copse and glided on the air currents towards Chisbury.

Suddenly, as she startled a flock of sheep grazing on the downs, between the trees, she spotted Fryxell dragging poor Johnny Chatterwell along the ground. The man was angry and was shouting at the boy. Johnny was doing his best to keep up but he was terrified and at the end of his tether. He simply had no more energy left to run.

Mabel turned and soared and with one huge flap, ducked her head and drove herself back the way she'd come.

She pulled in her tail; she lost height and with a huge roar she dived for the man and his captive.

Johnny looked up and screeched in surprise.

Fryxell took the back of his hand to the lad's cheek, unaware of what was bearing down on him.

"Look!" shouted Johnny, oblivious to the slap. Well, his mother gave him plenty of those and he was used to them. This slap wasn't as hard as one of her serious ones.

Fryxell looked up.

"Jesus Christ Almighty!" he yelled, letting go of Johnny. "God's Blood!"

Mabel, almost hovering, wheeled away as Fryxell ran for the close confines of the trees.

'Damn,' she'd not be able to get to him if he disappeared in there.

But she didn't think he wasn't quite going to make it to the safety of the woods.

Johnny rolled over onto his back and then stared up to the sky, motionless. It was almost as if he knew that the beast was not interested in *him*. He watched as the gryphon looped back and went for Fryxell once more, catching him by the shoulders of his tunic with huge talons. It lifted the man from his feet.

The man screamed and paddled his legs hoping to get away.

Mabel screamed with him "Grraragh' and lifted higher, grasping his clothing tighter. She didn't want to drop him until she was good and ready. She could feel that she had pierced his skin with her huge claws and was not in the slightest bit penitent.

She saw Johnny stand shakily and watch as the gryphon circled the woods, teasing the man she was holding by dropping and rising over the tops of the trees.

She flew off in the direction of Chisbury and she saw Johnny, with renewed vigour, set off to follow, keeping her in his sight.

Fryxell was writhing in the gryphon's claws, yelling and screaming out in pain and anger. Then he grew silent and ceased to move.

Mabel looked down. He'd lost consciousness. His head was lolling on his chest.

'Good!'

She looked over her shoulder to see Johnny stumbling along, not really knowing where he was going but following all the same.

Mabel realised that she'd have to let Fryxell down soon for her stamina was wearing thin.

She approached a bare piece of down, devoid of sheep and from a height of about ten feet, callously dropped Fryxell onto the grass. He fell with a thud and lay there in a heap. Johnny was rapidly approaching and so Mabel turned a circle and pulled the gaze of the young boy back the way he'd come, away from Fryxell.

He circled on the spot, his mouth open as she flew back the way they'd run.

The boy managed a spurt of speed and ran towards the outliers of Shawgrove Copse.

"Wait!" he cried. "Wait." But the gryphon was far ahead and far above him and was not going to stop until she had enough cover to turn deosil and become Mabel Wetherspring again.

*****

"Lord save me!" cried Gabriel, reaching up to cradle his head. After a moment he took away his hands and there was blood on them but he didn't think that he had been delivered a grievous blow.

He knelt giddily and felt instantly nauseous. He squeezed his eyes shut hoping it would soon pass. Then he began to recall what had happened and who had been there.

Mabel had pursued Fryxell who had taken Little Johnny Chatterwell hostage.

Gabriel blinked several times to get his head and eyes clear. Which way had they gone? Towards Shawgrove Copse, he thought.

He stood and staggered a little as his legs began to obey his wishes once more.

He searched the immediate farmyard where there was no sign of Godyth. Had she defied him and pursued the beast?

Sir Gabriel set off at a slow pace and rounded the end of the barn. Open downland greeted his view, as far as he could see. There was no sign of a gryphon, the felon or a small boy nor for that matter, Godyth.

He wove his way around the barn and set off at a stumbling jog-hop across the down.

*****

Mabel landed in a clearing in Shawgrove Copse. There was no doubt *that* had been fun. He deserved everything he'd got, this mad Fryxell man.

Then she realised that she'd been a gryphon a bit too long and the mind of the creature was infiltrating her own human brain. This happened sometimes. It was very difficult to keep one's own personality and brain separate from the animal she'd become.

She shook her eagle head.

Clumsily, on huge saffron coloured talons, she turned deosil and in her eagle head, she said, 'I wish to be Mabel Wetherspring again.'

After a heartbeat or two she fell to her knees with exhaustion.

But she had no time to recover, she had to find Johnny.

She stood, trembling for a moment and got her bearings. If Johnny had followed then he wouldn't be far behind her.

She took a deep breath and walked back the way she'd come.

She found Little Johnny Chatterwell sitting on an ivy covered tree stump, his chin on his chest.

"Mistress Mabel?"

"Oh Johnny, I am so glad to see you."

"And I'm glad to see you too."

"Did the man Fryxell hurt you?"

"No. But... but…"

"But what?"

"The Beast of Bedwyn has got him."

"Ah yes—I saw the beast rise up from behind the cottage at the farm. What happened? You were much closer than I was."

Johnny proceeded to tell her, without embellishment, exactly what had happened to him and to John Fryxell. "I think he might be dead."

"Where was he, when he fell?"

"Oh he was on the other side of the woods."

"And where did the beast go?"

"Over Shawgrove Copse. I think." He pouted. "I lost it."

"Then the beast is behind us. It's unlikely to come back now. Let's go and find Fryxell."

Mabel helped Johnny up. She could see that the poor boy was exhausted. She was none too lively herself.

They'd only taken four steps when they heard a voice calling them from the trees.

"Mistress Wetherspring! Johnny!"

"Oh look, it's Sir Gabriel!" cried Johnny happily. "If the beast comes back, he'll deal with it I'm sure."

"Hmmm," said Mabel with an enigmatic smile.

They waited while Gabriel staggered up to them out of breath. Mabel saw the blood in his hair and on his cotte.

"What happened to you?"

"I stumbled and hit my head." It was the way in which he said this which made Mabel very suspicious. Her brow furrowed.

"What are you doing here anyway?"

"I saw the beast, Mistress Wetherspring, and I followed in case you and Johnny were in danger."

"Hmmm."

"I told you Sir Gabriel would protect us," said the boy.

"I thought you were questioning people in Bedwyn."

"I was. I did."

Gabriel was scanning the surroundings, eyes on everything but the sky. He knew of course that the gryphon would not return.

"Oh Sir Gabriel..." began Johnny, "The beast picked up the Fryxell man like he was a rabbit and dropped him. I think he might be dead."

Sir Gabriel Warrener gave Mabel a sidelong look.

"The gryphon was acting as jurymen and judge then, Johnny. Do we know what the gryphon was thinking when it did such a thing?"

Mabel coughed. "I'm sure it was thinking nothing in particular, sir."

"It picked up the man to have a little fun with him and dropped him again when it'd had enough," said Johnny with an illicit giggle.

"Unlucky for Fryxell."

"It didn't try to eat him or nothing..." said Johnny.

"Lucky for Fryxell."

"It was wonderful!" said Johnny, his face glowing again. Then he yawned.

"I am so tired."

"Come on lad, you leap up on my shoulders and we'll get you home."

'We can't go home yet!"

"Why not?"

"We have to find Goddy."

"I saw Godyth at the farm." Gabriel's gaze flicked to Mabel. "I sent her home."

"What do we do with Fryxell?" asked Mabel.

"Well, by rights we should take him back to Bedwyn and attach him for the crimes we think he's committed. Mistress Hartshorn told me all about the Fryxells, that they are as mad as a bag of bats. But…"

"Ah—I think we should go and find out and make sure where he is. He should be alright but if he is unable to walk, we shall have to get someone out to fetch him," said Mabel.

Gabriel sighed.

"Alright—hop up Johnny and we'll go and look for this prey of the gryphon."

They set off with Johnny perched on Gabriel's shoulders. He kept up a commentary the whole way to the open patch of down where lay Master Fryxell.

When they got closer they called out.

"Fryxell. Get up, we will take you back to Bedwyn"

Johnny slipped from Gabriel's grasp and jumped down to earth. Running forward he kept up his banter.

"Haha! The monster got you, you horrible man. We saw it—you—" Johnny stopped a few feet from the man lying on the ground, halted in his tracks.

Mabel and Gabriel eventually caught up and looked down.

Mabel could see the injuries she had inflicted to the man's shoulder. Blood had soaked into the cloth of his tunic but it had not been a mortal wound.

However, it was the man's head which took their attention.

When Mabel gryphon had let go of the felon, he'd fallen to earth to land on his side on soft turf.

Now he lay on his front and the back of his head was a pulpy mess of blood, bone and brain.

Mabel turned to Gabriel and in an unguarded moment said, "I didn't do *this*."

"No—but I have an idea who *might* have done it," said Sir Gabriel, fingering his sore head.

CHAPTER FIFTEEN
~ AN ANSWER? ~

"Someone hit you with a stone?"

"They did."

"Why?"

"I don't know. But I think it might have been Godyth."

"You're sure it wasn't an accident? She knew you were there?"

"Oh yes. I had been facing her. I had just told her that I knew she had been lying about the flying beast. I told her that I knew she hadn't seen it."

Mabel sat down on the downland grass. Johnny sat with her and she put her arm around him. He was half asleep and his head slid down to her lap.

"But of course, you couldn't tell her why," she whispered.

"Of course not, that would be more than foolish," answered Gabriel.

He stood above them, turning over the short grass with the toe of his boot. Actually, the toe of *Bunce's* boot. They were silent for quite a while.

"Fryxell confessed to killing Gelle. But we don't really know *why*," said Mabel.

"And Fryxell swore that he hadn't killed any of the children," she added.

"And you believe him?"

"He had no reason to lie at that moment," she answered. "In fact he was kind of bragging and I think he'd have confessed to it if it were true."

"Why would Lovegrove tell such a lie for Fryxell?" said Gabriel, throwing up his hands in desperation. "Saying *he'd* killed Gelle. Killed his own wife."

"He wouldn't. He wasn't protecting *him*."

"Then who?"

"I think he was protecting Godyth from the truth. That her grandfather was also her father, maybe?" whispered Mabel so that Johnny didn't overhear.

Gabriel lifted his brow to Heaven and Mabel gazed at the scudding clouds.

"Oh—oh—I think I have it!" she said suddenly. "I think I understand."

Johnny looked up, he wasn't really asleep after all. "You alright Mistress Mabel?"

She squeezed him tight. "I am Johnny and I think I have just worked it all out."

"What? You know where the monster is?"

Gabriel laughed. "Mistress Wetherspring has known that all along, Johnny."

Johnny's eyes grew wide.

"I told that horrible man that you were clever and I was right," he said.

Mabel jumped up and offered him her good hand.

"Come, there are a few things we need to do."

"Aren't we going to catch the monster?" asked Johnny.

"Ah no. Not today, Master Chatterwell," said Mabel as they ran up the slight hill.

*****

It was the next day before they could get to the castle in Marlborough to release Master Lovegrove. At first, the constable and the sheriff's man were unhappy with their account of events. But Gabriel and Mabel managed to convince them that Master Lovegrove could not have killed his wife. Naturally they left out the part about the gryphon. They did confide their suspicions to the constable but, although he was in agreement with them, said they needed more evidence.

Mabel did not need to crawl through the grill into the gaol this time and she waited outside the castle on the bridge, for Gabriel to walk out with a rather dishevelled and dirty Phillip Lovegrove.

They'd brought a cart with them from Bedwyn and Peter Corngold was happy to drive it for them. On the way to Marlborough they'd turned over the facts as they saw them.

"Why did you become the Beast of Bedwyn again?" asked Gabriel when they were riding behind the cart and out of earshot.

"I had thought of becoming a wolf once more but I tried that before, remember, and was injured even so. A gryphon was going to be proof against most weapons. And I had to stop Fryxell."

"And it was very impressive I must say. Terrifying!" he said with a little chuckle.

Mabel grinned.

Philip Lovegrove, a little bewildered, climbed into the back of the cart and pulled a blanket around himself. Gabriel rode beside them on Bertran as Mabel took Lovegrove's shoulder in her hand.

"I am sorry that you have had to spend time in the gaol, Phillip. It could have been avoided if you had just been a little more forthcoming with information, before this. If you had told us the truth."

He shivered and his gaze drifted away. He looked a completely different man with several days-worth of beard and his hair plastered to his head. It seemed he had lost weight too. Not that he had had much to lose. His face was now gaunt and lined.

"We now know that it was John Fryxell who killed your wife. We got a confession from him."

Lovegrove looked at Mabel in disbelief.

"No! Never. He'd never confess."

"He did. He thought that I wouldn't be able to tell anyone because he tried to kill me too. Get me out of the way. He was bragging. And we have one more witness to his confession. Even if it is a child."

Lovegrove groaned. "He's an evil man."

"This is who Gelle was describing when she said that Godyth's father was a wicked man, wasn't it?"

Lovegrove nodded.

"Well—he can't hurt anyone now. He's dead, Phillip. We found him with his head smashed in yesterday, up on Bedwyn Common," said Gabriel.

"Dead?" he gulped. "No..? You're certain?"

"He was murdered," added Mabel.

Phillip was almost about to sob. Mabel thought it was in relief.

"Tell us Phillip... Godyth? She is Fryxell's daughter but I cannot see Gelle being a willing participant in..."

"He raped her. Several times. Godyth was the result."

Now Mabel understood why Gelle had hated her father so much, why she called him evil and why she could not look after the resultant child of their union.

"Then he went away and we didn't see him. Good riddance, we thought."

"For quite some time, I think."

"Years."

"And then he came back, didn't he?"

Lovegrove grabbed Mabel's poorly arm. She flinched.

"Oh Mistress Mabel! He was the very devil! He came back and he killed Master Leofric Stock and he came to find Godyth. And he... he..." He began to weep in earnest. "He did to Godyth what he had done to her mother."

Gabriel wiped his hand over his face.

"You are telling us that Fryxell raped his own nine year old granddaughter?"

"He did… and she was just eight then."

"Jesus aid us," said Gabriel in a shocked voice.

"Now we know the motive for Fryxell killing Gelle and trying to kill Godyth. He needed to keep them quiet. He needed to keep his incest a secret."

"Against the law of man and God—incest." said Gabriel in a small voice.

Mabel swallowed hard and then said, "When did he come back to see her?"

"It was last year, in the late summer. When we had the run of good, warm days."

"When Dunstan Durwald from Crofton was killed?"

"The same week."

Mabel looked up at Gabriel who'd gone very pale.

"He swore that he didn't kill or harm any of the children."

"He was a great liar and an evil man," said Lovegrove.

"You know, Phillip, I agree with you. He was an evil madman but I think I believed him when he said that the deaths of the children were not down to him," said Mabel.

Lovegrove was shaking his head. "No—no—no."

Mabel patted the man's knee. "Phillip, you will have to be very brave."

"No. No! You cannot question Godyth."

"We just have one or two more things to do and then we will know everything."

"Will we?" said Gabriel with a blank face.

*****

Mabel and Gabriel argued about how they were going to do the next thing it seemed necessary to do.

"We need a confession. We'll never get the crimes to stick if we don't get a confession," said Gabriel.

"How are we going to do that? You know full well we won't get any cooperation. All we have is a series of coincidences and circumstances."

"Circumstances do not directly prove guilt but it allows us to draw up a reasonable idea about a fact based on the evidence we have. It is different from direct evidence, which establishes guilt as a fact on its own."

"My goodness, Gabriel! Have you swallowed a book of the law?"

Gabriel looked affronted. "No. I'm just interested in it—you know that."

Mabel sat down and prodded her dinner with her spoon. She really wasn't hungry.

"So what *do* we have?" She pushed it away from her.

Gabriel paced up and down. "We have the culprit in the right places at the right times..."

"Mostly."

"We have a motive—now that Lovegrove has spilled the beans."

"Maybe."

"And we have a foolproof theory about how it was done."

"Unless of course it's sheer coincidence."

Gabriel lifted his hand to his temple. "This lump and graze is not a coincidence, believe me."

"The only thing we can do is try a confrontation and see what happens," said Mabel.

"Just don't turn your back eh?" Gabriel chuckled under his breath.

"Ah no—look on the bright side..."

"There's a bright side?"

"We have Eadric. I think we must first have a confrontation with Eadric Ceorlson. You know how terrified he is of *you*. He knows what is going on, Gabriel. He does. I'm sure."

"Question him again?"

"I am sure he will confess what he knows. We must use the age-old method of extracting information from him."

Gabriel blinked..."You mean torture?"

"Ah no—really Gabriel!" Mabel looked up to the Heavens. "I'll be sweet as honey and you be..."

"You mean I should be the bad investigator ready to use my fists and you the good one, all sweetness and...?"

"We can try it."

"Why can't I be the sweet one?"

*****

They encouraged the village reeve to let them into the lockup.

Master Head puffed up his chest and tried to look authoritative. "I'm not sure I can allow you to..."

Gabriel wanted to say, "Come on you pompous, witless peabrain, do as I say or..."

What he actually said was, "You need me to ride off to Rutishall, do you, where the Lord Stokke will be and tell him that you are not being cooperative, reeve?"

"Failing that we could go to Master Henry," said Mabel. "He has a key. I am sure he would..."

"Oh Lord save us—anyone but him." The reeve rubbed his temple with a podgy hand. "If we involve him, we shall be debating the merits of closing the door after us and putting Ceorlson in irons for a week ," said Head, "before we can even get in there."

"You know what an old biddy he can be," chuckled Mabel.

Reluctantly Master Head took the key from his purse. "Alright. But I need to be there."

"Oh yes, we need you there, John," said Mabel. "We need someone of authority who has a good grasp of what's going on."

Gabriel looked at her quickly. Had she really just said that?

"And I expect we'll need to get you to make a statement about what you hear."

"Oh well in that case..." said Henry Head, puffing up his chest even further, "I am at your disposal, Sir Gabriel."

*****

"Eadric, it's very important that you answer these questions as carefully as you can. If you tell us the absolute truth, we will be able to let you go home. Is that clear?" said Gabriel. "But if you are still bent on lying then I'm afraid it's another beating for you. Do you understand?"

Mabel looked askance at Gabriel. 'Steady on!' she thought. 'We have only just started!'

Eadric Ceorlson sniffled and nodded.

"We now know what has been happening, Eadric," said Mabel. "And we are very sorry you have been dragged into this."

Master Head stood by the door, his arms folded over his large belly, his nose in the air. "You won't be welcome in the village ever again, Eadric, if you do not confess. Even if you get off—the Lord will move you..."

"Thank you Master Head, we shall ask the questions," said Gabriel sharply.

Ceorlson began to shiver with fear. He stared at Gabriel with the eyes of a frightened rabbit before a stoat.

"Will you help us?" Mabel leaned forward and gave Master Ceorlson an endearing smile.

"I—I will if I can."

"We think we know that a year ago, Godyth's father came back to the area..."

"Master Fryxell..."

"Oh, you know about him?"

"He's a wicked, evil man."

"Yes. We know that is true," said Mabel.

"Did you know that he was living at Stock Farm?"

"I knew he was somewhere close by because I used to see him."

"Where?"

"He was following Godyth about when she went out, now and again."

"And did you follow him?"

"Aw no!" Eadric shivered again. "He's a wicked, wicked man. He's cursed and he might put a curse on us."

Mabel thought, 'In a way, he has.'

"Ah no, Eadric, he can't do that now, you see, because he's dead," said Gabriel casually, leaning back on his seat. "He's been killed."

"The devil take his soul!" said Eadric hastily and with venom. Then as an afterthought, he crossed himself.

"Oh no doubt he has. As sure as we all have two feet!" said Gabriel glibly.

"You're sure he's dead?"

"Yes. Absolutely dead. He left his brain—or most of it—out on the common..."

"Someone hit him with a rock, Eadric," said Mabel.

Ceorlson's eyes glazed over. "It weren't me."

"No, it can't have been you. You were locked up in here."

"But Eadric," said Mabel softly, "We know that you've been following Godyth."

Ceorlson shook his head.

Gabriel slapped the table in front of him hard.

Eadric jumped and so did Mabel. She gave Gabriel a sidelong look which was meant to mean, 'Not too much of the bad investigator, please.'

"Do not lie to us, Ceorlson."

"No, sir."

"You followed Godyth and you found the body of Dunstan Durwold at the bottom of the hill."

Ceorlson nodded.

"And then you followed Godyth again and you found little Archard Tapscott?"

Eadric began to cry but gave an infinitesimal nod.

"You covered him over with stones, didn't you?" said Gabriel.

"You tried to protect him, I know," said Mabel. "You mounted a guard outside his house and that is why your shoes were covered in the fruit from the crab apple tree there."

Eadric nodded. "But I couldn't stay there the whole time."

"And then you rescued little Johnny Chatterwell from the forest. How did you know where he'd gone?"

Ceorlson wiped his nose on his sleeve. "I found them, him and Goddy and took Johnny away and brought him home. Goddy had taken him into the forest."

"And you did the same with little JohnFour, Master Head's son, didn't you?" asked Mabel.

The village reeve made a strange sucking noise. "No—no. That's not right, he took John away and..."

"Please, Master Head," said Mabel. "You'll see in a moment what has been happening."

"You rescued him and kept him safe, didn't you?"

"Yes, I did."

"But you were very sad that you couldn't keep your nephew, Henry, from harm, weren't you Eadric?"

The man sobbed. "Aye... aye... I was."

Mabel leaned further over the table. "Why did you keep this to yourself, Eadric?"

"I wanted to tell—I wanted to. But I couldn't..."

"You confronted him, confronted Master Fryxell, didn't you? Godyth's father."

"He just gave me a bang around the head and kicked me down and said I could never tell because..."

"Because of Godyth."

"Aye." Ceorlson threw his head in his hands. "Cursed. Cursed. All the Fryxells are cursed!"

Mabel gave Gabriel a final knowing look.

"Eadric. All these children. Godyth took them didn't she? And she killed some of them and you—you thwarted her with those you could save."

"Aye, aye I did."

Mabel took hold of his grubby hand.

"Will you say it out loud so that Master Head and Sir Gabriel can hear clearly?"

His red rimmed eyes, full of tears, bored into hers.

"Aye. Goddy killed all those littluns and if I hadn't taken them away she would have killed the others."

"She pushed Archard Tapscott down the hill, she threw Dunstan Durwood over the cliff and she killed her brother, didn't she?"

"Yes—...yes, she did. But she can't help herself—she can't."

Master Head's mouth was open so far, Mabel thought it might be possible to drive a cart into it.

"Godyth?" he whispered at last.

"Yes. Godyth," said Mabel

The reeve crossed himself and swallowed as if he was quaffing a huge draught of ale.

"The devil is loose in Bedwyn," he said.

*****

"Of course I didn't!"

"You had a stone in your hand and you struck me over the head with it, Godyth," said Gabriel.

"You have been seeing things. Why would I do that to you?" she said with a toss of her head. The dark curls bounced around her shoulders.

They'd found Godyth at home alone in Mistress Ceorlson's cottage and they were quite surprised she was still there.

At last Mabel stepped in between Godyth and Sir Gabriel who were nose to nose by the fireplace.

"When you left Sir Gabriel, whether you hit him or not, where did you go, Godyth?"

"I was afraid of the beast, I ran all the way home."

Mabel smirked at the girl. "You weren't afraid before."

"I hadn't seen it before— it was huge and horrible and I was frightened it would come back."

"And you left Johnny Chatterwell?" said Gabriel.

"Not a very kind thing to do," said Mabel, "was it?"

"I didn't leave him," insisted the girl, "I knew he was with you. Safe."

Mabel raised her voice. "Godyth, we know that you have lied. You told me before that you'd seen the Beast of Bedwyn. You told me that it was the cause of your brother's death."

"I... I..."

"That was a lie? You hadn't seen it flying about then or attacking Henry, had you?"

"I thought it... probably... had."

"And you told Johnny that you'd seen it out at Chisbury to encourage him to go with you."

"No!" Godyth cried out. "If he is saying that then he's a liar. I told him that I had heard that was the last place it had been seen. Not that it was definitely there."

"Where did you hear that?"

"From my Uncle Eadric."

Gabriel turned to Mabel. "Blaming Eadric again. It's everyone's fault but her own."

Gabriel took hold of the girl's arm,

"You doubled back after you hit me and you found Master Fryxell lying injured on the ground and then, no doubt, with the same rock with which you hit me, you killed him."

"No!"

Mabel looked the girl over.

"Tell me, Godyth, what were you doing at Crofton when you found little Dunstan Durwood?"

"I didn't find him."

"Your uncle Eadric said you told him where to find the body."

"I've told you before, my uncle is a drunkard. He hardly knows what he is doing some days."

In an exasperated strut, the young girl stomped across the cottage and threw herself down on her bed.

Mabel softened her voice.

"We know that Fryxell killed your mother, Godyth, we heard him confess it."

Mabel was certain that Godyth had heard him confess it too.

"If you did kill him, we understand why you would do it."

"NO!"

"That is the kirtle you were wearing when you went to see your mother, isn't it, Godyth?"

The girl was thrown off guard for just a moment and then, recovering her poise, sneered. "Of course. I only have two kirtles. This one and my red Sunday one."

"This was the dress you say was muddied and torn on the day you went to Chisbury to meet Gelle."

Mabel followed the girl across the room and stood looking down at her.

She reached out and fingered the neck.

"I remember you have a small brooch which keeps the two pieces of the neck together."

Godyth's hand went up to the front of her brown-yellow kirtle where there was now a gap at the throat.

"I—I—lost it."

"Yes, I know you lost it."

Mabel fiddled in her purse. "Where did you lose it?"

"I don't know," said the sullen girl.

"I know. Goddy, I know exactly where you lost it." Mabel pulled out the little silvered brooch.

"I found it in the pond when we were looking for little Johnny, the day he went missing. The day he went into the woods with you to look for the Beast of Bedwyn."

Godyth stared at Mabel from the tops of her eyes. It was a very unfriendly expression. Gabriel recognised it as the look she'd also given him.

"I told you I lost it."

"In the pond?"

"I must have lost it in the pond if that is where you found it."

Mabel sat down next to the girl on the bed. Gabriel watched from a distance. He'd let Mabel deal with Godyth. He felt her so absolutely evil he almost couldn't bring himself to speak to her further.

"I have a very good memory, Godyth."

The girl scoffed.

"I do. And I remember that the day that Sir Gabriel and I found the body of your mother, there had been no rain for quite some time. Yet you say you fell in some mud. I couldn't find any mud anywhere around there, at Chisbury."

"It. Was. Muddy."

"You had washed your kirtle in places, hadn't you? As you have now. It's damp."

"Mud."

"Not mud—blood." There was a tiny silence.

"I had forgotten, it was my mother's blood."

"Oh yes. Of course. You found her first, before we did, didn't you?" There was an icy silence.

"Have you washed Master Fryxell's blood from it now, Goddy?" The girl merely harrumphed and turned away.

"The day your brother died, your shoes were wet. It didn't rain. Why were they wet? Because you had been by the river bank hadn't you?

"No."

Mabel sighed. This was like squeezing a walnut for milk

"You knew that Fryxell was your grandfather and that he had killed your mother. You also knew that he was your father. Your real father."

The evil look was back.

Mabel rose and took a deep breath.

"The Fryxells are cursed, did you know that, Godyth?"

"Your mother was a Fryxell," said Gabriel quietly. "Your brother Henry was a Lovegrove. Your Uncle is a Ceorlson. But you now—you alone are a Fryxell."

Suddenly Godyth had risen from her bed, her hands two tight fists, her face pink and angry.

"You are all mad. All of you. If I am a Fryxell then I can bring down the curse on you all—every one of you."

Gabriel shivered.

Mabel smiled.

"It doesn't frighten us, Godyth," she said.

*****

They tried and failed to get Godyth to admit to the abductions and murders of the little children and in the end they had to put the girl in the lockup overnight to give them time to inform the constable and the local coroner. Eadric would have to be released for he had committed no real crime.

Mistress Ceorlson screamed at them when they took Godyth to the lockup. The reeve, Master Head, had explained why they were doing it but Mistress Ceorlson would not accept his explanation. He had always had it in for their family, she said. Going back years, when her husband, Adam Ceorlson and he had fought over her. Mabel and Gabriel learned that the reeve had courted the woman in his younger days but Master Ceorlson had won. Head had never forgiven her for accepting the other man, she said.

In the end Eadric offered to stay in the lockup with Godyth but Mabel thought this a bad idea. She didn't trust the girl at all.

Gabriel and Mabel were somewhat miserable that evening. They were absolutely sure that Godyth was their killer but just could not prove it and it was unlikely they'd get a confession from Godyth herself.

"The girl is completely mad. What are we to do with someone who is completely mad?"

"Out of her right mind she may be Gabriel, but she knows what she is doing and knows right from wrong."

"Then she will be twelve in a short while. If they accept our evidence such as it is, she must face trial as an adult and if found guilty she must hang," answered Gabriel. "If the justices wish it."

He pushed away his plate of food virtually untouched and wiped his knife, hanging it once more on his belt.

"Why—tell me why she wants to kill these children?"

The deaths had started once her father had come back to the area. Mabel tried to explain to Sir Gabriel why she thought Mabel's brain was hopelessly disturbed.

"I think she only took boys because she saw them as a threat."

"What? Tiny boys like JohnFour?"

"JohnFour would grow into a man one day. They all would and they could inflict pain and suffering on women. Like her father had done on her grandmother, her mother and of course, on her. She couldn't really tackle men, so she killed boys."

"That is completely deranged. Surely they cannot hang someone who is so unsound of mind?"

"That of course will be up to the justices."

"And tell me this. Why, if Fryxell committed rape on Mistress Ceorlson and on Gelle Lovegrove, did they then conceive children? Correct me if I'm wrong but I thought that it wasn't possible."

"What?"

"Well, I was always taught that if a woman is raped and she conceives a child then...well..."

"That she has not been raped? She must have enjoyed the experience?" said Mabel with a tinge of scorn.

"That's what I have heard."

Mabel sat in front of Gabriel over her trestle table and joined her hands together.

"You are a knight, Gabriel and you must have heard some tales of war, even if you have not as yet been to war yourself."

"Well—no—not yet. The Lord Stokke hasn't been called to...'

"And if you have heard tales of war you have no doubt heard about the terrible things which are done by soldiers—to civilians."

"We try to stop it. There is a code."

"Pah! Code! I am sorry Gabriel, but if you think that men with their blood on fire, searching for treasure or pleasure will stop to weigh up a code of conduct before they rape, steal or kill, then you are sadly mistaken."

"But..."

"I remember the tales my grandfather used to tell when I was younger, about the poor women of the enemy he had seen when accompanying his lord off to war."

Gabriel was silent and still.

"The screams and the pleadings, the terrible sights, were with him until his dying day. No, Gabriel. No woman enjoys rape. No matter what the doctors say. They are wrong and any woman who has been raped and lived, will tell you, it was the most awful experience of her life."

"You sound as if you know someone who...?"

"I do. A couple of years ago, a girl I know was raped by a man in her village. A village not too far away from here. He was a known troublemaker and someone subsequently murdered him."

"Murdered him?"

"Not solely because of the rape but for another reason. This girl I know, she got pregnant by him and believe me, if you were to talk to her, you would understand that it wasn't something she'd invited nor enjoyed."

"Is she...?"

"She married the village blacksmith and they are very happy, I'm told."

"Rather like Master Lovegrove marrying Gelle when she was already with child."

"Just the same. There are some good men in the world."

Gabriel felt duly ticked off and so that night, he went to the hall in the manor to play merrells with anyone who'd play with him. He was so distempered about Godyth he couldn't stay at Mabel's and needed a diversion. As it happened, it was master steward Henry Buttermere who agreed to engage him in a game. Afterwards Gabriel would sleep in the hall in his usual place.

Four hundred and forty four feet and four inches away, Mabel lay on her bed and looked up into the rafters. It was a very bright night, for the sky was clear, the stars were shining and the moon was quite bright through the open shutters. Her room was lit up as if she was burning a dozen candles. Perhaps she'd have one last fly around the village. It might clear her head and allow her to sleep.

A little bat went scooting out of her open window and made for the river. By rights, if she was a real bat, she should be hibernating at this time in the winter but she knew this one fly around wouldn't hurt her.

She careered over the oak tree and turned to the river, following it for a short distance.

Her wings beat dozens of times before she glided on them, the membranes outstretched and taut. She steered herself down to the small landing stage where Master Atwater kept his little boat.

Landing on the horizontal post, she wriggled her way underneath and hid in the dead and dying plants still twining up the bank and covering the posts, her claws catching hold of the wooden rail. There she happily hung upside down.

Master Atwater was the man responsible for making sure that the river was well kept in the village. It wasn't his only job, for he was also the miller's assistant.

Mabel pictured the affable man with his contagious grin and his shiny bald head. His brother, who was the miller himself, was very like him and the two of them might be mistaken for each other at a glance.

Mabel looked down at the pool, black in the night. With the moon shining, she could see her figure on the shimmering surface of the water clutching the rail and squeezing herself into the spaces between the plants.

'I could be any small bat. They all look alike. Unlike people, even if they are related. They all look different in some small way. But tiny bats are all the same.'

A picture of Little Johnny came into her head. He was one of four children and looked completely unlike the rest.

The other children all had their father's square chiselled face, his stocky figure, his brown hair and eyes, but Johnny, he was his mother's son. His eyes were blue grey and his hair a dark blond and straight. His face was round and apple cheeked like his mother and his ears stuck out a little, just like hers.

Mabel smiled a bat smile.

She was fond of Johnny and thinking about him sent a flicker of an idea through her bat brain.

If she was so fond of Johnny, could she make herself put him in peril? Her heart started to race as she mulled over the idea—a dangerous idea.

It was one way to make sure that they had the right person for the crimes.

Would Johnny go for it? She was sure he would if there was a promise of flying pigs or the chance to see a gryphon.

She and Sir Gabriel would have to keep him safe. They'd have to. Or she would never live with herself.

"Someone hit you with a stone?"

"They did."

"Why?"

"I don't know. But I think it might have been Godyth."

"You're sure it wasn't an accident? She knew you were there?"

"Oh yes. I had been facing her. I had just told her that I knew she had been lying about the flying beast. I told her that I knew she hadn't seen it."

Mabel sat down on the downland grass. Johnny sat with her and she put her arm around him. He was half asleep and his head slid down to her lap.

"But of course, you couldn't tell her why," she whispered.

"Of course not, that would be more than foolish," answered Gabriel.

He stood above them, turning over the short grass with the toe of his boot. Actually, the toe of Bunce's boot. They were silent for quite a while.

"Fryxell confessed to killing Gelle. But we don't really know why," said Mabel.

"And Fryxell swore that he hadn't killed any of the children," she added.

"And you believe him?"

"He had no reason to lie at that moment," she answered. "In fact he was kind of bragging and I think he'd have confessed to it if it were true."

"Why would Lovegrove tell such a lie for Fryxell?" said Gabriel, throwing up his hands in desperation. "Saying he'd killed Gelle. Killed his own wife."

"He wouldn't. He wasn't protecting him."

"Then who?"

"I think he was protecting Godyth from the truth. That her grandfather was also her father, maybe?" whispered Mabel so that Johnny didn't overhear.

Gabriel lifted his brow to Heaven and Mabel gazed at the scudding clouds.

"Oh—oh—I think I have it!" she said suddenly. "I think I understand."

Johnny looked up, he wasn't really asleep after all. "You alright Mistress Mabel?"

She squeezed him tight. "I am Johnny and I think I have just worked it all out."

"What? You know where the monster is?"

Gabriel laughed. "Mistress Wetherspring has known that all along, Johnny."

Johnny's eyes grew wide.

"I told that horrible man that you were clever and I was right," he said.

Mabel jumped up and offered him her good hand.

"Come, there are a few things we need to do."

"Aren't we going to catch the monster?" asked Johnny.

"Ah no. Not today, Master Chatterwell," said Mabel as they ran up the slight hill.

*****

It was the next day before they could get to the castle in Marlborough to release Master Lovegrove. At first, the constable and the sheriff's man were unhappy with their account of events. But Gabriel and Mabel managed to convince them that Master Lovegrove could not have killed his wife. Naturally they left out the part about the gryphon. They did confide their suspicions to the constable but, although he was in agreement with them, said they needed more evidence.

Mabel did not need to crawl through the grill into the gaol this time and she waited outside the castle on the bridge, for Gabriel to walk out with a rather dishevelled and dirty Phillip Lovegrove.

They'd brought a cart with them from Bedwyn and Peter Corngold was happy to drive it for them. On the way to Marlborough they'd turned over the facts as they saw them.

"Why did you become the Beast of Bedwyn again?" asked Gabriel when they were riding behind the cart and out of earshot.

"I had thought of becoming a wolf once more but I tried that before, remember, and was injured even so. A gryphon was going to be proof against most weapons. And I had to stop Fryxell."

"And it was very impressive I must say. Terrifying!" he said with a little chuckle.

Mabel grinned.

Philip Lovegrove, a little bewildered, climbed into the back of the cart and pulled a blanket around himself. Gabriel rode beside them on Bertran as Mabel took Lovegrove's shoulder in her hand.

"I am sorry that you have had to spend time in the gaol, Phillip. It could have been avoided if you had just been a little more forthcoming with information, before this. If you had told us the truth."

He shivered and his gaze drifted away. He looked a completely different man with several days-worth of beard and his hair plastered to his head. It seemed he had lost weight too. Not that he had had much to lose. His face was now gaunt and lined.

"We now know that it was John Fryxell who killed your wife. We got a confession from him."

Lovegrove looked at Mabel in disbelief.

"No! Never. He'd never confess."

"He did. He thought that I wouldn't be able to tell anyone because he tried to kill me too. Get me out of the way. He was bragging. And we have one more witness to his confession. Even if it is a child."

Lovegrove groaned. "He's an evil man."

"This is who Gelle was describing when she said that Godyth's father was a wicked man, wasn't it?"

Lovegrove nodded.

"Well—he can't hurt anyone now. He's dead, Phillip. We found him with his head smashed in yesterday, up on Bedwyn Common," said Gabriel.

"Dead?" he gulped. "No..? You're certain?"

"He was murdered," added Mabel.

Phillip was almost about to sob. Mabel thought it was in relief.

"Tell us Phillip... Godyth? She is Fryxell's daughter but I cannot see Gelle being a willing participant in..."

"He raped her. Several times. Godyth was the result."

Now Mabel understood why Gelle had hated her father so much, why she called him evil and why she could not look after the resultant child of their union.

"Then he went away and we didn't see him. Good riddance, we thought."

"For quite some time, I think."

"Years."

"And then he came back, didn't he?"

Lovegrove grabbed Mabel's poorly arm. She flinched.

"Oh Mistress Mabel! He was the very devil! He came back and he killed Master Leofric Stock and he came to find Godyth. And he... he..." He began to weep in earnest. "He did to Godyth what he had done to her mother."

Gabriel wiped his hand over his face.

"You are telling us that Fryxell raped his own nine year old granddaughter?"

"He did... and she was just eight then."

"Jesus aid us," said Gabriel in a shocked voice.

"Now we know the motive for Fryxell killing Gelle and trying to kill Godyth. He needed to keep them quiet. He needed to keep his incest a secret."

"Against the law of man and God—incest." said Gabriel in a small voice.

Mabel swallowed hard and then said, "When did he come back to see her?"

"It was last year, in the late summer. When we had the run of good, warm days."

"When Dunstan Durwald from Crofton was killed?"

"The same week."

Mabel looked up at Gabriel who'd gone very pale.

"He swore that he didn't kill or harm any of the children."

"He was a great liar and an evil man," said Lovegrove.

"You know, Phillip, I agree with you. He was an evil madman but I think I believed him when he said that the deaths of the children were not down to him," said Mabel.

Lovegrove was shaking his head. "No—no—no."

Mabel patted the man's knee. "Phillip, you will have to be very brave."

"No. No! You cannot question Godyth."

"We just have one or two more things to do and then we will know everything."

"Will we?" said Gabriel with a blank face.

*****

Mabel and Gabriel argued about how they were going to do the next thing it seemed necessary to do.

"We need a confession. We'll never get the crimes to stick if we don't get a confession," said Gabriel.

"How are we going to do that? You know full well we won't get any cooperation. All we have is a series of coincidences and circumstances."

"Circumstances do not directly prove guilt but it allows us to draw up a reasonable idea about a fact based on the evidence we have. It is different from direct evidence, which establishes guilt as a fact on its own."

"My goodness, Gabriel! Have you swallowed a book of the law?"

Gabriel looked affronted. "No. I'm just interested in it—you know that."

Mabel sat down and prodded her dinner with her spoon. She really wasn't hungry.

"So what do we have?" She pushed it away from her.

Gabriel paced up and down. "We have the culprit in the right places at the right times..."

"Mostly."

"We have a motive—now that Lovegrove has spilled the beans."

"Maybe."

"And we have a foolproof theory about how it was done."

"Unless of course it's sheer coincidence."

Gabriel lifted his hand to his temple. "This lump and graze is not a coincidence, believe me."

"The only thing we can do is try a confrontation and see what happens," said Mabel.

"Just don't turn your back eh?" Gabriel chuckled under his breath.

"Ah no—look on the bright side..."

"There's a bright side?"

"We have Eadric. I think we must first have a confrontation with Eadric Ceorlson. You know how terrified he is of you. He knows what is going on, Gabriel. He does. I'm sure."

"Question *him* again?"

"I am sure he will confess what he knows. We must use the age-old method of extracting information from him."

Gabriel blinked..."You mean torture?"

"Ah no—really Gabriel!" Mabel looked up to the Heavens. "I'll be sweet as honey and you be..."

"You mean I should be the bad investigator ready to use my fists and you the good one, all sweetness and...?"

"We can try it."

"Why can't I be the sweet one?"

*****

They encouraged the village reeve to let them into the lockup.

Master Head puffed up his chest and tried to look authoritative. "I'm not sure I can allow you to..."

Gabriel wanted to say, "Come on you pompous, witless peabrain, do as I say or..."

What he actually said was, "You need me to ride off to Rutishall, do you, where the Lord Stokke will be and tell him that you are not being cooperative, reeve?"

"Failing that we could go to Master Henry," said Mabel. "He has a key. I am sure he would..."

"Oh Lord save us—anyone but him." The reeve rubbed his temple with a podgy hand. "If we involve him, we shall be debating the merits of closing the door after us and putting Ceorlson in irons for a week ," said Head, "before we can even get in there."

"You know what an old biddy he can be," chuckled Mabel.

Reluctantly Master Head took the key from his purse. "Alright. But I need to be there."

"Oh yes, we need you there, John," said Mabel. "We need someone of authority who has a good grasp of what's going on."

Gabriel looked at her quickly. Had she *really* just said that?

"And I expect we'll need to get you to make a statement about what you hear."

"Oh well in that case..." said Henry Head, puffing up his chest even further, "I am at your disposal, Sir Gabriel."

*****

"Eadric, it's very important that you answer these questions as carefully as you can. If you tell us the absolute truth, we will be able to let you go home. Is that clear?" said Gabriel. "But if you are still bent on lying then I'm afraid it's another beating for you. Do you understand?"

Mabel looked askance at Gabriel. 'Steady on!' she thought. 'We have only just started!'

Eadric Ceorlson sniffled and nodded.

"We now know what has been happening, Eadric," said Mabel. "And we are very sorry you have been dragged into this."

Master Head stood by the door, his arms folded over his large belly, his nose in the air. "You won't be welcome in the village ever again, Eadric, if you do not confess. Even if you get off—the Lord will move you…"

"Thank you Master Head, we shall ask the questions," said Gabriel sharply.

Ceorlson began to shiver with fear. He stared at Gabriel with the eyes of a frightened rabbit before a stoat.

"Will you help us?" Mabel leaned forward and gave Master Ceorlson an endearing smile.

"I—I will if I can."

"We think we know that a year ago, Godyth's father came back to the area…"

"Master Fryxell…"

"Oh, you know about him?"

"He's a wicked, evil man."

"Yes. We know that is true," said Mabel.

"Did you know that he was living at Stock Farm?"

"I knew he was somewhere close by because I used to see him."

"Where?"

"He was following Godyth about when she went out, now and again."

"And did you follow *him*?"

"Aw no!" Eadric shivered again. "He's a wicked, wicked man. He's cursed and he might put a curse on *us*."

Mabel thought, 'In a way, he has.'

"Ah no, Eadric, he can't do that now, you see, because he's dead," said Gabriel casually, leaning back on his seat. "He's been killed."

"The devil take his soul!" said Eadric hastily and with venom. Then as an afterthought, he crossed himself.

"Oh no doubt he has. As sure as we all have two feet!" said Gabriel glibly.

"You're sure he's dead?"

"Yes. Absolutely dead. He left his brain—or most of it—out on the common..."

"Someone hit him with a rock, Eadric," said Mabel.

Ceorlson's eyes glazed over. "It weren't me."

"No, it can't have been you. You were locked up in here."

"But Eadric," said Mabel softly, "We know that you've been following Godyth."

Ceorlson shook his head.

Gabriel slapped the table in front of him hard.

Eadric jumped and so did Mabel. She gave Gabriel a sidelong look which was meant to mean, 'Not too much of the bad investigator, please.'

"Do not lie to us, Ceorlson."

"No, sir."

"You followed Godyth and you found the body of Dunstan Durwold at the bottom of the hill."

Ceorlson nodded.

"And then you followed Godyth again and you found little Archard Tapscott?"

Eadric began to cry but gave an infinitesimal nod.

"You covered him over with stones, didn't you?" said Gabriel.

"You tried to protect him, I know," said Mabel. "You mounted a guard outside his house and that is why your shoes were covered in the fruit from the crab apple tree there."

Eadric nodded. "But I couldn't stay there the whole time."

"And then you rescued little Johnny Chatterwell from the forest. How did you know where *he'd* gone?"

Ceorlson wiped his nose on his sleeve. "I found them, him and Goddy and took Johnny away and brought him home. Goddy had taken him into the forest."

"And you did the same with little JohnFour, Master Head's son, didn't you?" asked Mabel.

The village reeve made a strange sucking noise. "No—no. That's not right, he took John away and…"

"Please, Master Head," said Mabel. "You'll see in a moment what has been happening."

"You rescued him and kept him safe, didn't you?"

"Yes, I did."

"But you were very sad that you couldn't keep your nephew, Henry, from harm, weren't you Eadric?"

The man sobbed. "Aye… aye… I was."

Mabel leaned further over the table."Why did you keep this to yourself, Eadric?"

"I wanted to tell—I wanted to. But I couldn't…"

"You confronted him, confronted Master Fryxell, didn't you? Godyth's father."

"He just gave me a bang around the head and kicked me down and said I could never tell because…"

"Because of Godyth."

"Aye." Ceorlson threw his head in his hands. "Cursed. Cursed. All the Fryxells are cursed!"

Mabel gave Gabriel a final knowing look.

"Eadric. All these children. Godyth took them didn't she? And she killed some of them and you—you thwarted her with those you could save."

"Aye, aye I did."

Mabel took hold of his grubby hand.

"Will you say it out loud so that Master Head and Sir Gabriel can hear clearly?"

His red rimmed eyes, full of tears, bored into hers.

"Aye. Goddy killed all those littluns and if I hadn't taken them away she would have killed the others."

"She pushed Archard Tapscott down the hill, she threw Dunstan Durwood over the cliff and she killed her brother, didn't she?"

"Yes—...yes, she did. But she can't help herself—she can't."

Master Head's mouth was open so far, Mabel thought it might be possible to drive a cart into it.

"Godyth?" he whispered at last.

"Yes. Godyth," said Mabel

The reeve crossed himself and swallowed as if he was quaffing a huge draught of ale.

"The devil is loose in Bedwyn," he said.

*****

"Of course I didn't!"

"You had a stone in your hand and you struck me over the head with it, Godyth," said Gabriel.

"You have been seeing things. Why would I do that to you?" she said with a toss of her head. The dark curls bounced around her shoulders.

They'd found Godyth at home alone in Mistress Ceorlson's cottage and they were quite surprised she was still there.

At last Mabel stepped in between Godyth and Sir Gabriel who were nose to nose by the fireplace.

"When you left Sir Gabriel, whether you hit him or not, where did you go, Godyth?"

"I was afraid of the beast, I ran all the way home."

Mabel smirked at the girl. "You weren't afraid before."

"I hadn't seen it before— it was huge and horrible and I was frightened it would come back."

"And you left Johnny Chatterwell?" said Gabriel.

"Not a very kind thing to do," said Mabel, "was it?"

"I didn't leave him," insisted the girl, "I knew he was with you. Safe."

Mabel raised her voice. "Godyth, we know that you have lied. You told me before that you'd seen the Beast of Bedwyn. You told me that it was the cause of your brother's death."

"I... I..."

"That was a lie? You hadn't seen it flying about then or attacking Henry, had you?"

"I thought it... probably... had."

"And you told Johnny that you'd seen it out at Chisbury to encourage him to go with you."

"No!" Godyth cried out. "If he is saying that then he's a liar. I told him that I had heard that was the last place it had been seen. Not that it was definitely there."

"Where did you hear that?"

"From my Uncle Eadric."

Gabriel turned to Mabel. "Blaming Eadric again. It's everyone's fault but her own."

Gabriel took hold of the girl's arm,

"You doubled back after you hit me and you found Master Fryxell lying injured on the ground and then, no doubt, with the same rock with which you hit me, you killed him."

"No!"

Mabel looked the girl over.

"Tell me, Godyth, what were you doing at Crofton when you found little Dunstan Durwood?"

"I didn't find him."

"Your uncle Eadric said you told him where to find the body."

"I've told you before, my uncle is a drunkard. He hardly knows what he is doing some days."

In an exasperated strut, the young girl stomped across the cottage and threw herself down on her bed.

Mabel softened her voice.

"We know that Fryxell killed your mother, Godyth, we heard him confess it."

Mabel was certain that Godyth had heard him confess it too.

"If you *did* kill him, we understand why you would do it."

"NO!"

"That is the kirtle you were wearing when you went to see your mother, isn't it, Godyth?"

The girl was thrown off guard for just a moment and then, recovering her poise, sneered. "Of course. I only have two kirtles. This one and my red Sunday one."

"This was the dress you say was muddied and torn on the day you went to Chisbury to meet Gelle."

Mabel followed the girl across the room and stood looking down at her.

She reached out and fingered the neck.

"I remember you have a small brooch which keeps the two pieces of the neck together."

Godyth's hand went up to the front of her brown-yellow kirtle where there was now a gap at the throat.

"I—I—lost it."

"Yes, I know you lost it."

Mabel fiddled in her purse. "Where did you lose it?"

"I don't know," said the sullen girl.

"I know. Goddy, I know exactly where you lost it." Mabel pulled out the little silvered brooch.

"I found it in the pond when we were looking for little Johnny, the day he went missing. The day he went into the woods with you to look for the Beast of Bedwyn."

Godyth stared at Mabel from the tops of her eyes. It was a *very* unfriendly expression. Gabriel recognised it as the look she'd also given him.

"I told you I lost it."

"In the pond?"

"I must have lost it in the pond if that is where you found it."

Mabel sat down next to the girl on the bed. Gabriel watched from a distance. He'd let Mabel deal with Godyth. He felt her so absolutely evil he almost couldn't bring himself to speak to her further.

"I have a very good memory, Godyth."

The girl scoffed.

"I do. And I remember that the day that Sir Gabriel and I found the body of your mother, there had been no rain for quite some time. Yet you say you fell in some mud. I couldn't find any mud anywhere around there, at Chisbury."

"It. Was. Muddy."

"You had washed your kirtle in places, hadn't you? As you have now. It's damp."

"Mud."

"Not mud—blood." There was a tiny silence.

"I had forgotten, it was my mother's blood."

"Oh yes. Of course. You found her first, before we did, didn't you?"

There was an icy silence.

"Have you washed Master Fryxell's blood from it now, Goddy?"

The girl merely harrumphed and turned away.

"The day your brother died, your shoes were wet. It didn't rain. Why were they wet? Because you had been by the river bank hadn't you?

"No."

Mabel sighed. This was like squeezing a walnut for milk

"You knew that Fryxell was your grandfather and that he had killed your mother. You also knew that he was *your* father. Your *real* father."

The evil look was back.

Mabel rose and took a deep breath.

"The Fryxells are cursed, did you know that, Godyth?"

"Your mother was a Fryxell," said Gabriel quietly. "Your brother Henry was a Lovegrove. Your Uncle is a Ceorlson. But you now—you alone are a Fryxell."

Suddenly Godyth had risen from her bed, her hands two tight

fists, her face pink and angry.

"You are all mad. All of you. If I am a Fryxell then I can bring down the curse on you all—every one of you."

Gabriel shivered.

Mabel smiled.

"It doesn't frighten us, Godyth," she said.

*****

They tried and failed to get Godyth to admit to the abductions and murders of the little children and in the end they had to put the girl in the lockup overnight to give them time to inform the constable and the local coroner. Eadric would have to be released for he had committed no real crime.

Mistress Ceorlson screamed at them when they took Godyth to the lockup. The reeve, Master Head, had explained why they were doing it but Mistress Ceorlson would not accept his explanation. He had always had it in for their family, she said. Going back years, when her husband, Adam Ceorlson and he had fought over her. Mabel and Gabriel learned that the reeve had courted the woman in his younger days but Master Ceorlson had won. Head had never forgiven her for accepting the other man, she said.

In the end Eadric offered to stay in the lockup with Godyth but Mabel thought this a bad idea. She didn't trust the girl at all.

Gabriel and Mabel were somewhat miserable that evening. They were absolutely sure that Godyth was their killer but just could not prove it and it was unlikely they'd get a confession from Godyth herself.

"The girl is completely mad. What are we to do with someone who is completely mad?"

"Out of her right mind she may be Gabriel, but she knows what she is doing and knows right from wrong."

"Then she will be twelve in a short while. If they accept our evidence such as it is, she must face trial as an adult and if found guilty she must hang," answered Gabriel. "If the justices wish it."

He pushed away his plate of food virtually untouched and wiped his knife, hanging it once more on his belt.

"Why—tell me *why* she wants to kill these children?"

The deaths had started once her father had come back to the area. Mabel tried to explain to Sir Gabriel why she thought Mabel's brain was hopelessly disturbed.

"I think she only took boys because she saw them as a threat."

"What? Tiny boys like JohnFour?"

"JohnFour would grow into a man one day. They all would and they could inflict pain and suffering on women. Like her father had done on her grandmother, her mother and of course, on her. She couldn't really tackle men, so she killed boys."

"That is completely deranged. Surely they cannot hang someone who is so unsound of mind?"

"That of course will be up to the justices."

"And tell me this. Why, if Fryxell committed rape on Mistress Ceorlson and on Gelle Lovegrove, did they then conceive children? Correct me if I'm wrong but I thought that it wasn't possible."

"What?"

"Well, I was always taught that if a woman is raped and she conceives a child then...well..."

"That she has *not* been raped? She must have enjoyed the experience?" said Mabel with a tinge of scorn.

"That's what I have heard."

Mabel sat in front of Gabriel over her trestle table and joined her hands together.

"You are a knight, Gabriel and you must have heard some tales of war, even if you have not as yet been to war yourself."

"Well—no—not yet. The Lord Stokke hasn't been called to...'

"And if you have heard tales of war you have no doubt heard about the terrible things which are done by soldiers—to civilians."

"We try to stop it. There is a code."

"Pah! Code! I am sorry Gabriel, but if you think that men with their blood on fire, searching for treasure or pleasure will stop to weigh up a code of conduct before they rape, steal or kill, then you are sadly mistaken."

"But…"

"I remember the tales my grandfather used to tell when I was younger, about the poor women of the enemy he had seen when accompanying his lord off to war."

Gabriel was silent and still.

"The screams and the pleadings, the terrible sights, were with him until his dying day. No, Gabriel. No woman enjoys rape. No matter what the doctors say. They are wrong and any woman who has been raped and lived, will tell you, it was the most awful experience of her life."

"You sound as if you know someone who…?"

"I do. A couple of years ago, a girl I know was raped by a man in her village. A village not too far away from here. He was a known troublemaker and someone subsequently murdered him."

"Murdered him?"

"Not solely because of the rape but for another reason. This girl I know, she got pregnant by him and believe me, if you were to talk to her, you would understand that it wasn't something she'd invited nor enjoyed."

"Is she…?"

"She married the village blacksmith and they are very happy, I'm told."

"Rather like Master Lovegrove marrying Gelle when she was already with child."

"Just the same. There are *some* good men in the world."

Gabriel felt duly ticked off and so that night, he went to the hall in the manor to play merrells with anyone who'd play with him. He was so distempered about Godyth he couldn't stay at Mabel's and needed a diversion. As it happened, it was master steward Henry Buttermere who agreed to engage him in a game. Afterwards Gabriel would sleep in the hall in his usual place.

Four hundred and forty four feet and four inches away, Mabel lay on her bed and looked up into the rafters. It was a very bright night, for the sky was clear, the stars were shining and the moon was quite bright through the open shutters. Her room was lit up as if she was burning a dozen candles. Perhaps she'd have one last fly around the village. It might clear her head and allow her to sleep.

A little bat went scooting out of her open window and made for the river. By rights, if she was a real bat, she should be hibernating at this time in the winter but she knew this one fly around wouldn't hurt her.

She careered over the oak tree and turned to the river, following it for a short distance.

Her wings beat dozens of times before she glided on them, the membranes outstretched and taut. She steered herself down to the small landing stage where Master Atwater kept his little boat.

Landing on the horizontal post, she wriggled her way underneath and hid in the dead and dying plants still twining up the bank and covering the posts, her claws catching hold of the wooden rail. There she happily hung upside down.

Master Atwater was the man responsible for making sure that the river was well kept in the village. It wasn't his only job, for he was also the miller's assistant.

Mabel pictured the affable man with his contagious grin and his shiny bald head. His brother, who was the miller himself, was very like him and the two of them might be mistaken for each other at a glance.

Mabel looked down at the pool, black in the night. With the moon shining, she could see her figure on the shimmering surface of the water clutching the rail and squeezing herself into the spaces between the plants.

'I could be any small bat. They all look alike. Unlike people, even if they are related. They all look different in some small way. But tiny bats are all the same.'

A picture of Little Johnny came into her head. He was one of four children and looked completely unlike the rest.

The other children all had their father's square chiselled face, his stocky figure, his brown hair and eyes, but Johnny, he was his mother's son. His eyes were blue grey and his hair a dark blond and straight. His face was round and apple cheeked like his mother and his ears stuck out a little, just like hers.

Mabel smiled a bat smile.

She was fond of Johnny and thinking about him sent a flicker of an idea through her bat brain.

If she was so fond of Johnny, could she make herself put him in peril? Her heart started to race as she mulled over the idea—a dangerous idea.

It was one way to make sure that they had the right person for the crimes.

Would Johnny go for it? She was sure he would if there was a promise of flying pigs or the chance to see a gryphon.

She and Sir Gabriel would have to keep him safe. They'd *have* to. Or she would never live with herself.

CHAPTER SIXTEEN
~ PLANS ~

Gabriel was not winning. Master Buttermere had won three games of merrells and Gabriel only one. He knew he was good at the game. What was the matter with him? Why could he not concentrate? His mind was simply not on the challenge.

"Sir Gabriel, if I might make a suggestion...?"

"Huh?"

"Mistress Wetherspring..."

"What about her?"

"You don't think that it's—well—unseemly to allow her to accompany you on..."

"She has an excellent mind and memory, Buttermere. And the Lord Stokke insists that her excellent mind and memory is employed upon..."

"I am sure that the Lord Robert does not really *know* what it is she *actually* does."

Gabriel's heart gave a lurch. He moved one of his pieces into place to complete a mill, trying to keep a straight face.

"Oh, Master Steward, and what *does* she do?"

Henry Buttermere moved one of his white pieces to take one of Gabriel's black counters.

"She spies upon people, for a start."

"You have seen her at this spying, have you?" said Gabriel, moving a piece out of harm's way.

"I have."

"So it's alright for *you* to spy on Mistress Wetherspring or for me to spy when I need information but not for Mabel?"

Henry took another of Gabriel's pieces. "But my good sir, *we* are men."

"You think that women do not make good spies, Henry?" said Gabriel, chuckling.

"I think that Mistress Wetherspring should stick to her job. She is housekeeper here. And lately she has been very lax in her duties."

"Well, perhaps you should have it out with the Lord Robert, Henry," said Gabriel, rising from his seat. "He is the one who specifically asked for her help."

Buttermere looked up at him. "Investigating crime and in particular murders, sir, is no job for a woman. Spying is a man's job."

"But Master Buttermere, you have been doing just that for quite a while, I think. Spying."

Buttermere grimaced, not quite sure if this was a compliment or not.

"By your own admission, you have had Mistress Wetherspring in your sights," said Gabriel.

"I am in no doubt that she has—shall we say—certain special qualities. But..."

Gabriel's heart gave another lurch. Lurchier than the last.

"Oh what qualities might those be?"

Henry's lips formed a rather nasty smile. "Oh Sir Gabriel, I'm sure you know what I mean. We are both men of the world are we not?"

"No, I don't, you are going to have to spell it out."

Henry came closer to Gabriel and lowered his voice. "As I have said before, you spend a lot of time in her cottage—alone together. That is not a gentlemanly thing to do. I fear it might be—misinterpreted."

"Oh, by whom?"

"Your reputation, my lord will be virtually untouched by—anything that might be said—but Mistress Mabel's...?

"Said by whom, Henry?"

"Anyone, Sir Gabriel."

Gabriel turned his back.

"Leaving, sir? Before you have had a chance to get even at merrells?"

"Yes. I have some more *spying* to do."

Gabriel marched across the hall. Turning back he shouted, "And as far as getting even is concerned, Buttermere. If I catch you spying upon Mistress Wetherspring again, I will give you a good thrashing. Is that clear?"

Henry looked shocked but he gave no answer. The hall had gone silent. Everyone was looking at him.

Wearing a shamefaced expression, he speedily fled to his office and locked the door.

Gabriel was furious. How dare Buttermere suggest that there were secret things of an illicit romantic nature going on between him and Mabel. Even if it was true. Which it wasn't of course. Ahem.

He walked slowly back to Mabel's cottage in the moonlight and whispered at the door.

"Mabel, it's me. Let me in, we need to talk."

The locking bar went up and the door opened a crack. Gabriel squeezed through the space.

"I thought you were going to..." began Mabel.

"Yes, well I have something to tell you."

"Oh?"

"Henry Buttermere has been spying on you."

"Whatever for?"

"I warned you before, you remember? Well to be truthful, he's been spying on us both."

"And he will have seen nothing, will he?"

"The odd kiss—perhaps."

"What does he hope to achieve with his spying?"

Gabriel sat down wearily. "He says he is worried for your reputation."

Mabel scoffed. "Never!"

"Do you know what I think? I think he finds you very attractive. I think he wishes that you'd pay him more attention. He has a fancy for you!"

"No, surely not?" Her expression was so horrified, Gabriel had to chuckle.

"He wants me out of the way so he can..."

"Then he will be completely disappointed, Gabriel. He's old and—and—pernickety and pedantic and thin and—ugly. And completely useless."

Gabriel chuckled again. "I am glad to hear this is what you think of him. But still—you have to be careful."

"I really thought he was far too lazy to put himself out to spy."

"If he caught you transforming..." Gabriel came closer to Mabel, "I would probably have to kill him in order to keep him quiet. But you did not hear me say that."

"Say what, Sir Gabriel?" she said as she grinned, seated herself, and began to comb her hair. He watched as her fingers deftly moved about the locks to braid them again.

"I've been thinking," she said suddenly.

"We need to do a deal of thinking if we are to prevent the death of any other small boys around here. I don't think Godyth will be able to stop. She'll carry on, won't she?"

"If she can kill her own brother—and not bat an eyelid..."

"Little JohnFour, those boys Godyth has tried to hurt and failed; it is just possible that she'll try again. Johnny Chatterwell is one of those who escaped her clutches, of course."

"It is little Johnny that I have been thinking about."

Mabel then told Gabriel what she thought they might be able to do.

"It's dangerous Mabel."

"If there are enough of us, I doubt it will be as perilous as we think."

"Then we shall have to let her out of the lockup and that goes against the grain. Do we need to involve the authorities?" asked Gabriel.

"Perhaps Master Head will do. He is already involved."

"You think he'll be a good enough witness?"

Mabel crossed her fingers. "Let's hope so."

She took hold of Gabriel's sleeve "But just to make sure, I think we need a few others to 'appear' at the right time."

*****

Gabriel sauntered over to the house of the reeve.

The man came out of the door, a mug of ale in his hands. "Ah, Sir Gabriel…"

"I want to speak to Godyth…"

"Godyth, sir? You are not finished talking with her?"

"I want to see if I can get her to confess."

"Again?" Master Head peered around with an exaggerated gesture. "No Mistress Mabel with you today?"

"Ah no. She's busy with little Johnny Chatterwell."

"What can she possibly want with him?"

"She needs to check his story before we talk to Godyth. After all it was little Johnny who saw her at Stock Farm with Master Fryxell."

"Of course the testimony of a child of eight or nine cannot be…"

"No, we know this."

Master Head sighed. "This will be a waste of time, m'lord. Although Johnny might be able to tell us what happened, his testimony won't be admissible…"

"Not a lord, reeve, just a sir."

"Ah yes."

Master Head breathed an exaggerated sigh.

"The wife has gone to the lockup to feed Godyth. She has the key."

"Right. One other thing, Master Head."

"Yes?"

"If I can't get her to confess then I'm afraid we shall have to let Godyth go as we have no actual evidence against her."

The reeve, shaking his head, peered into his empty ale cup. "The word of a knight is not good enough?"

"I'm afraid not. We need hard evidence or a confession."

"The confession and word of her uncle is not sufficient?"

"At present it's thought that he is the killer of the children. Mistress Wetherspring and I are not so sure. He is, sadly, not a reliable witness."

"No. A mind befuddled with drink, I fear," said the reeve.

"We need help, Master Head. Do you think you can bring some folk to the cliff at Crofton and have them hide in the bushes?"

Henry Head grimaced. "Well, I suppose I can try... What are you going to do?"

Gabriel shook his blond locks. "We just need you to be there and to listen and remember."

Master Head smiled. "I have an excellent memory, my lord."

"Not a lord, reeve—just a knight."

*****

Master Head had been busy. Very busy, he'd said, earlier that day. He simply didn't have the time to go to the lockup to take Godyth something to eat, a task which was usually his, when there was a prisoner in the tiny building.

A little while before, his wife, Alys, had organised the plate of food and the mug of ale and she'd purposefully put it down in front of him.

"Here—it's time to take something to Godyth—poor girl." It was obvious that his wife thought that Godyth was innocent and shouldn't be incarcerated in the lockup.

"She'll be starving. And she'll be cold." She took up a large blanket and folded it. "And take this to her too, if she has to be there another night. I doubt the constable or the sheriff's man will stir themselves today to talk to an eleven year old girl… so she probably will. I bet…"

"Will you stop wittering, woman!" said Henry Head. "I know you think she shouldn't be there but don't blame me."

"You put her there, you pea brain."

"The Lord Stokke's man put her there. I simply hold the key."

"Oh for Heaven's sake, give me the key and I'll go and feed her."

"It's woman's work anyway," said the bad-tempered reeve. "Food and drink and visiting—children."

As she picked up the blanket and tray of food and drink, and passed him, she caught her husband a slight blow to the head.

"Oi!"

"And I'll have that apple you are just about to bite into."

And she snatched the wizened apple from the reeve's hand before he could set his teeth into it.

Mistress Head threw the blanket over her arm and steadied the tray as she carefully made her way to the lockup. In order to lift the bar and get the key into the lock, she put down the tray outside the door.

"Here we are Goddy. It's Mistress Head come to see you. I've brought you something to eat and drink."

She opened the door wide and went into the dark interior, bending to pick up the tray again.

Godyth was sitting with her knees drawn up to her chin, her hair making a dark curtain over her eyes.

"It was cold last night. I expect you were freezing. Pah! Trust the men to put you in here without a warm blanket…"

She laid it over the girl's back.

As swiftly as a minnow darts from a frond of weed, Godyth grabbed the apple on the tray and threw it with all her might at the unsuspecting woman. It bounced into her eye and Mistress Head shrieked, throwing up her hands to her face. The tray went flying. Then the blanket was swung from the prisoner's shoulders and thrown around mistress reeve's head.

Godyth pushed her to the back of the lockup and slammed the door.

Laughing, she turned the key in the lock and ran for the trees, throwing the key into the bushes. In a heartbeat, she was gone.

*****

Gabriel rounded the corner just as Mistress Head recovered and started screeching from the lockup and pulling off the blanket which had obstructed her vision.

"Argh! The monster!"

"Monster?" Instinctively he looked up into the sky. He could see no monster.

"Mistress Head, is that you?"

"That girl is a monster!"

"Godyth?"

"Who else?"

"Where's the key?"

"Gone!" wailed the woman. "She stole it."

Gabriel took a hard kick at the door with his foot and on the third kick it flew in.

Mistress Head was standing rubbing her eye socket. "She threw an apple at me."

Gabriel tutted.

"The reeve was too lazy to come and feed the girl. So I did," she sobbed.

Gabriel sighed. "What happened? She fled?"

"Aye, she pushed me."

"In which direction did she run?"

"How do I know?" Then Mistress Head realised that she was

talking to a knight of the realm and that she had better watch how politely she addressed him.

"Oh I'm sorry, m'lord. It's just I'm right put out."

"Understandably, Mistress Head."

"To think I have looked after that girl as if she was me own daughter. And she goes and does this to me."

Gabriel leaned in to look at her. "You'll have a black eye ere long I suspect."

The woman straightened her head cloth. "She'll have more than a black eye when I see her next. I'll give her a sore a...."

"Have you any idea which way she went?"

"Well, she likes that Chisbury place they say. My Henry says she's drawn to it like a bee to woodbine! But on the other hand..."

Gabriel hovered. He had better go and tell Mabel that now they had no need to let Godyth out of the lockup. She'd done it for herself. But they did need to know where she'd gone. Gabriel remembered Mabel had said that she'd be talking to Little Johnny.

He came to the back of the Chatterwell house to see Johnny looking up at Mabel with huge eyes.

"The beast?" the lad was saying with feeling.

"It's been seen flying around Crofton. I thought that you and I could maybe go and have a look," said Mabel.

"Us two?"

"But if you'd rather..."

"Oh no—I want to—but dada said I has to stay home."

"Oh he did?"

"Just now."

"Mabel! Our prisoner has flown," cried Gabriel, running up. "She managed to escape the lockup."

"Has she indeed? Has she hurt anyone?"

Gabriel shook his blond locks. "Only Mistress Head's pride."

"Do you think she's gone looking for the beast?" said Johnny, excitement in his voice.

"I really wouldn't be at all surprised. But on the other hand, she told me she was afraid of it," said Mabel.

"I'm not afraid of it."

"Oh I know. And neither am I," said Mabel with a smile.

"And neither is Goddy—*really*."

"Well then, let's beat her to it. Sir Gabriel?"

"Can you come and help us, Johnny?"

The boy's eyes glittered. "If you need my help…"

"Are you with us, Sir Gabriel?" said Mabel.

"I am indeed."

"On foot?"

"Why not?"

"Which way will she have gone, do you think? To Crofton?"

"If she had run to Chisbury, she'd have to run right through the village and she'd be seen too readily. My guess is she's heading for Crofton. We can't be far behind her," said Gabriel.

Johnny stooped to tie up his shoes. "I'll just tell Gertie where I've gone."

"Oh she'll know, I'm sure," said Mabel, biting her inner cheek. "She'll guess. C'mon! We've no time to lose."

'Oh Mabel,' she said to herself, quashing her grave misgivings. 'I hope Johnny will be alright. I must protect him at all costs.'

They ran off across the meadow hand in hand until Johnny had to stop and put on his shoe again.

*****

It took a while to get a party of people together to search for Godyth. Many folk had no wish to go and look for a Fryxell child. Word had got round the village that Godyth was the incestuous daughter of an incestuous mother and everyone knew that the Fryxells were touched in the head.

Later that morning, the reeve's wife, Mistress Alys, went amongst her gossips with her black eye and told her tale. The women were appalled that the girl could behave so badly to someone who had been so kind to her. They nagged their menfolk until in the end, Alys Head's husband managed to make up a small group of men and lead them through the trees and onto the river lane to Crofton. Here in a bunch, they stalled, protesting and moaning out of the sight and hearing of their womenfolk.

"She's a murderer, lads!" said the reeve. "We can't let her escape."

"To be fair, reeve, we don't really know that," said Master Corngold.

"Aye, it's just a lot o' gossip," said John Swineherd.

"Sir Gabriel and Mistress Wetherspring think she is a killer," added the reeve.

"But there in't no evidence is there?" said John Whitelock.

"Only the word of her drunken uncle," said Corngold again.

"My Johnny says she enticed him out to the forest and then abandoned him there," said Master Chatterwell. "If Eadric hadn't come along..."

"Aw c'mon Chatters!" said Stephen Meadow. "If we were to take everything your littl'un said as gospel, we'd all be searching for flying pigs! He's eight for goodness sake."

There was an outbreak of laughter.

"If I could see it with my own eyes, then I'd believe it," said Geoffrey Miller. "I must say, I don't think Mistress Wetherspring is wrong very often."

"About flying pigs?" said a bemused Stephen Meadow.

"No, idiot. About murder. You remember Edward Greathouse and ol' Sweetcheeks back in the summer? She was right about them."

The men shuffled their feet and mumbled a bit.

"Alright," said Corngold eventually. "We go to Crofton cliff but if there's no evidence then we come back home. With or without Godyth Lovegrove."

They all nodded and in single file picked their way along the riverside lane, not really with any haste.

*****

It had begun quite a still calm day with one or two little fluffy clouds flying along on high. By midday it was dull and the clouds had scudded in along with a gusty wind which tossed the tops of the trees along the Crofton road.

Mabel kept hold of Johnny's hand and grasped her skirts with the other, for they were being tossed about her knees by the brisk breeze.

"Johnny, when we find Goddy, do you think you might ask her some questions? Could you do that for me?" said Mabel, drawing Johnny to her side as they walked.

"Why can't *you* ask her Mistress Mabel?"

"Oh, it's just that, I think she'll be a little angry with me and she will certainly be angry with Sir Gabriel here for locking her up."

"Goddy gets angry pretty quick if you don't do what she wants."

Mabel tried to laugh. It came out as a few wobbly vowels.

"Do you remember telling me that you thought she was bossy but that it didn't matter to you because you have bossy sisters and she was just the same as they were?"

Johnny Chatterwell managed a perfect titter. "Yees!"

"Except she isn't, is she Johnny? Tell the truth."

The boy grasped his lip with his teeth. "She can be really nasty."

"I know."

"I know that too, Johnny. She was angry with me and she hit *me* with a rock," said Gabriel who had backtracked after forging ahead. "All because I told her she'd told a lie about the Beast of Bedwyn."

Johnny drew back and stood still. "She told me if I didn't do what she asked, she'd hit me with a rock."

Gabriel and Mabel exchanged a furtive glance.

Mabel leaned back, took hold of him and cradled the lad in her arm. "And that is why you went with her?"

"I didn't believe she'd hit me. She's my friend—she was my friend."

"Well, I want you to still be friends with her," said Mabel with a smile. "But I'd like you to see if you can get her to tell you the truth about Little Dunstan and also Archard. And of course her brother Henry."

"You want me to ask her if she killed them?"

There was no point in hiding the facts now.

"Oh Johnny—will you do this for me? We shall be close by but we don't want her to see us. We think she'll speak more freely to you."

"Because she's my friend?"

"Of course," said Gabriel.

"And if she won't tell me?"

"Then we'll have to take her back to Bedwyn and lock her up again."

"And then," said Gabriel, "the constable and the coroner will talk to her and they won't be as nice as we would be."

"Oh!" said Johnny. His face screwed up. "Will *they* hit her with a rock?"

"No. I don't think they'll do that but they will definitely shout at her," said Mabel.

"Very loudly," said Gabriel. "And I'll have a go at her too. I've learned some pretty effective methods of getting information from people over the..."

Mabel and Johnny stared at him wondering what he'd meant by that and then Johnny moved off again, his fine blond hair streaming out in the wind.

"What else do you want me to ask her?"

"Johnny, you are a very clever boy," said Mabel, giving him a quick kiss on the cheek. "I knew you'd understand."

Johnny blushed to the roots of his hair which was at that moment cascading over his forehead in the stiff wind.

Mabel took hold of his hand again and as they walked, she told him what they needed to know.

*****

They battled against the wind and at last the gorse bushes at the top of the cliff above the river at Crofton came into view. Of Godyth there was no sign.

"Perhaps she fled to Chisbury after all," said Gabriel. "Folk worry about *that* place and are wary of it. It might prevent them from following her. She'd feel safe there"

"It wouldn't prevent *us* from following and anyway, she's desperate to see the gryphon and *that* was last seen here, remember?" said Mabel, her tongue in her cheek.

"It's haunted at Chisbury, isn't it, Mistress Mabel?" said Johnny.

"Well Johnny, that's what they say but I have been there several times on my own and I must say, although I think it's a sad place, I don't think it's haunted. And obviously neither does Goddy because she likes it there."

Johnny took a quick look round. "Does that mean we have to walk all the way to Chisbury now?"

"No. We'll wait here a little while. After all, we are told this is where the gryphon was last seen. Sir Gabriel and I will sit here and you go and sit under that big bush where it isn't so windy. We'll be watching all the time."

"Are you sure?"

"You are a brave lad."

Johnny walked slowly away from them, every so often throwing a worried look over his shoulder.

"Here?"

"That's perfect. Now we must be quiet. If the gryphon is going to come, he won't come if he knows we are here."

"Won't he smell us?"

Mabel and Gabriel exchanged a glance.

"I happen to know, Johnny, that gryphons haven't got a very good sense of smell," said Sir Gabriel, smiling to himself. Johnny really was a clever young lad.

Mabel and Gabriel hunched together out of sight, close by the gnarled bole of an old birch tree, their backs to its grey flecked bark.

"Can you see Johnny from here?" asked Mabel, whose vision was a little impaired by the tangle of branches.

"I can see him clearly." Gabriel squeezed Mabel's shoulder. "Don't worry."

The wind howled above them, tossing the sparse branches of the birches and swirling the leaves on the ground into piles. Mabel thought it looked as if they were dancing. Small twigs were flying through the air like little bats.

"She should have been here before us," she whispered. "Where can she be hiding?"

Gabriel brought his head close to hers. It was impossible to be heard with all the noise and he didn't want to raise his voice.

"She's come by a different route. One which isn't the usual. So that folk don't follow or intercept her, I suppose."

"She knows this forest like the lines on her hand. She knows every little animal path and trail. When I came back from Chisbury with her, the night she went missing, she brought me back to Bedwyn through lanes *I* didn't know existed."

"I suspect that's how she's managed to get the children away from their villages. On little known paths."

Mabel shivered.

"Are you cold?"

"No—it's just—the thought of what that girl has done makes my hair curl."

Gabriel moved closer to her and put his arm more firmly around her shoulder. "Is that better?"

She lifted her face to his. "You know it is."

She stared into his light blue eyes for a while, and then traced the path of the scar which was becoming a pinkish white thread from the edge of his eye to the crease of his lips.

His fair hair was gently blowing in the wind, even though they were not in the teeth of the gale there.

Gabriel looked down on Mabel and saw a terrible sadness in her face. Sadness at the horrible things a young girl had done to boys who had trusted her, who had thought her their friend. Sadness for a young girl whose mind had soured. And another sort of sadness which he could not really fathom.

He bent and kissed her gently and quickly and she closed her eyes so that the sense of sadness faded.

When he next looked up, Godyth was standing gazing down at Little Johnny Chatterwell who had fallen asleep under his gorse bush.

Gabriel tensed and squeezed Mabel's arm and she looked up sharply.

"She's here," he whispered into her ear.

"What are you doing here, Johnny?" said Godyth harshly.

Johnny jumped, suddenly startled awake, but he betrayed no fear of her. "Hello Goddy. What are you doin' here?"

"I'm looking for the gryphon."

"I have been looking for the gryphon too. It lives round here and it will come soon, they say."

"Who says that?"

"Mistress Mabel. She knows a lot about the gryphon. Sir Gabriel says that she's known a lot about it from the very beginning."

Godyth picked a yellow flower from the gorse bush beside her and held it to her nose. She sniffed. "I'll help you look."

"Well you have to sit down and be very quiet."

Godyth sat close by Johnny. "Where are they?"

"Mistress Mabel and Sir Gabriel? Oh back in Bedwyn, I suppose."

"Why do we have to be quiet?"

"Mistress Mabel says that the gryphon is a very shy creature and is rather afraid of people."

"It wasn't afraid of my grandfather when it took him up in its claws."

"I think it knew that your grandfather was a very wicked man."

"How would it know that, silly?"

"It's a very special beast. It knows a lot of things."

"Like what?"

"Oh probably like—like—that you killed your grandfather with a rock."

Mabel, sitting by the birch tree, held her breath.

"You think it knows that?" said Godyth wistfully.

"I think it probably saw you."

Godyth didn't answer but continued to sniff her gorse flower.

"You did, di'n't you? You 'it him on the back of the head with a rock when the beast dropped him."

"*He* killed my mother."

"I heard that horrible Fryxell man say that he'd killed Mistress Gelle. He told Mistress Mabel and me that he had murdered her."

"I heard him say it too. But I have known about it for a while. I was there shortly after he did it."

"And so you killed him because you knew they'd never catch him to hang him, didn't you?"

"Someone had to kill him. So I did it. Yes. In revenge."

"Did you have to kill Henry too? Did he know what you had done to Dunstan and Archard?"

"He was stupid. He said he was going to go to the steward and tell him that I had killed our mother."

"No! Why would he do that? It wasn't true."

"No. It wasn't. So I had to stop him."

"But you did kill Dunstan and Archard didn't you?"

"They were boys. I don't like boys."

For the first time, Johnny seemed uncertain and a soupçon of fear crept into his voice. "You wouldn't kill me, would you? I'm your friend and I'm a boy."

Godyth looked at Johnny under her eyebrows. "I know."

The girl jumped up and searched the sky with her dark eyes.

"Come on, let's see if the gryphon is flying around over there." She grabbed Johnny's arm.

He resisted. "No, we have to stay here and keep still and quiet."

Godyth pulled the boy up. "Who says we do? Do as you are told, you stupid boy."

"Oh Goddy—don't!"

Mabel craned her neck to see Godyth pull Johnny through the gap in the gorse bushes to the edge of the cliff where not too long ago, Sir Gabriel had slipped on the uncertain soil of the defile.

"Gabriel!" she whispered loudly.

"I see them."

Godyth took a deep breath and yelled out into the wind, "Come on gryphon! Let's see you! I *command* you to come!"

Johnny was struggling in her grasp. "You can't just tell it to come—just like that!" he said.

"Well then, how do we get it to come, Master silly Chatterwell?"

"It will only come—if you tell the truth." He wrenched his arm away.

"What truth?"

"Well, it's a thing isn't it?"

"What thing?"

"That you can get a gryphon to obey you if you are truthful and never tell a lie."

"Only those who don't hang onto a lie can summon a gryphon?" asked Godyth.

"Yes. Or if you confess to a lie. Like a unicorn can be captured by a maiden and only a maiden."

Godyth faced Johnny with the wind tossing their hair and clothing this way and that. "Well then, *you* summon it. You don't tell lies do you?"

"Well…"

"Go on…"

"You first. You tell the truth. Did you kill little Archard and Dunstan?"

"Yes of course I did. And I covered their faces with leaves so that they couldn't see me."

Suddenly Godyth lifted her arms up to the heavens and yelled. "I killed them all. And I would have killed little JohnFour and even you if my uncle hadn't stopped me!"

"Oh Goddy, you wouldn't have killed me, would you? I thought we were friends."

"You silly boy! You aren't a girl. I only like girls and only girls are my friends."

Mabel crept to her knees and inched forward for a better look, her heart hammering.

"Come on gryphon! Let's see you," shouted Godyth to the sky as she shook poor Johnny like a threshing flail.

One moment Johnny was at the top of the cliff and the next both he and Godyth had disappeared.

"Oh Sweet Saints!" cried Gabriel, leaping up. "She's gone over the cliff top! And she's taken Johnny with her!"

CHAPTER SIXTEEN
~ RESCUE! ~

They rushed to the precipice and with great care peered over. Gabriel fell immediately to his knees. The soil had given way and a great gouge had appeared at the edge.

"They're here. Hanging on."

Mabel peeped over. Godyth was hanging from a projecting root which had caught hold of the cloth of her kirtle by the belt at her waist like a pin. She struggled and tried to free herself.

Johnny was flattened against the chalky soil of the slope holding the hem of Godyth's kirtle. His feet were scrabbling for a purchase on the cliff face.

He looked up and saw Sir Gabriel surveying the scene quickly. The knight saw panic in his eyes.

"Keep still Godyth. If the fabric tears you will fall down the rocky slope," he yelled.

She continued to writhe as if he had not spoken.

Gabriel watched as she tried to kick out at Johnny to dislodge his grip. He screeched as she made contact with his arm and he let go with one hand.

Mabel's heart felt as if it had tightened in her chest. How could this girl be so wicked?

She knew that this time, it wasn't going to be possible to become a

251

goat and pull the two children up to safety. She could hear the Bedwyn villagers as they began to come up behind them, through the bushes and trees, the noise of their progress pulsing on the wind. There was no way she could turn withershynnes here.

"Gabriel, I am going down to get them."

"What?"

"Cover for me. I am going down there." She pointed to the little river happily chuckling its way over its stony bed forty feet below, oblivious to the drama being played out above it.

Gabriel flattened himself and leaned over the edge trying to catch hold of the cloth at Godyth's shoulder. Only two fingers could reach her. He stretched some more and his shoulder muscles protested. Now he had three fingers and a thumb but no real purchase on the girl's kirtle.

He gritted his teeth and braced his chest with as much breath as he could take in.

He heard Master Corngold asking "Sir Gabriel—sir, what has happened?" as he ran up. But Gabriel wasn't able to answer.

Corngold took a brief look over the cliff.

"Jesus! What's going on?"

All of a sudden there was a great noise of rushing like the cascading of a river in spate.

Gabriel wasn't able to lift his head but from the top of his eyes, he saw a huge brown wing glide through his vision.

"Mabel!"

Instantly the gryphon rose over the cliff in one movement, like a huge cloud and wheeled back out into the empty air.

"Johnny, Goddy! Hold on!" cried Gabriel. "Hold on tight!"

Master Corngold paddled backwards, and swearing at the top of his voice, rose and ran off yelling.

Master Head and his body of men standing on the grass a few feet from the edge, looked up to see a gigantic bird-like creature circling the cliff edge not feet from their heads. They panicked.

"Arhghhh!" they cried as one and ducked. All but one or two fled back into the protection of the trees. Master Swineherd flattened himself to the grass and protected his head with his hands. Master Miller bravely stood, his mouth opening and closing and rotated, watching the beast as it circled.

"Holy Mother of God," he said as he crossed himself.

The gryphon took off, defying the fierce winds which buffeted the cliff top and sent the gorse bushes dancing and bowing. A few yellow gorse petals went cascading down the slope.

The beast drew close to the cliff face.

"Not too close," shouted Gabriel, not caring if people heard him giving instructions to a gryphon. "The draught may dislodge them."

The gryphon circled again, this time closer to the cliff face. Small stones and pieces of chalk, clods of earth with grass attached, tumbled down the slope.

The Beast of Bedwyn rose higher and then dropped. Godyth hid her face in her arm. Johnny screeched as his grasp began to slacken. Again Godyth tried to kick Johnny away from her.

Two evilly clawed and pointed feet lurched out and the beast almost hovered, with vast leathery wings slowly beating back and forth, setting up a draught that rivalled the tumultuous wind.

A large clod of earth came loose and the children dropped another foot. Godyth's kirtle tore at last.

One of the claws took hold of Johnny's tunic and jolted him up. It rolled on itself slowly and secured him in its grasp. The eagle head came close to Johnny's gaze and the wickedly pointed beak gently took hold of the neck of his tunic and pulled. The young lad gazed into gentle and warm eyes.

Johnny felt himself lifted as one of his loose shoes fell from his foot and bounced down the slope.

Then they all heard Godyth screaming. "No—not him—me—save me. Not him!"

The eye of the gryphon swivelled to the girl's gaze. Now there was a distinct loathing in *this* expression.

"I *admitted* it! I did! I took the boys and I killed them. And I killed my brother and grandfather. Take me up first," she screeched. "I command you."

The gryphon rose on its monstrously powerful wings and jolted as he was, Johnny let go of Godyth's kirtle.

Godyth screamed at the top of her voice in anger and frustration and yes, fear.

The gryphon soared up over the cliff top and deposited Johnny gently on his feet on the grass to the other side of the gorse bushes before roaring in contentment and wheeling off again and throwing itself once more into the abyss.

The gryphon gained height again and then dropped, extending those sharp yellow talons once more and made to grasp Godyth's kirtle.

The branch which had so far secured the girl to the slope gave way at last as her clothing tore further and it tumbled down the slope. She fell about four feet, flailing out with hands and feet for a purchase on the cliff face.

One of the huge wings of the gryphon bowed underneath the girl and as Godyth fell again, the beast rose to catch her. Now only one wing was employed in keeping the gryphon up in the air and it was obvious that it was finding flying difficult.

Godyth thrashed and squirmed.

"You stupid beast!" she cried, as she attempted to wriggle her way onto its back.

The gryphon roared again and lifting a taloned foot it made a grab for the girl.

The sharp points struck Godyth in the side and grasped her kirtle.

The girl screamed.

"Keep still, Godyth!" yelled Gabriel from the top of the cliff. "Let it help you."

Godyth's threadbare kirtle began to tear once more. The gryphon rose higher with one sweep of its wing but Godyth would not let go of the rocks of the cliff face.

"Let go, Godyth. Let it lift you," cried Gabriel.

The girl took one hand from the chalky and stony surface.

But then, with a terrible rending sound the gryphon's talon broke through the wool of Godyth's old and worn kirtle and grabbed for thin air.

They would never forget the terrible screech made by the girl as she left the cliff face and bounced down the scree slope like a tossed rag landing in a heap at the bottom. Several yellow gorse petals landed on her and settled.

No one moved for quite a long time.

*****

They had all heard Godyth yelling. They had all heard her confess to the killings. They had all seen the gryphon rescue Little Johnny Chatterwell and attempt to save Godyth Lovegrove.

Eventually the gryphon soared up into the grey sky and as the men of Bedwyn came cautiously out from their protecting trees they watched as it vanished, a speck amongst the scudding clouds.

Johnny was gathered up by his father who shook him, hugged him, kissed him and took him up on his shoulders like a hero.

Ever after Little Johnny Chatterwell would be known as the boy who was rescued by a gryphon. Little Johnny Gryphon.

He smiled shyly at Gabriel. "She pushed me off."

"I know. We saw her, lad."

"Why did she do that?"

"I don't really think we'll ever know, Johnny," said Gabriel.

The young boy looked round the party and asked worriedly, "Where's Mistress Mabel?"

Gabriel dusted down his cotte and combed back his hair with his fingers. "She's gone down there to see if Godyth is..."

But they all knew that she wouldn't be alive.

No one wanted to look over the edge but they'd have to go and take up the body at some point.

After a while, the reeve peered over the precipice and saw Mistress Mabel Wetherspring straightening the broken limbs and bloodied and maimed body of young Godyth Lovegrove.

No one asked how Mabel had got down there so quickly.

They all began to troop down the hill by the path which snaked down the side of the little valley.

Gabriel stayed at the top with Master Chatterwell and Little Johnny who was so tired out by his adventure that he was falling asleep with his arms hooked around his father's neck, mumbling gently and incoherently.

"Take him home, Arnulf," said Gabriel at last. "We'll follow."

He stood with his head bowed for a few heartbeats looking down at the river; a silver thread winding its way through a green sward. He saw Mabel rise from her knees and look up at him. She lifted her arm in acknowledgement. He saw her bow her head and look down at the body of Godyth Lovegrove. He watched the path for a sign of the villagers working their way down the slope.

Then, inexplicably, there came an unusual sound—a swooshing, windy sound. A sound rather like that which he had just heard as Mabel had flown out to rescue Johnny and Godyth; the sound of a great beating starting up behind him, atop the forest trees. He looked up. Over the great oaks came a large bird-like beast, smaller than Mabel had been but huge nevertheless.

Sir Gabriel looked down to the river. There was Mabel talking to Master Head whilst the other men made to collect branches to weave into a hurdle to accommodate Godyth's body and take it back to Bedwyn. They'd seen nothing of this new beast yet and Master Chatterwell and Johnny were now out of sight. They wouldn't see it. In fact no one else saw it.

Gabriel raised his hand to his brow to shield his eyes. He stared with a thumping heart and a dry mouth. Yes. It *was* a gryphon. It *was*. A male gryphon with beautiful glossy tan plumage to its head and neck, rough buff hair to its body and huge wings like a pair of blacksmith's bellows. With its yellow beak open, horridly sharp, and its talons outstretched, it circled the forest oaks and then with one languid flap of its strong, brown wings it rose up and glided out over Savernake until it too was a speck in the sky.

'The Beast of Bedwyn!' thought Gabriel grinning to himself. 'I wonder if that was what Godyth saw? Perhaps she wasn't lying after all?'

He shouted after it. "Please, don't come back. I really *don't* want to have to deal with *you!*"

*****

It was going dark by the time they got home. It took a while to carry Godyth's ruined body along the river path on its makeshift bier, to the village.

As they walked, they all talked. And talked. Talked about what they had seen. They must get their stories straight. There must be no deviation or they would not be believed. Little Johnny had been rescued by a kindly gryphon. It had not been a dangerous beast at all. They had, every one of them, seen it and what it had done. As they neared the village, all talking ceased. The shock of events overtook them all.

It was difficult to believe that an eleven year old girl could be the murderer of so many people but it was even more difficult to believe that they had all seen the Beast of Bedwyn. It really existed and it was not hostile as they'd all thought.

There was much scratching and shaking of heads that evening in Bedwyn village as the tale was told over and over in different households.

Godyth was taken to her father's house but he would not open the door nor would he answer the reeve when he yelled.

"Lovegrove—Phillip. Open the door. We have your daughter here. I am afraid she is dead."

Eventually Lovegrove shouted back through the door, with a sob in his voice. "She is no daughter of mine." Which of course was quite true, though he had always treated her as his well-beloved daughter. Until now.

Godyth was laid in the lockup, until she could be prepared for her grave and that was that.

Master Head went trudging off to the steward to give him a report about the afternoon's events. Henry Buttermere would write to the Lord Robert to apprise him of the goings on. Gabriel followed Master Head just to make sure that everything went smoothly. He had been a witness to the whole thing and with the testimonies of all the men of Bedwyn they pieced together an account which would satisfy the authorities.

Mabel went home. She was so exhausted and despite her hard heart towards Godyth, she was upset that she hadn't managed to save the girl.

Gabriel scratched on the door some while later. She sleepily answered him, "The door is open."

"It's all done. Master Corngold offered to take his cart to Rutishall tomorrow with a letter for Lord Robert."

"But you will go instead?"

"I…" Gabriel came in and shut the door. "I think I must. A letter is all very well but a first hand account from one of his knights…"

"Yes, of course, you must." She rolled her blankets around her and sat up in bed.

"Mabel, you mustn't blame yourself. The girl was her own worst enemy. She was selfish and unkind—not to mention cruel…"

"And she deserved the death she got?" Mabel swallowed. "Godyth was not in her right mind, Gabriel."

"Better that, than months of waiting for trial in poor conditions at the castle gaol, then a harrowing trial for everyone concerned and a death by strangulation. At least it was quick."

"Yes, I know."

"It is better this way, I think."

Gabriel came to sit on her bed. "It wasn't your fault. You did everything you could. Godyth just wouldn't be helped."

"She was a strange girl. At least now we know why she was so strange," said Mabel. "And her mother."

"The curse of the Fryxells. There are none left now?"

"No. Not around here," said Mabel.

Gabriel came a little closer, "But I tell you what *is* left."

"Oh...?"

"Flying around over the trees north of Crofton..."

"Yes?"

"A gryphon. A male gryphon."

"Oh Gabriel don't be so..."

"No. Truthfully. I saw it."

Mabel sniggered. "No."

"A beautiful beast, a male gryphon. It circled overhead. Perhaps it was looking for a mate?"

"What *do* you mean?"

"Well, perhaps it knew that you had been flying about the area and came to find you."

"Aw no..." said Mabel, her face draining of colour..

"And when you had 'disappeared', the poor beast took off sad and lonely again. Disappointed and lonely."

"Oh don't be daft."

"I am telling you Mabel, I saw it. I was feet away."

"A gryphon? You aren't joking? A real one? "

"A real one."

"Oh dear." At last her brow crinkled in amusement. "I do hope he doesn't cause any difficulties locally."

"Well, if he does, I will just have to come back and deal with him," said a grinning Gabriel.

"What?"

Gabriel leaned over her and planted his lips on hers. Her arms came over his shoulders and she pulled him to her. After a few heartbeats, they came up for air.

"After all—I can't have competition like that, can I?"

"Competition?"

"Such an amazing rival for your affections."

Mabel pushed him off the edge of the bed with a giggle.

*****

When his duties allowed, Johnny Chatterwell spent many hours staring up at the sky hoping to catch a glimpse of his gryphon. He had longed for it to fly by and that he would be able to give it his heartfelt thanks for saving his life. But Johnny was to be disappointed. The Beast of Bedwyn was never again seen over the little village nestled in the forest trees of Savernake.

And of the male gryphon, even though they searched, no one was ever able to find it.

No one ever saw it again.

FIN

GLOSSARY

Attach - to arrest.

Bairns - children

Basilisk - a legendary reptile reputed to be a serpent king, who can cause death with a single glance.

Besom - a brush made of twigs bound together on a long handle.

Bier - a rudimentary bed for the laying out of corpses.

Bullneck disease - diphtheria

Burh - an Old English fortification or fortified settlement.

Coif - a cap made of linen worn by men and women.

Coracle - a small boat paddled with a single oar.

Coroner - a medieval official who was tasked to record all cases of sudden and unnatural deaths including suicides, accidents and homicides.

Cotte - long garment belted at the waist worn by both men and women.

Cott - cottage

Cow byre - cow barn

Cubit - the distance between thumb and outstretched finger to the elbow

Cuckold - husband of an adulterous wife.

Crab apples - small wild apples which are very sour.

Crepuscular - relating to twilight

Daub - A mixture of dung, mud and straw for building walls.

Defile - steep-sided narrow gorge, valley or passage

Deosil - clockwise

Drop spindle - suspended spindles used to twist fibres into a workable thread or yarn

Dudgeon - a feeling of offence or deep resentment.

First Finder - the person who first finds a dead body. They must report to the authorities.

Furlong - imperial measurement one eighth of a mile, equivalent to 660 feet, 220 yards, 40 rods, 10 chains or approximately 201 metres.

Gambeson - padded wool and wool stuffed jacket worn under maille.

Garth - garden for growing food.

Green woodpecker - *(Picus viridis).* A medium woodpecker with distinctive green and red plumage.

Gryphon - composite mythological creature with a lion's body (winged or wingless) and a bird's head, usually that of an eagle.

Hoglet - a young pig

Heriot - a death-duty in late Anglo-Saxon England and early Mediaeval era which required that at death, a nobleman provided to his king a given set of military equipment, often including horses, swords, shields, spears and helmets. It later developed into a kind of tenurial feudal relief due from villeins.

Hippocras - wine mixed with sugar and spices, usually including cinnamon, and possibly heated.

Interdict - ecclesiastical censure, or ban that prohibits persons, certain active Church individuals or groups from participating in certain rites

Keep - type of fortified tower built within castles during the Middle Ages.

Kirtle - A dress worn by women in the Medieval era.

Kite - *(Milvus milvus)* a bird of prey which feeds on carrion. These were the refuse collectors of the Middle Ages.

Locking bar - a wooden bar which is pushed into a bracket to secure a door.

Merrells - Nine Mens' Morris. A game played with counters the object of which is to form 'mills' horizontally and vertically to remove the opponents counters.

Mouldwarp - ancient dialect word for a mole

Napery - collective name for linens for the table.

Palliasse - a straw mattress.

Potage - a soup made of vegetables cooked in a pan over an open fire.

Pricket - a spike for a candle.

Plantain - *(Plantago major)* a large leaved herbaceous plant which can be eaten.

Preaching cross - a free-standing upright stone cross erected in a churchyard to designate a preaching place.

Roach - *(Rutilus rutilus)* a fresh- and brackish-water fish of the family Cyprinidae, native to most of Europe

Routiers - mercenary soldiers of the Middle Ages with a fearsome reputation for violence.

Saker - a large species of falcon.

Samhain - a Gaelic festival marking the end of the harvest season and beginning of winter or "darker-half" of the year. It is held on 1 November but with celebrations beginning on the evening of 31 October

Scree - an accumulation of loose stones or rocky debris lying on a slope or at the base of a hill or cliff.

Sexton - a church officer or employee who takes care of the church property and performs related minor duties (such as ringing the bell for services and digging graves

Shippon - a barn for animals.

Saffron - spice derived from the flower of (Crocus sativus) which stains bright yellow.

Soupcon - a tiny amount.

Supertunic - a sleeveless garment usually of wool or silk worn over the cotte.

Terce - a service forming part of the Divine Office of the Western Christian Church, traditionally said (or chanted) at the third hour of the day (i.e. 9 a.m.).

Threshing flail - an agricultural tool used for threshing, the process of separating grains from their husks.

Tincture - a medicine consisting of a substance in a solution of alcohol.

Tun - a large beer or wine cask.

Twelfth Night - festival on the last night of the Twelve Days of Christmas,

Villein - a peasant tied to the land and a master usually a nobleman.

Yule log - a specially selected log burnt on a hearth as a winter tradition in regions of Europe.

AUTHOR'S NOTE

Most Mediaeval people believed in magic and in magical beings of all kinds. Werewolves and vampires are just two types often discovered in the pages of manuscripts and in legends.

Shapeshifters are people who are able, simply by wishing it to be so, to change into any animal they wish and back into human form. This change must be voluntary for them to be considered true shapeshifters. Transformation must not be accidental and it must not be subject to any particular rule or set of circumstances. They must retain their human mind.

This series of books came about by me watching a fly land on my car windscreen when I was sat in a traffic jam. Moments later I had the germ of the idea for Withershynnes - In the Dark, book 1.

I had long wanted to write another series of Mediaeval books where my 'detective' is female and not noble.

There are, of course, other writers whose tales have female investigators at their heart. I loved some of those books but they just never quite ring true for me, for it's highly unlikely that a woman could do the things they are allowed to do in those centuries before emancipation. Women were at the beck and call of men and would never be allowed to roam freely gathering information about crimes. I wanted a woman who could come and go at will, never be beholden to anyone (except her lord, at times) and be free to investigate when and how she wished.

So Mabel Wetherspring was born; an independent, clever, literate, practical, woman who is from common stock, and with a special skill which proves extremely useful.

I am at heart a murder mystery writer. I am a Mediaevalist. And so I chose to set Mabel down at a time I am interested in, the beginning of the thirteenth century, in a place I know well, Savernake Forest.

Belief in fantastical beasts like the gryphon was rife in the 13th century. One just needs to read the chronicles and peruse the pages of bestiaries (books of beasts) written at the time. It's no surprise that the village of Bedwyn has its own creature. Even if it does arrive by accident. One wonders what mediaeval folk were 'on' in order to report seeing these amazing beasts! The best place to see them nowadays, of course, is in the margins of manuscripts. Here gryphons, basilisks, manticores and unicorns abound.

The name Fryxell is a local Wiltshire name mentioned in manuscripts and is pronounced Frizzel.

WITHERSHYNNES BOOK 4: WEAVE WALKER
WILL BE OUT SOON.

SAMPLE CHAPTERS AND MORE CAN BE FOUND AT
SUSANNAMNEWSTEAD.CO.UK

USE QR CODE FOR SUSANNA'S SITE
JOIN HER EMAIL LIST FOR NEWS & BONUSES

ABOUT THE AUTHOR

Susanna, like Mabel has known the Forest of Savernake all her life. After a period at the University of Wales studying Speech Therapy, she returned to Wiltshire and then moved to Hampshire to work, not so very far from her forest. Susanna developed an interest in English history, particularly that of the 12th and 13th centuries, early in life and began to write about it in her twenties. She now lives in Northamptonshire with her husband and a small wire haired fox terrier called Tabor.

Susanna hopes to return fairly soon to her beloved Wiltshire downs where she will continue to write the Withershynnes series, the Savernake Medieval murder series and her Kennet Valley mystery romances set in the area around Marlborough, Wiltshire.

ALSO BY SUSANNA M. NEWSTEAD

The Savernake Medieval Murder Mysteries

ALSO BY SUSANNA M. NEWSTEAD

WITHERSHYNNES MEDIEVAL FANTASY

Withershynnes : In The Dark

Withershynnes 2: Cat's Cradle

Withershynnes 3: Cheating the Wind

Withershynnes 4: Weave Walker (coming soon)

KENNET VALLEY MEDIEVAL ROMANCES

Forceleap Farm

Hunting the Wren

The Harmonious Blacksmith

Please visit her website for further information
https://susannamnewstead.co.uk/

Printed in Great Britain
by Amazon

22767621R00158